*A good name is rather to be chosen than great riches,
and loving favour rather than silver and gold.*

—Proverbs 22:1 (KJV)

LOVE'S A MYSTERY

Love's a Mystery in Sleepy Hollow, New York
Love's a Mystery in Cape Disappointment, Washington
Love's a Mystery in Cut and Shoot, Texas
Love's a Mystery in Nameless, Tennessee

Love's a Mystery

in

NAMELESS TN

LESLIE GOULD & ELIZABETH LUDWIG

Guideposts

Published by Guideposts
100 Reserve Road, Suite E200
Danbury, CT 06810
Guideposts.org

Cover and interior design by Müllerhaus.
Cover illustration by Dan Burr at Illustration Online LLC.
Typeset by Aptara, Inc.

ISBN 978-1-961441-38-5 (hardcover)
ISBN 978-1-961441-39-2 (softcover)
ISBN 978-1-957935-83-6 (epub)

Printed and bound in the United States of America.

FIDDLIN' WITH LOVE

by

LESLIE GOULD

…I have called thee by thy name; thou art mine.

—Isaiah 43:1 (KJV)

ᴄᴏ Chapter One ᴄᴏ

Nameless, Tennessee
Monday, September 3, 1945

Shifting the Bantam convertible into third gear, Iris Pitts kept her eyes wide open for Nameless, Tennessee. Mr. Scott Parker, president of the Nameless school board, had written in his offer letter, *Don't blink or you'll miss it.*

Iris had taken Highway 70 from Memphis to Nashville and then headed north. She'd driven on smaller and smaller roads, crossed the Cumberland River, and then turned onto an unpaved back road.

Now, as she gained elevation, the trees became thicker and the curves more frequent. Mr. Parker had called Nameless a "hilltop settlement," and that seemed accurate. Just ahead, the general store, with a gas pump and a shed, was on her right. On her left was a café. Then some sort of office. And a handful of houses. Mr. Parker had written there were fewer than two hundred people in the town. He'd also written, *I know you're wondering how Nameless got its unusual name. Our founding fathers couldn't agree on what to call the community, so the post office declared it "Nameless." And it stuck.*

There was the two-room school. *Her school.* At least for a year. She turned in to the lot, shifted into first, and came to a stop. She'd never heard of Nameless, Tennessee, until her neighbor mentioned they had an opening for a teacher. The previous one left to get married. Four months ago, Iris thought she'd be marrying Will McCrae, home from fighting in Europe, by now—or at least soon. Instead, she was arriving in his car as a nobody from nowhere who had ended up in Nameless, Tennessee. On a wing and a prayer.

She climbed out of the convertible, untied the scarf holding her hair in place, and walked toward the school. She'd be teaching grades one through eight, all in one room. She'd spent the last two weeks preparing.

"Miss Pitts!"

She shaded her eyes. A man wearing a fedora came toward her. "Mr. Parker?"

"Indeed it is." He took off his hat, showing a head of thick, gray hair. His hazel eyes shone as he spoke. "I'm delighted to meet you." He extended his hand, and she took it. His grip was firm but not too tight.

"You made good time." He nodded to the convertible. "That's some car you have there. A '39 Bantam, correct?"

She smiled. "That's right. It's fun, but not much good in a move." Both the front passenger seat and the back area were packed with her belongings, as was the trunk.

"I'll show you inside the school and then your new home."

"Will my things be safe out here?"

"Oh my, yes," he answered. "We don't have any crime in Nameless. No one locks their doors even. You could have the Hope Diamond in that convertible of yours, and it would be safe."

She trusted that meant Will's beloved fiddle was safe in the trunk then. She doubted he was coming back—she would have heard from him by now if he was. Not knowing was as hard as anything she'd ever gone through. But just in case he did return, she'd keep his fiddle safe.

Mr. Parker turned the knob of the schoolhouse door and flung it open. He motioned for her to enter. She stepped into a large area with hooks for the students to hang their coats and a row of shelves for their lunch buckets. There was a stack of wood at the far end of the room. There were two doors across from each other and a third door to the right, at the end of the hall.

"As I told you in my letter, the school has two rooms, but we're only using one at this time. Quite a few of our families left during the war to work in cities. We'll gain some back over the next year, but others will go to the Jackson County schools in Gainesboro. In time, all our students will." Mr. Parker sighed. "But for the time being, we'll carry on here and do the best we can. As I said, you'll have all the grades in one room, thirty students in total. First through eighth grade, although several of the students are older than thirteen."

"Oh?"

"We don't have a bus to take them to Gainesboro, and their families don't want them to be out of school yet."

"How old are the oldest students?"

"Fifteen, I believe. Try to challenge them as best you can." He motioned to the door on the left.

Iris hadn't prepared for older students. She exhaled as she stepped through the doorway and then walked down the center aisle between the desks to the large teacher's desk up front.

Mr. Parker followed her. "I've put a list with the students' names and grades on your desk, plus the textbooks for each grade. The students' books are on the shelves over there."

Iris glanced at the shelves along the wall. The books appeared old and ratty. She focused on her desk again. It was large, and the chair looked comfortable. There was a chalkboard behind it, maps to the right, and an iron stove in the corner.

"You'll notice we don't have electricity yet. Putting up lines in the mountains was slowed down by the war. Hopefully, that will change soon." He glanced toward the south-facing windows. "The light is good in this room. There are lamps in the cupboard." He motioned to the far wall. "If you ever need them."

Charleston, Asheville, and Memphis had all had electricity.

"Do you have any questions?" Mr. Parker asked.

Iris looked around the room. There was a slate on each desk with chalk. She hadn't used a slate twenty years ago when she started school in Charleston, but Nameless was small and remote. "Are there paper and pencils available for the students?"

"Most families can't afford those for their children, so the school board provides the slates."

"I see." She glanced around the room again. "What about cleaning supplies?"

"There's a broom, mop, and bucket in the closet in the cloakroom. Plus a jug of ammonia. Work out a cleaning schedule for the students."

"All right." She smiled at him. "Thank you."

"Would you like a little background on the area?"

"Please," Iris said.

"The county seat is Gainesboro, which is ten miles from here. Traveling is better than it was in the olden days but can still be a problem. Many of our students live out in the country and will have a hard time getting to school when the weather turns. You came over the Cumberland River to get here—"

Iris nodded.

"There's good fishing in it and the Roaring River too—catfish and bass—and also in the creeks all through the mountains." Mr. Parker gestured to the windows. "The rivers used to be the main means of transportation, and there's plenty of people who still get around using them. Of course, the hunting is good too. Lots of deer and quail." He grinned. "Not that I expect you to hunt for game."

She smiled. "I'd be willing to give it a try."

"No need," he said. "No doubt the older boys will be bringing you a bird now and then. Most of the students live on farms. Tobacco and corn are the common crops. Lots of livestock. Lumber is another source of income, and there are several mills in the area."

It would clearly be a different life than Iris was used to.

"Some of our students lost loved ones in the war—brothers, fathers, uncles."

Iris blinked a couple of times, fighting back her own grief. No doubt, everyone had been affected in some way.

"How long have you lived in Nameless, Mr. Parker?"

"I grew up here," he said. "Then moved around quite a bit for business. I returned a couple of years ago to the family farmhouse, but I lease out the land. I'm no farmer." He smiled. "I'm ready for a quieter way of life, now that I'm growing older."

"Well," Iris said, "this is a lovely place to return to."

"That it is." He held her gaze for a long moment and then said, "I'm pleased you're here, Miss Pitts." Before she could respond he added, "I'll stop by tomorrow after school. I'm sure you'll have more questions then."

"I'm guessing I will."

"Now, let's take a look at the gymnasium and then go look at your new home."

When they returned to the cloakroom, he nodded to the door at the end of the hall. "That's where the gymnasium is. Basketball was king around here a few years ago." He chuckled. "We had students repeating eighth grade just so they could keep playing. During the war, as we lost students, the team hasn't done as well, but it's still the favorite sport."

Will had loved basketball.

Mr. Parker opened the door. The gym had a polished wood floor. "Of course, you won't be responsible for cleaning in here. Basketball practice won't start for a couple of months. We haven't hired a coach yet, but when we do, this will be his responsibility. When the weather gets cold, you can use the space for recess."

Benches lined the gymnasium, and high windows let some light in. There were five rows of bleachers on the far side.

"Now let's take a look at your new home."

Iris followed Mr. Parker out of the school. He pointed to a small building in a grove of white pines on the back property of the school. "Your cottage is right there."

As she followed Mr. Parker, Iris squinted. When they reached the building, it was clear it wasn't in very good shape.

"I'm sorry the accommodations aren't better," Mr. Parker said. "I'll hire someone to shore it up a little before winter—repair the roof, clean out the latrine, that sort of thing." It had been a while since she'd had to use an outhouse.

He opened the door to the one-room cottage and again ushered Iris in first. There was a small table with a lamp atop it, two chairs, a kitchen area, and a bed with a bare mattress.

"Well," Mr. Parker said, "I imagine you have some unpacking to do. Like I said, I'll stop by tomorrow after school to see how the first day went." He started toward the door, leaving Iris alone in the middle of the room. But then he turned back to her and said, "If you have some extra time tonight, there's a gathering at the Nameless Grange Hall." He pointed east. "There'll be music, maybe some dancing. It's just a short way past here—but I would drive. You don't want to walk home on the road in the dark."

"Thank you," Iris said. "I'll think about it."

As she unpacked the car, Iris felt unsettled. She'd grown up in Charleston, gone to the teachers college in Asheville, and then moved to Memphis to be close to Will before he shipped out to Europe. Then, instead of getting a teaching contract, she'd taken a job at the Memphis Ordnance Plant, determined to do her part. By the time the war in Europe ended in May, production began to slow and she'd needed another job—a teaching job. Although Nameless was small and out of the way, she was thankful for the opportunity.

Just yesterday, the surrender document for the end of the war with Japan was officially signed. It truly was over. And yet, Will wasn't home. She'd last heard from him in March, six months ago. She'd written the War Department but received a form letter saying no information could be released, since she wasn't kin. She'd tried to track down an uncle Will had mentioned by contacting people with the last name of McCrae all over Tennessee, but she couldn't locate him.

Living in Nameless, a place with no memories of Will, would be the best thing for her. She carried in her clothes, bedding, and her few kitchen items—a Dutch oven, cake pans, a frying pan, and a kettle. Then a box with a few plates and bowls. And a box of staples— flour, sugar, spices. She grabbed the box of school things—her calendar and lesson plans and the books she'd kept from college—and placed it on the table so it would be ready for the morning.

She decided to leave the fiddle in the trunk for now. At least it was secure. The cottage barely had a doorknob, let alone a decent lock.

After making the bed, Iris glanced around, trying to decide whether to go to the grange hall or not. By the time she finished her supper of leftover fried chicken from lunch, she'd decided. It would be good to meet some of the people in the community.

She changed into her only new garment in the last four years. A navy-blue Kitty Foyle dress with a white collar and cuffs. She'd bought it last March, thinking she'd wear it the day Will came home. She might as well wear it now. She pinned her dark hair into a victory roll style, two rolls on top and long in the back, and then slipped into her red pumps. She applied bright red lipstick. Had Will not contacted her on purpose? Or because he couldn't? Would she ever know if he had even survived the war?

Tears threatened. She grabbed a sweater.

As she drove toward the grange hall, a man stopped and stared. Then he shouted, "Where'd you get that car?" She was used to people—especially men—staring when she drove Will's convertible, and sometimes they shouted, mostly things she ignored, but no one had shouted a question before.

She kept driving. By the cars and trucks and buggies parked around it, she knew when she found the grange hall. She shifted down and made the left-hand turn. An older man started to wave but then his hand froze in midair, and he shook his head. What was going on? Perhaps someone in town owned a Bantam convertible— or had. It was sad to be the new teacher in town and have people already disappointed to see her.

She found a place close to the hall to park the car but couldn't hear any music. Once she turned off the engine, she debated about leaving the fiddle in the trunk. She wasn't worried someone would take it—but then, she was worried someone might take the entire car. She chastised herself. Mr. Parker had said the place didn't have any crime. She climbed out of the car and headed to the front door of the grange hall.

Several people standing on the porch turned toward her and then stepped aside, allowing her to enter. Mr. Parker waved from the middle of the hall and motioned for her to join him. Just as she reached the group, three musicians took to the stage—an elderly man on the guitar, a middle-aged man on the banjo, and a young man—who was taller than the other two—on the fiddle. He wore a pair of patched overalls and had a surly expression on his face. He also had a boyish face. Perhaps he was younger than she thought.

The guitar player said, "This will be our last set. I hope you've enjoyed the music."

The crowd clapped, and the fiddler pushed his instrument against his chest as if he planned to drive it through his body. The music to "Medley of Reels" began.

Mr. Parker offered Iris his hand, and she took it as people began to pair off in groups of four. It had been a long time since she'd danced. Since Will had gone off to war. The music, the beat that came down from above and up from the floor, and the movement of dancing around the square sparked something inside of her. She bounced on her feet, pivoted, and sashayed around the square, smiling at Mr. Parker and the others as she passed. The faces of the musicians floated by—all three had smiles on their faces as they played, even the young man. As Iris twirled around, she felt a hint of joy. It'd been so long! It wasn't the harmony she'd felt with Will, but it gave her hope.

For just a moment. Until, on the closing note of the song, the fiddle groaned, and Iris turned toward the stage, reminded of how very quickly life could change. A war. A last letter. A move. An end to harmony and hope. And joy.

The fiddler held his bow out in one hand and his fiddle up in the other. Iris gasped. The back of the fiddle had cracked.

The other musicians stopped, and the guitar player put down his instrument and spoke softly to the young man. A few words were exchanged and then the fiddler stormed off the stage.

Iris's heart ached for him.

The guitar player stepped to the edge of the stage. "Young Judson's had some bad luck. Say a prayer for him—we all know that was his daddy's fiddle." The man bowed his head and clasped his hands together. Iris thought he was going to pray out loud, but then he raised his head and said, "We need another fiddler." He squinted as he looked into the audience. "Do we have another? Anyone? You don't have to be that good."

Iris glanced around the group on the floor and those who stood along the sidelines. She hadn't played in public for years, but she still practiced every day. She felt her hand go up, slowly, perhaps inspired by the music and the dancing and the hope she could feel something besides despair again.

The guitar player met her eyes. "Miss? Do you play?"

She nodded. "Give me a minute to collect—um, my instrument—and I'll join you on the stage."

When she reached the convertible, Judson stood at the hood of the car, the bow and broken fiddle still in his hands. Iris said, "Hello," and then opened the trunk and pulled out Will's case.

"Where'd you get this car?" Judson asked.

"It belongs to a friend of mine."

Judson's eyes narrowed.

"I'm sorry about your fiddle," Iris said. "Do you have someone who can repair it?"

He scowled, his dark eyes narrow and his chin down. Instead of answering, he asked, "Did you steal the car?"

"I did not." Iris pointed to the back of the hall. "Is there a door that leads to the stage?"

Judson nodded. "I'll show you."

She followed him up a few steps to the door.

"Go on through it," he said. "You'll see the stairs."

She made her way in the dim light up onto the stage. Behind the curtain, she took the fiddle out of the case, holding it tenderly for a moment as she gazed at the carving of hummingbirds and irises on the back. Will had the fiddle long before he'd ever met her. When she'd told him her name was Iris, he took notice.

She tuned the fiddle while the two remaining musicians played "Maiden's Prayer." When they finished, she stepped through the curtain. Then she tucked the fiddle under her chin and joined in with the other two. As she played, she noticed one particular couple. The woman wore her auburn hair on top of her head, a red dress, red varnish on her nails, and black dancing shoes. The man was tall with his light brown hair cut short. He wore a suit and held his partner with a tenderness that made Iris's heart ache. *Will!* But it wasn't. The man was heavier and a few years older. But still, he resembled Will.

As she kept playing, the music came to life and filled her soul. After eight more songs, the guitar player turned to Iris and asked, "Do you know 'Haste to the Wedding'?"

"Yes," she answered. It was one of her favorites. The guitar player counted out the beat, and Iris joined in. *Come haste to the wedding ye friends and ye neighbors.* As she played, she fought back tears as she searched the crowd for the man who reminded her of Will, but he and his partner were gone.

She closed her eyes as she played. The music coursed through her. It was time to let go of Will. *No Care Shall obtrude here, our Bliss to annoy... Which love and innocence ever enjoy.* She held the bow on the strings, drawing out the last notes as the crowd began to cheer. It was time to make Nameless, Tennessee her new home, at least for a season.

CHAPTER TWO

Once Iris was back in her cottage, she took Will's violin in with her, not wanting to leave it in the car after all. She scooted it under the bed, to the far corner, then put on her nightgown and climbed under the covers.

She'd taken violin lessons in Charleston from the time she was ten until her senior year of high school, at her mother's insistence. She played Bach and Beethoven, Mozart and Brahms. When she went to Asheville to attend the teachers college, she left her violin behind. She'd mastered the instrument but didn't enjoy it.

At the beginning of Iris's second year, Will played for a dance at the school. Watching him made her miss her violin. Could she feel what he felt? The joy on his face radiated around the room as he tapped—or stomped—his foot while playing and swaying to the tune. He seemed to create music as easily as other people breathed.

Her roommate Sara must have sensed that Iris was enraptured with him. "He gives lessons," she said. "Here at the college."

"Really?"

"You can rent a fiddle."

Iris did just that and began taking lessons from Will. Of course he was impressed with everything she knew. It turned out the only difference between a fiddle and a violin was the music—Irish ballads and Scottish hymns instead of Mozart. Drinking songs and African blues instead of Bach.

The other difference was that Will held his fiddle against his chest, while she placed her violin under her chin.

After her first lesson, Will began to play Brahms's Concerto in D Minor. She'd smiled and then played along.

The memories were bittersweet, and Iris felt tears on her cheeks before she dropped off to sleep.

The next morning, she woke with a start and quickly checked her alarm clock. It was six. School started at eight. She relaxed. She had plenty of time.

After lighting the lamp, starting the coal stove, and heating the water she'd pumped the night before for washing and coffee, she readied herself. At seven o'clock, she stepped out in a misty morning, carrying her stack of papers and books along with a couple of leftover biscuits and an apple from the tree by the pump.

Iris entered the building, sat at her desk, and then bowed her head and asked the Lord to bless her work as a teacher and to bless her students. She had felt His presence and comfort the last few years, especially since Will's letters stopped. Iris would trust Him now for the next step in her life, and she hoped He would use her to serve her students.

She worked quickly, going over the list of names and grade levels, making a seating chart, and then placing the right textbooks on each desk. There was an eighth-grade student named Judson Johnson. Surely he wasn't the Judson from the night before. He was certainly older than fifteen. Clearly, there were at least two people named Judson in town.

She wrote her name on the chalkboard. *Miss Pitts.*

The first three students arrived ten minutes early. They were quiet and tentative. "Come in!" Iris called out. "Find your desk."

One of the children approached and gave Iris a quick hug. "My name is Hannah," she said, "and I'm in the first grade."

"Welcome, Hannah! I'm so glad you're here." Iris patted her shoulder. "We're going to have a great year."

A group of older girls arrived, chatting and laughing. One of them said, "Hello, Miss Pitts! I'm Marjorie Johnson. Everyone calls me Marj." She had brown curly hair that bounced around her shoulders.

"Hello, Marj." Iris had to fight to keep from smiling. That was one thing she remembered from teachers college. *Don't smile until Thanksgiving if you want your students to respect you.* "I'm pleased to meet you." She clapped her hands together. "Check the seating chart on the board and find your seats, girls."

Marj groaned when she saw where she'd be sitting. "Can we switch?"

Iris squared her shoulders. "Absolutely not."

By eight o'clock every desk in the room had a student at it—except Judson Johnson's. Iris went through the roll call, marking each student present when he or she responded. When she called out Judson's name, Marj said, "He's helping Grannie get the cow back in the pen. He'll be along shortly."

"Thank you, Marj." Iris guessed Judson and Marj were siblings. They were both in the eighth grade. Perhaps they were twins.

The morning progressed better than she'd expected. The older students worked on a math assignment while Iris started a reading lesson with the younger ones. After a half hour, she began a writing assignment with the older students while the younger ones wrote their numbers. Near the end of the morning, Judson—the one whose fiddle cracked the night before—sauntered in. He was younger than he'd looked last night in the dim grange hall. Apparently, he was young enough to be her student.

He stopped in the middle of the aisle and gawked at her. "You're the fiddle gal."

Her face grew warm. "That's right. I recognize you too. How are you?"

"All right. Where do I sit?"

"Right there." Marj pointed to the empty desk beside her.

"Great." Judson shuffled toward it. As he sat down, he raised his head and said, "I'm Judson Johnson, and the last place I want to be on earth is here, in this forsaken school, in this forsaken town."

Shocked that Judson-the-fiddler, who towered over her, was a student of hers, it took a few moments for Iris to remember her plan for the morning. She had to check her notes. A geography lesson. For the entire school.

"Students." She picked up thirty pieces of paper from her desk. "We have a special activity."

She passed out mimeographed copies she'd made in Memphis of a map of the US without the states labeled and divided the students into several groups. "Start with Tennessee," she said, "and then our neighboring states. Fill in as many of the states as you can and help each other. We'll see which group finishes first."

The students worked well together for ten minutes. But then a rustling in the back distracted everyone. Judson stood and stretched. Iris ignored him. He sat down and began speaking to the boy next to him.

Marj looked up from her work. "Judson, be quiet," she ordered.

"Knock it off, Marj," he growled.

"You knock it off," Marj retorted.

Judson reached over and cuffed her on the head.

"That's enough." Iris started down the aisle. "We'll have none of that in our classroom."

"I didn't ask to sit by him," Marj muttered.

Judson leaned back in his chair and yawned. "This is getting boring."

"I need to talk to you," Iris said to Judson. "Outside."

He shrugged, stood, picked up his piece of paper, and handed it to her. She looked it over. Each state was labeled correctly in perfect cursive.

He started toward the cloakroom.

Iris said, "Students, continue with your work. I'll be right back."

She hurried after Judson. He was already out the door.

"Wait," she called out.

He stopped and turned at the bottom of the stairs.

"What's going on?" she asked.

He crossed his arms. "I shouldn't be here, but Grannie's making me come. I'm fifteen. I should be working."

Although she'd thought he was older, he didn't behave as if he were any older than fifteen. If anything, he acted younger. "An education is important," Iris said. "You'll be starting high school soon."

"Marj will. I won't." He raised his voice. "Besides needing to support Grannie and Marj, I need to buy a new fiddle." He balled his hands into fists and started back up the stairs.

Iris stepped aside to let him pass. Did he think their talk was over? "It's noon," he shouted into the building. "Time for lunch." Then he turned to Iris and said, "Ma'am."

Iris watched as he descended the stairs, two at a time, and then sauntered out to the road, heading toward the grange hall. The children began streaming out of the cloakroom with their lunch pails.

Marj came out with hers in one hand, a ball in the other, and a bat tucked under her arm. "He'll be back soon," she said. "Otherwise, Grannie will make him regret it."

The children ate quickly. Iris saw butter sandwiches, cold chicken, dry biscuits, apples, and slices of ham disappear quickly. Then they organized a game of baseball. A few mitts appeared. The teams seemed evenly matched, with Marj the captain of one and BJ, a boy who sat near the back of the classroom, the captain of the other. Iris guessed whichever team Judson had been on, had he stayed, would have dominated the game.

At ten minutes before one, Iris blew her whistle. "Time to wash up," she called out. The students quickly ended the game and took turns at the pump.

As the students filed back into the classroom, Iris sat at her desk and pulled the book *Five on a Treasure Island* from her stack. "It's time for read-aloud," she said.

It was warm in the schoolroom. All the windows and the door were open, but the afternoon was breezeless. As Iris read, the children began to fall asleep one by one, their faces red from the ball game. The heat grew thicker, and even Iris started to grow drowsy. She hadn't intended for the children to fall asleep, but she guessed many of them needed a rest. All of them had their heads on their desks, except for Marj. She was wide awake. When she reached the end of the first chapter, Iris put the book down, stood, and clapped her hands. "It's time to move on to our next lesson."

Several of the older children raised their heads. Most of the younger ones did not. She was just about to clap again when Judson sauntered back into the classroom. "What did I miss?" he asked.

"A boring story," BJ said.

A couple of the students snickered.

"Please take a seat," Iris said to Judson. "We're ready to finish our geography lesson." The younger children began to stir and raise their heads. Hannah was the last to wake. With blurry eyes, the students turned their attention to Iris. "Judson," she said, "would you please come to the blackboard and lead the class in naming all of the states?"

He leaned back in his desk and crossed his arms.

"Judson, come on up."

He shook his head. "I have a nonparticipation policy."

"Well, I don't." She regretted asking him. Clearly, he was a stubborn young man.

"I'll do it," Marj said.

Iris felt her irritation rising but was afraid that standing her ground with Judson would only make things worse. "Thank you,

Marj," she said. "But I'll lead the class." Having Marj take over wasn't going to work either.

Iris grabbed the pointer from its place in the corner and a piece of chalk and then called on BJ to help her. "I need you to be our scribe."

As BJ started up the aisle, Judson put out his foot. BJ tripped and crashed into Marj's desk before he fell to the floor.

Iris suppressed a groan. What had made her think she could teach eighth graders? Before she could say anything, Marj shot out of her desk, yanked BJ to his feet, and began scolding Judson. "Get out," she said. "Don't come back until you can behave yourself."

Judson laughed. He stood and headed for the cloakroom.

"No," Iris called out. "Come back!" But Judson kept going, out the door. She inhaled deeply, trying to calm herself and regain control. "All right, students," she said, "this is what we're going to do." She pointed to the state of Washington. "I need three facts about this state in the far northwest corner of our nation. BJ will record what you say."

"Its western border is the Pacific Ocean," a middle-grade student called out.

"Correct." Iris pointed to Hannah.

"There are lots of mountains."

"Very good," Iris said as BJ continued to write.

The lesson continued. The children knew quite a bit about the states. Erasmus, another eighth grader, said that Crater Lake, the deepest lake in the US, was located in Oregon. Temperance, who was also an eighth grader, said that Hollywood could be found in California. Hannah blurted out that potatoes grew in Idaho.

After they finished the geography lesson, Iris taught a science lesson, focusing on the solar system. A couple of times the sound of a truck going through town or someone honking distracted her, but Iris guessed she'd get used to the noises in the community.

The rest of the afternoon went smoothly but only because Judson didn't return. At two forty-five Iris gave each grade level their assignment for the next day, and then at three o'clock she announced the school day was over. "I'll see y'all tomorrow," she called out.

"Thank you, Miss Pitts," the students said in unison and then filed out of the classroom, leaving Iris relieved. Marj gave her a wide grin. She didn't seem upset that Iris hadn't allowed her to fill the role she'd asked Judson to do. It hadn't been a perfect day, but she'd survived.

Iris had forgotten to have the children sweep and clean their desks before they left. She'd remember to do that tomorrow. She filled the bucket with water from outside, added ammonia, and washed the desks down. Then she found the broom and dustpan in the cloakroom and began sweeping, expecting Mr. Parker to interrupt her at any minute. But he didn't. She carried her papers and books to the cloakroom and mopped the schoolroom floor. Then she dumped the water from the bucket, gathered up her things, pulled the door shut behind her, and headed to her cottage. She'd enjoyed being with the children, but here she was, by herself again. She'd spent so much time alone over the last four years, even while working in the ordnance plant.

She opened the cottage door and stood a moment as her eyes adjusted to the dim light. She squinted. Had an animal gotten into her little home? The quilt was pulled off the bed. The cupboard doors in her kitchen were wide open. The drawers of her bureau were pulled open, and the bottom ones were on the floor. No, an animal wouldn't have done this.

Someone had broken into the cottage.

Her engagement ring! She dropped her papers and books on the table, rushed to the bureau, and dug through the open top right drawer. The box was there. Relief flooded through her as she opened it. The two-tone gold ring with chips on either side of the diamond was safe.

The fiddle! She dropped to her knees and then her belly and scooted underneath the bed. She reached for the far corner. The fiddle was gone.

She rolled out from under the bed and dusted herself off. She'd drive to the general store and call the sheriff—or whatever lawman was available—from there.

As she hurried out the door, a Studebaker with running boards stopped in the schoolyard. A man wearing a suit climbed out of the car. He was tall and thin. Too thin. Will? Will McCrae?

Could she trust her eyes?

Yes, it was Will.

She froze. Was he happy to see her?

A smile spread across his face, and he opened his arms as wide as the sky behind him.

"Will!" she cried out as she rushed to him.

CHAPTER THREE

Will wrapped his arms around her and lifted her in a tight embrace. "I found you!" he shouted as he swung her around.

"I can't believe it," she said. "I was afraid you were dead."

He lowered her to the ground. Her feet touched, but she still felt as if she were spinning. She said, "Tell me everything." But then she remembered the fiddle. "Wait, I have to tell you something. I was on my way to find the sheriff."

He grabbed her hand. "What happened?"

"My place was ransacked sometime today while I was teaching. And your fiddle was stolen."

"Stolen?"

"Well, taken at least. Stolen, I assume."

He paused for a moment but then said, "That doesn't matter. I've found you."

"I'll find your fiddle, I promise." She squeezed his hand and led him to the steps of the schoolhouse. As they sat, she said, "Where have you been? I tried to find you, but the War Department wouldn't give me any information."

"Because you're not my wife."

She took both of his hands. "What happened?"

"I was captured at the end of March, put in a POW camp, and then released in May. I spent about a month in a hospital in England."

"Were you injured?"

"Yes. I took a bullet in my stomach, but I've healed up since."

She put her head on his shoulder. "I'm sorry. Was it horrible in the camp?"

He paused and then said, "It wasn't too bad. After I recovered, I shipped to New York, to Pine Camp Cantonment. You didn't get any of my letters?"

"No. The last letter was written in March and arrived in my mailbox in May. Did you get mine?"

"The last letter I received was written in March."

"I wrote to you every day until June...until I was sure I would have heard from you..." Her voice trailed off. Finally, she asked, "How did you find me?"

"I took the train to Nashville to see my uncle and aunt and then headed to Memphis in their car. Your apartment was empty."

"I moved out a few days ago so I wouldn't have to pay more rent and stayed with a woman from the ordnance plant for a couple of nights. I arrived here yesterday."

"That makes sense. It's a good thing your neighbor knew you'd headed to Nameless for a teaching job."

"Betty is the reason I got the job," Iris said. "She told me about it."

"I wondered how you ended up in Nameless. I didn't think you even knew it existed."

"I didn't. But here I am." She raised her head. So much about Will was the same. The suit. The pressed white shirt. The gold cuff links and tie clip. His square jaw. Blue eyes. But there was a sadness in his eyes, with good reason. He'd fought through Europe. He'd been shot and captured. He'd seen untold suffering.

Will put his arm around her, and she shivered. She'd do whatever she could to help him keep healing.

They sat in silence for several minutes until a sheriff's car turned into the schoolyard. "Well, look at this," Iris said. "I didn't even have to go to the store and place a call." Perhaps the fiddle had already been found.

She stood and started down the steps. Will followed.

The sheriff parked his car and climbed out. "Good afternoon!" he called.

"Good afternoon," Iris said.

"I'm guessing you're the new schoolteacher."

"Yes, sir." She extended her hand. "I'm Iris Pitts."

"Miss Pitts." He shook her hand. "Glad to have you. The young'uns around here need a good teacher, which I'm sure you are."

Her face grew warm. Perhaps he was here about Judson being truant for the afternoon.

The sheriff looked past her to Will. "And who do we have here? I like to talk with strangers as soon as they arrive in town."

Iris turned to Will, who had his mouth open. But before he could speak, the sheriff hooted and then said, "Will McCrae? Is that you?"

"Yes, sir."

"By gum, you made it home."

"I did indeed."

Now it was Iris's mouth that was open. "Home?" she said. "Did you used to live here?"

"No, but my maternal grandparents did. And my uncle, my mom's brother."

"You never mentioned Nameless. Not once."

He shrugged. "I thought I did."

"Believe me," Iris said, "I would have remembered."

"Wait," the sheriff said. He crossed his arms. "You're the gal who played the fiddle last night at the grange hall."

"That's right," she answered. "And speaking of that fiddle, someone stole it out of my cottage today while I was teaching."

"Sheriff!" someone called out. "Sheriff Whitaker!"

A man clutching a straw hat was running toward them. He waved his hand. "There's an accident in front of the café. You're needed."

"All right." Sheriff Whitaker walked to his car. "Stop by the office and report the missing fiddle," he said. "The sooner the better." He climbed into his car, started the motor, and put the vehicle in gear. Then he spun around and pulled onto the highway, headed south.

Iris turned to Will. He had a puzzled expression on his face. "You played my fiddle at the hall last night?"

"That's right. The fiddler's instrument broke, and the lead musician asked for another fiddler. When no one else volunteered, I did."

"And you just happened to have my fiddle with you?"

She nodded. "It was in the trunk of your car."

"There could have been plenty of people there who might want my fiddle."

"Plenty?" Iris asked, incredulously. "There are fewer than two hundred people in the entire town."

"And half of them want my fiddle."

She wasn't sure if he was having delusions of grandeur or if he was paranoid. Perhaps he'd suffered mental trauma along with his injury during his time in the POW camp. She took a deep breath. "Why would half the town want your fiddle when not once in the five years that I've known you have you ever mentioned Nameless, Tennessee?"

"It wasn't relevant," he said. "Nothing happened here I wanted to talk about."

"Something happened here." She pointed at him. "If you'd mentioned Nameless, I would have come here looking for your relatives. I would have known in May if you were dead or alive."

"I told you, my uncle moved to Nashville." He headed toward the Studebaker.

Dumbfounded, Iris asked, "Where are you going?"

"Somewhere to think."

What had gotten into him?

Will drove the Studebaker out of the schoolyard and then turned right, in the direction of the grange hall, having no idea where he was going.

What had he just done? He was overjoyed to find Iris. He was ready to marry her—something she'd refused to do before he left. Yes, she'd accepted his proposal before he shipped out, but she'd been adamant they should wait until he returned to marry.

That had been hard for him to accept. Nevertheless, having her as his fiancée was what had gotten him through the war. Now he'd run off like a fool and hurt her. Sure, he cared about the fiddle. His grandpappy had made it and left it to him when he died. But Will cared about Iris far more than he did the fiddle.

He slowed as he passed the grange hall and then accelerated again, bumping along the gravel road, keeping his eyes fixed straight ahead. He hadn't told Iris about Nameless, because he'd wanted to pretend the year before he'd met her never happened. He wanted to forget he'd become engaged to Charlene Morrison and then went on the road with his band. He wanted to forget how, after the second week, her letters stopped even though he'd given her his exact itinerary and the address of each location.

But when he returned three months later, Charlene acted as if nothing had happened, told him her letters had been lost. But she was different. Distant. Distracted. Dodgy.

Will glanced in the rearview mirror at the cloud of dust behind him and then shifted his eyes ahead, gripping the steering wheel even tighter.

Soon after, Charlene moved to Nashville, and when Will visited her, it became obvious she'd been lying to him. Even though he hadn't figured out who she was seeing, he knew there was someone else.

He'd fled to Asheville Teachers College, brokenhearted, vowing to never return to Nameless, where everyone knew his heartache. His grandparents passed away while he was overseas. Only his uncle and aunt remained. The only reason he'd returned was to find Iris.

His only consolation now was that Charlene had remained in Nashville over the last five years, a fact his uncle had confirmed.

He'd never told Iris a word of what happened with Charlene. At the time, he figured he'd forgive and forget. And although he was sure he'd forgiven Charlene, he obviously didn't forget, because when Iris's letters stopped, he feared she had dumped him too. Other prisoners in the camp received letters from their loved ones, but not one letter arrived for Will.

He'd told Iris the POW camp wasn't that bad because he didn't want to think about it. Maybe if he didn't tell her how horrible it was, it would be easier to forget.

Will shuddered and slowed the car again. Then he pulled over to the side of the road and pressed his forehead against the steering wheel as the dust caught up with him and billowed around the car. He rolled up the window.

Could he trust Iris? She seemed genuinely happy to see him. But he'd thought the same thing about Charlene all those years ago. He couldn't go through that again.

After turning the car around, he rolled the window down again and headed back to the school. He needed to apologize. He needed to do better.

And yet, if he had no reason *not* to trust Iris—why did he feel so fearful?

Iris fought back tears as she tidied up the cottage. She closed the cupboard door, put the drawers back in the bureau, and made her bed. Then she stood in the middle of the room and prayed out loud. "Lord, I thought Will was dead—or that he dumped me. Then he shows up, only to drive away again." She shook her head. "It seems I was right not to marry him before he left. He didn't come back the same man."

Her mother had told Iris a time or two, or ten or twenty, that her father wasn't himself when he came back from the Great War. Iris had never wondered, until now, what had happened to him.

She turned toward the door and spotted something under the table. A plain silver cuff link. It hadn't been there before she left this morning. She picked it up and put it in her purse.

Had the thief left anything else?

She got down on her knees and looked under the bed. She couldn't see anything. She went through each of her drawers. There wasn't anything that didn't belong.

Finally, she grabbed her purse and headed out the door just as the Studebaker pulled back into the schoolyard.

She froze.

Will climbed out. "I'm sorry."

She tried to smile.

"Want a ride to Gainesboro?"

"That's about ten miles from here, right? At least, that's what Mr. Parker said."

"Right. That's where the sheriff's office is."

"That's not far." She squinted into the western sun. "Want to drive your car?"

He smiled. "Of course."

She handed him the key.

He went to the driver's side and then stopped. "What happened?"

"What do you mean?"

He stared at the side of the car.

She headed around to stand beside him. There was a scrape down the side of the car. Iris gasped and put her hands to her face. "Oh no. That must have happened today while I was in school."

He shook his head. "The fiddle's gone. The car's wrecked."

"The car can be repaired. And I'll find the fiddle."

He rubbed the side of his head and then pointed at her left hand. "Where's your ring?"

"Inside, in the bureau drawer. I took it off yesterday, on my way here. I didn't want people asking questions."

He stared at her as if he was trying to decide whether to believe her or not.

She stepped toward him. "Are you all right?"

"I think so," he said. "But maybe you should go to Gainesboro by yourself. The car's fine to drive."

"No." She reached for his arm. "I'm going to stay with you."

He shook his head. "I have a room…near the store. I haven't gotten my strength back completely. I should go rest." He tossed the key to the convertible at her.

She caught it.

"I'll stop by tomorrow," he said. "After school."

She reached for his arm. "Do you think I did something with your fiddle? That I wrecked your car? That there's some other reason I don't have your ring on my finger?"

"No," he answered. "I believe you. Someone around here took the fiddle, no doubt. And someone hit the car. Maybe the same person. We just need to figure out who." He waved and started walking away. Without turning around, he added, "And I understand not wanting to answer questions."

CHAPTER FOUR

Iris ran her hand along the scrape on the car. Who would have done such a thing? She examined the dirt. There were tire tracks, but she couldn't decipher what kind.

She pulled her scarf from her purse, tied it around her head, and then climbed into the car. She started the motor, backed into the schoolyard, and turned left onto the road. She passed the café, slowed for a chicken crossing the road, and then passed the store. At the junction, she turned north toward Gainesboro.

As she shifted into third gear, she leaned back in the seat, still tense from her interactions with Will. As she passed by a field of corn, the car began to pull to the left. She held the steering wheel steady, took her foot off the accelerator, and shifted into second and then first, pulling off the road as much as she could. She enjoyed driving the convertible, until she got the inevitable flat tire. She'd had at least twenty in the three years she'd been driving the car.

Just as she was tightening the spare, a Model T with a dent in the passenger door stopped, and an older woman with gray braids wrapped around her head leaned over, rolled down the window, and chuckled. "Looks like I got here just in time."

Iris stood and smiled. "I appreciate you stopping. If I didn't have a spare, I'd need a ride."

"So, everything's all right?"

"Yes, ma'am," Iris said. "The spare is on. I'll get the tire repaired in Gainesboro."

"There's a filling station on the outskirts of town."

"Thank you."

The woman smiled, and Iris gave her a wave. Soon she was back on the road. The pungent smell of wild garlic growing along the road kept her alert. Ancient oak trees, ones too big and gnarly for farmers to extract, dotted the fields. A stray dog darted under a fence and yapped at her tires. She accelerated and left him behind.

When she reached the edge of Gainesboro, Iris stopped at the filling station. As the attendant, Bert, fixed the flat, Iris said, "I'm looking for the sheriff's office. Is it right downtown?"

"Yes, ma'am," he said. "In the courthouse. You can't miss it. The sheriff's office is on the first floor. Use the side door."

"Thank you."

When she reached the Jackson County Courthouse—a yellow and white three-story building with a cupola on the top—she parked out front and then followed Bert's instructions to go to the side door. It was five thirty, and she guessed the front offices were closed. The sign by the door read Jackson County Sheriff, Robert Whitaker.

Iris opened the door and walked inside. A young man sat at the desk. "May I help you?"

"Yes, sir," Iris said. "I'm looking for Sheriff Whitaker. He's expecting me."

The man stood. "He just arrived. What's your name?"

"Iris Pitts. The new teacher in Nameless."

"All right. Hold on." He stepped away from his desk, into a hallway, and then into another room. A few minutes later he returned and said, "Go on back. First door on the right."

Iris followed the man's directions and knocked when she reached the door.

"Come on in."

She opened the door and stepped inside.

Sheriff Whitaker looked up over his glasses from the work on his desk. "Will didn't come with you?"

"No, sir," Iris said.

Sheriff Whitaker opened a ledger. "Tell me what happened, starting at the beginning."

Iris told him about having Will's fiddle in her possession, playing it the night before, and then hiding it under the bed in her cottage. "When I returned after teaching, the place had been ransacked. The cupboard doors were open, the bureau drawers pulled out, the bed stripped, and the fiddle gone." She pulled the cuff link from her purse. "I found this under the table."

Sheriff Whitaker reached for cuff link and examined it. "That's not going to help much. Did you find anything else?"

"Someone hit Will's car, the blue convertible, this afternoon too. There are tire tracks next to it."

"Can you prove the tracks weren't there before this afternoon?"

"I didn't notice them yesterday."

"We usually don't." He put the cuff link in an envelope and labeled it. Then he wrote in the ledger. When he finished, he met Iris's gaze. "Any suspects?"

"Will said half the town wanted his fiddle."

Sheriff Whitaker looked over his glasses at her. "Any suspects in particular?"

She lowered her voice. "I hesitate to say this because I certainly don't have any evidence…."

The sheriff took off his glasses. "But?"

"Judson Johnson."

Sheriff Whitaker groaned. "What's Judson done now?"

She told him about Judson's fiddle cracking the night before.

"I saw that," the sheriff said.

"At school today, Judson was insolent and left during the lunch hour and then again halfway through the afternoon. He told me he needed to get a job to buy a new fiddle."

"Well, that's not a crime."

Iris leaned back in her chair. "I'm not saying he committed the crime, but it might be worth questioning him."

"Do you think he sideswiped the car too?"

"I wouldn't know about that," Iris said.

"Do you think whoever scraped Will's car also stole the fiddle?"

She shrugged. "I have no idea."

"Well, whoever took the fiddle must have seen you at the grange hall last night."

"Most likely."

"All right," Sheriff Whitaker said. "Are you sure you can't think of anyone else in particular who might have taken the fiddle?"

Iris shook her head.

"What about Will McCrae?"

"Will?" Iris leaned toward the desk. "Why would Will steal his own fiddle? All he needed to do was ask for it. I've taken care of it for him since he left to go overseas, and I've been waiting and wanting to give it back to him."

"He might have his reasons not to ask for it." Sheriff Whitaker put his glasses on again and wrote some more. "You never know what a person might do, especially someone who's just returned from war."

By the time Iris arrived back in Nameless, she was famished but decided that before she ate she would drive around town to find the Studebaker Will had been driving. She wanted to know where he was staying. It didn't take long to find the car parked next to a two-story house behind the café. A sign hung over the door read NELLIE's BOARDINGHOUSE.

Iris returned to the cottage, lit the lamp, and started the coal stove. Then she cut up a potato and a sausage she'd brought from Memphis and fried them on the stovetop.

After she ate, she sat at the table and graded the students' math tests and maps of the US. She stared at Judson's for a long while. He might not like school, but he wasn't dumb. What had happened to make him so angry? Surely it was more than a cracked fiddle.

She went over her lesson plans for the next day and then readied herself for bed. Before she crawled between the sheets and under her quilt, she knelt beside the bed and clasped her hands together. She prayed for Will. "I don't know what he went through, but something's changed in him. I'm not going to hold it against him. Please show me what I can do to help him. Amen." She looked up at the ceiling for a moment and then dropped her head again. "Oh, and help me not to take personally what Judson Johnson does and how he treats me. I'm afraid he's hurting too."

She crawled into bed and stared at the ceiling for what seemed like hours. But when her alarm clock clanged at six, she struggled out of a sound sleep.

She woke thinking about Judson. What if he'd been working with someone else, someone who met him at the cottage? Perhaps that person accidentally scraped Will's car. Maybe Judson sold the fiddle to get money to fix his. Will's fiddle was too unique for Judson to use. It was too unique for anyone to use, at least around Nameless, Asheville, Memphis, and probably Nashville too.

She got dressed, cooked a couple of eggs for breakfast, grabbed another apple and her last biscuit for her lunch, collected her books and papers, and headed back across the schoolyard.

As she stepped into the schoolhouse, she silently prayed. *Lord, I'll be honest. I'd rather Judson Johnson doesn't show up—but if he does...* She wasn't even sure what to ask for. *Make him a different kid? Give me the perfect way to deal with him? Provide a miracle?*

Iris distributed the corrected assignments from the day before onto the students' desks. As she did, she said a prayer for each child, praying for Judson a second time.

At eight o'clock every student was in his or her seat—except for Judson. When she called his name, Marj called out, "Absent."

"I saw him fishing down by the creek," BJ said.

Iris didn't respond to that. "We'll start with math again today." She pointed to the board. "Grades one to three, there are problems for you on the board. Use your slates. Grades four to six, open your math books and do pages four to seven. Grades seven and eight, we'll meet in the back corner for your algebra lesson. Bring your books and slates."

The morning continued without incident. Everyone did their work as asked. After she'd completed the algebra lesson, she moved between the younger groups, helping with addition and subtraction, multiplication, and long division.

At lunchtime, the students again played baseball after they finished eating. Not long into their game, clouds gathered over the trees and the sky grew dark. A few minutes before it was time to go back inside, Marj—who'd just hit a home run—sauntered over to the steps and sat down beside Iris. She pointed to Will's car. "The talk of the town is that Will McCrae's in town. So why are you driving his car?"

"Does the whole town recognize Will's car?" Iris asked, astonished.

"Pretty much." Marj's freckles practically danced across her nose. "So why, if he's in town, do you have his car?"

"Because I was taking care of his car while he was overseas."

"You didn't do a very good job."

"Apparently not," Iris answered.

"And what about his fiddle? Why do you have that?"

Present tense. Marj didn't know the fiddle was stolen. "Same as the car. I was taking care of it for him."

"Why were you playing it?"

"He said I could. Just like he said I could drive his car." Iris hesitated a moment and asked, "Were you at the grange hall Monday night?"

"Of course," Marj said.

"Did you recognize the fiddle?"

"You bet I did."

"When was the last time you saw it?"

"Oh, five or six years ago. Will used to play here a lot. Everyone misses him and hopes he'll come back to stay."

Again, this mystery. Why hadn't Will ever mentioned Nameless? "So, six years later," Iris said, "you still remember Will, his music, and his fiddle?"

Marj folded her hands over knees, tugging her skirt down a little as she did. "With those hummingbirds and irises, it's hard to forget the fiddle. And he was the best musician who ever played in Nameless, which is saying a lot." She stole a look at Iris. "So, are you and Will sweethearts?"

Iris chuckled. "How old are you, Marj?"

"Fifteen. We'll be sixteen in January."

"We?"

"Judson and me."

That meant they would have been ten or so when Will was last in Nameless. "So, you are twins."

"That's right. I'm doing the eighth grade for the second time. I'm hoping you can give me some harder work than I did last year. Then maybe there'll be a bus next year to Gainesboro for high school and I can test to start as a sophomore."

"What about Judson? Is he doing eighth grade for the second time?"

She shook her head. "For the first time. He was out for a year when we were younger."

Just as Iris tried to craft her next question, the rain began. And then thunder crashed.

Iris jumped to her feet. "Students! In the school, now! BJ, grab the bat and ball."

Iris hoped Judson wasn't still down at the creek fishing. Regardless of how disruptive he was, she wished he was safe at the school, ready for the next lesson.

Chapter Five

The rain stopped by the time Iris had the students cleaning the schoolroom. At three o'clock they left, tiptoeing their way through the muddy schoolyard. As Iris told the students goodbye, she was thankful they were leaving and not coming and tracking mud all through the building. She guessed that would happen soon enough.

Iris went back to her desk to gather her things, expecting Mr. Parker or Will or both to come through the door. Fifteen minutes later, neither had appeared. She decided to go home. Both knew where to find her.

As she came out the front door, the sun slipped from behind a cloud. Hopefully, the mud would dry up soon. She walked down the steps and saw someone by Will's car. It was Marj, sitting on the bumper.

"Marj," Iris called out. "Do you need something?"

"Just to speak with you."

"All right." Iris picked her way carefully through the mud.

"You should go talk to my grannie about Judson."

"Does your grannie want to talk with me?"

"Of course."

"Could she come here?"

"Well, she could, but it would be better if you'd go there." Marj grinned. "You could give me a ride home, in Will McCrae's convertible."

Iris laughed. "I could."

"How about you bring his fiddle too?"

"How about I don't."

Marj crossed her arms and shrugged. "Suit yourself."

Iris wanted to meet the twins' grannie and see if she could broach the topic of Judson entering the cottage—unless Sheriff Whitaker had already stopped by to question Judson. Iris would have to see what kind of person their grandmother was before making such a judgment. Marj didn't seem to cater to Judson. Hopefully Grannie didn't either.

"I'll put these things away," Iris said. "And then I'll give you a ride home."

When Iris got to the cottage, her shoes were covered with mud. She guessed it wouldn't do any good to change them—a new pair would be covered with mud by the time she reached the car. She opened the door, slipped out of her shoes, and stepped into the room. She put her books and papers on the table and then grabbed two apples from the bag on the shelf.

As she turned back, Marj stuck her head in the door. "Nice place."

"Thank you." Iris held up one of the apples. "Want one?"

"Sure."

Iris tossed it to Marj, who caught it with a flourish.

"Let's go," Iris said. "Just make sure and scrape the mud off your shoes before you get in Will's car."

Marj directed Iris to go past the café and store and then turn right onto the highway toward Gainesboro. As she accelerated, Marj pointed ahead. "Who's that?"

A man wearing a suit was walking their way.

Iris slowed. "It's Will."

Marj hooted. "Will McCrae?"

"Yes," Iris said.

"This day just keeps getting better and better."

By the time Iris stopped, she could see Will's Studebaker up ahead on the opposite side of the road. His car must have broken down. "Need a ride?" she asked when he came up to the car. Perhaps he hadn't stood her up—maybe he was on his way to the school.

"Back into Nameless?"

"What's wrong?" Marj asked.

"Engine problems."

"My grannie might be able to help. Or at least give you a tow into town," Marj said. "We're just a mile up the road. Hop in."

"I don't know if I'll fit."

Marj scooted over. "Sure you will."

Iris inched over as far as she could as Will opened the door. Marj ended up so close that Iris wasn't sure she'd be able to shift. Once Will closed the door, Iris eased off the clutch and accelerated and then managed to shift into second.

Marj said, "I'm Marj Johnson."

"Nice to meet you. I'm Will McCrae."

"I know," she gushed. "I remember your car from when I was little. Judson remembers your fiddle."

Will sighed. "Sadly, the car is wrecked, and the fiddle's gone."

"The fiddle's gone!" Marj turned to Iris. "You wrecked his car *and* lost his fiddle?"

"I didn't wreck the car. Someone hit it. And the fiddle was stolen," Iris said. "Yesterday during school."

"Oh no," Marj said. "That's awful. Who do you think took it?"

"I don't know," Iris said, shifting around Marj's leg into third. "And I'm not pointing any fingers."

"But Judson would have had the opportunity when he stormed out of class." Marj groaned. "And the desire. He still talks about that fiddle."

"Do you think he might have taken it?" Iris ventured.

Marj frowned. "Honestly, anything is possible when it comes to Judson. I wouldn't be surprised at all." She pointed suddenly and shouted, "Turn left here!"

Iris pushed in the clutch and slammed the brake, swinging widely, barely making the turn. Will let out a low sound of protest.

"Sorry," Marj said. "Take the next right."

Iris turned again, bumping along a dirt road full of ruts. Ahead was a cabin and a barn.

"Park next to Grannie Mae's Model T."

It was the same Model T with the dent in the passenger door Iris had seen the evening before.

As Marj led the way to the cabin, Grannie Mae came down the porch steps, wiping her hands on the apron that she wore over a pair of overalls. "Where's Judson?" she called out.

"He didn't go to school again today," Marj answered. "BJ said he saw him fishing, but with that storm we had, I bet he didn't spend the whole day at the creek."

"That stinker." Grannie Mae stopped on the bottom stair. "Who do you have with you?"

"My teacher, Miss Pitts."

Iris stepped forward. "I met you yesterday. On the road. I'd just changed a flat."

Grannie Mae grinned. "That's right. You were driving Will McCrae's car." Grannie turned her attention to Will and squinted. "And who are you?"

Marj skipped forward. "Grannie, it's Will McCrae! You need to wear your glasses!"

"Will McCrae? Well, I'll be." She pointed past the three of them to Will's car. "I thought you'd sold your car to the new schoolmarm."

"No ma'am," Will said. "I'm only loaning it to her."

"Mr. McCrae needs help with his other car," Marj informed her. "It broke down on the highway."

"Really." Grannie Mae looked at Iris. "Y'all taking turns with car problems?"

"It seems that way," Iris said.

"And Miss Pitts needs to talk to you about Judson."

Grannie Mae wiped her hand across her forehead. "About him skipping school today?"

Marj nodded. "And Will McCrae's fiddle. Judson stole it."

"No," Iris said quickly. "We don't know that. I just have a couple of questions for him."

"Is that why Sheriff Whitaker was out here looking for him today?"

"The sheriff's after him too?" Marj put her hands on her hips.

Grannie Mae shrugged. "He said he wanted to ask him some questions." She turned to Iris. "Do you have any evidence Judson is involved in all of this?"

"No ma'am," Iris said. "He left school twice yesterday. I wondered if he saw anything."

"Put it this way," Marj said. "He knew Miss Pitts had the fiddle. The whole town did, after she played it at the hall Monday night."

Iris's face grew warm.

"And he had the opportunity to take it," Marj added, "because he can't keep himself at his desk like every other kid in the school. But I have to say, school is much better when he doesn't come at all."

"That's not true," Iris said. "I want Judson to come to school."

Marj harrumphed.

"That bad?" Grannie asked her.

"Worse. He was never as bad last year as he was yesterday."

Grannie Mae sighed. "I'll go check the barn to see if he's hiding in there." She turned to Will. "Then we'll go take a look at your car."

"Thank you, ma'am."

"Hopefully it'll be an easy fix," she muttered as she headed to the barn.

They watched her go, and then, when she was about halfway, Marj yelled, "Tell Judson that Will McCrae's here."

Iris doubted that would do much good if Judson had stolen the fiddle. But, just like that, Judson came ambling out of the barn.

Iris whispered, "Well, I'll be."

Grannie walked back to the other three and said, "Judson and I'll go with Will in case there's more wrong with the vehicle than an over-heated radiator. I have a few jugs of water in the Model T, so if that's what the problem is, it'll be more than enough. Then we'll come back for pie and coffee and have a chance to talk." She turned to Marj. "You put coffee on and cut the pie. Miss Iris, you can help Marj."

Iris followed Marj into the house. The living room was well furnished around a river rock fireplace, and the logs that made up the walls were hand hewn.

Marj motioned to Iris. "This way."

The kitchen was large. Pine cupboards lined three walls. There was a sink with a faucet and a wood range—all much nicer than Iris expected for a log cabin. At the grange hall, the guitarist mentioned that Judson's fiddle had been his father's. It seemed perhaps he was deceased, but Iris didn't feel she should ask Marj about him, nor about the children's mother. No one had mentioned her, or a grandfather either. Iris got the idea that it was just Grannie Mae and Judson and Marj.

"You can get the plates." Marj pointed to the cupboard to the left of the sink. "There's a tray above the stove. I'll start the coffee."

Iris grabbed the tray and then the plates. She opened the drawer to the left of the sink and found the forks. Then she checked to the right of the sink and found the mugs.

"You can get the chess pie from the springhouse," Marj said. "I made it last night." She motioned to the back door. "You'll see it."

Iris stepped out the back door. About thirty yards away was the springhouse on a knoll. Beyond it, downhill, was a pasture with goats. Stones lined the foundation of the little house. Iris opened the springhouse door. Inside, the spring was encased in more stones. As she stepped into the small area, the temperature dropped considerably. Shelves with jars of milk, cheeses, eggs, produce, and a chess pie lined the wall closest to the spring.

When Iris returned to the kitchen, she asked Marj, "Is the milk in the springhouse goats' milk?"

"That's right. Grannie raises goats and sells the milk. Plus, she makes cheese to sell."

Iris smiled. Being a city girl, she didn't know much about goats—except she'd heard they were a handful.

"Dish up the pie," Marj said. "And then place the plates on the tray."

Iris did as she was told.

The pot on the back of the stove began to percolate, filling the kitchen with the homey aroma of coffee.

Once it was done, Marj filled the mugs and grabbed three in one hand and two in the other.

Iris carried the tray out to the porch. They put the pie and coffee on the table and sat down. Between sips of coffee, they swatted flies.

"You can go ahead and ask me," Marj said.

"Ask you what?"

"What happened to our folks."

"Do you want to tell me?"

Marj held her mug close. "Do you want to know?"

Iris hesitated a moment and then said, "Yes. Yes, I do."

"Our mother died after I was born—Judson was born first. Grannie delivered us, right here in this cabin." Marj took a sip of coffee.

"I'm sorry."

Marj smiled a little. "I wish I could remember her. There's only one photo, and it's a little fuzzy."

Iris thought of her own father. She didn't even have a photo. She suspected her mother did at one time—several—but she probably destroyed them.

"Judson really hates still being in school," Marj said, "as you can tell. When he was twelve, he broke his leg working with the team of horses after Pa left. It was a bad break, and he missed another year. He loved playing basketball but couldn't anymore. He probably could now, if he tried." Marj took another drink of coffee. "Grannie won't let him drop out like he wants. He doesn't feel like he belongs."

Empathy filled Iris.

"As far as our daddy—" The sound of a car distracted Marj. She stood and stepped to the porch railing, leaning over it to see the driveway. "Oh, good. They're back." She shouted, "Wash up. The coffee's getting cold!"

"We didn't get dirty," Judson called back.

"You're always dirty," Marj shot back.

The three of them, including Judson, washed up at the outside pump and came to the porch shaking the water off their hands.

"Where's the car?" Iris asked.

"Back in Nameless," Will answered. "Grannie Mae towed it to Olly—he has a little repair place by the store."

After everyone sat down, Grannie Mae said, "I don't usually say a prayer before pie, but I feel compelled to. Let's bow our heads." She paused for a long moment while everyone obeyed, and then said a prayer of thanks. She ended with, "We need Your guidance, Lord. Every minute of every day." Then she added a hearty, "Amen."

Iris raised her head and opened her eyes.

"Let's eat," Grannie Mae said.

Judson wolfed down his piece in a few bites and then said, "I'm going to get my fiddle."

Something was different about Judson. He seemed younger than he had at the hall and at school. He seemed eager for once. Excited to share something. Willing to please.

Iris told Marj that the pie was delicious.

"Yes, it most certainly is," Will said. "And so is the coffee." He glanced from Marj to Grannie Mae. "I can't thank y'all enough for your help and hospitality."

Judson came bursting through the door, holding the fiddle to show the crack in the side of the instrument.

"Here it is."

Will stood. "I'm so sorry that happened."

Judson extended the fiddle and Will took it, turned it over, and examined the wood. "I think it can be repaired."

"Really?"

Will nodded. "I'm not certain, but it's worth a try."

"It was Pa's," Judson said.

Will met the young man's gaze. "Where's your pa now?"

"Gone."

In the awkward silence that followed, Iris waited to hear the rest of the story.

CHAPTER SIX

Grannie Mae put her cup down hard on the tray. "We have some questions for you, Judson. We just need answers—not reactions."

Judson placed his fiddle in the middle of the table and folded his hands.

"Go ahead," Grannie Mae said to Iris.

"I have something to tell you before I ask you a couple of questions. Please don't take offense."

Judson sat up straight and crossed his arms. "All right." He leaned back in his chair.

"Yesterday, sometime during the day while I was teaching, someone entered my home behind the school and took Will's fiddle."

He leaned forward. "And you think I took it?"

Marj blurted, "Did you take it?"

Judson stood. "I'm fixin' to come unhinged."

Grannie Mae grabbed the back of his overalls and pulled him back into his chair. "You can come unhinged later. Settle down and answer Miss Iris's questions." She nodded at Iris. "Go ahead."

"Did you see anyone lurking around the yard when you left the school?"

He shook his head.

"Did you see anyone enter the cottage?"

"No, ma'am."

"Did you see a vehicle in the yard? Did you see someone hit Will's car?"

He hesitated but then smirked. "I thought you did that."

"You noticed the scrape yesterday?"

"No, ma'am. I saw it today."

Grannie Mae began putting the dishes on the tray. "Let's search all of your hidey places, just to be sure."

Judson looked as if he might cry. "Grannie. Sheriff Whitaker found me down at the creek and already asked me about all of this."

"Well, I'm glad he questioned you. But we need to make sure. It's not that I think you did it. I don't. I want to prove that to all of us. And, because you haven't been honest about other things—like skipping school—the only way to prove your innocence is to take a look around."

"How about if I clean the dishes," Iris said, "while the rest of you look."

"All right." Grannie Mae stood. "Judson, do you want to go along with us or help Miss Iris in the kitchen?"

"I'll wait here."

"No, sir," Grannie Mae said. "Either with one of us or Miss Iris."

Judson grunted and stood. "I'll go with Will. We'll go through the house, including my room and Pa's. You and Marj can go through your own rooms."

Iris headed to the kitchen with the tray of dishes. She filled the large kettle on the back of the stove with water and turned on the burner. Then she found the soap.

She could hear Will and Judson down the hall, although she couldn't make out their words. Marj and Grannie Mae were looking together in another room.

The water grew hot, and Iris poured it in the pans. A few minutes later, as she finished drying the plates and mugs, Marj came into the room and said, "We're going out to the barn. Want to come with us?"

"Sure." Iris put the dish towel back on the hook and followed Marj and Grannie Mae out the door.

"I don't think Judson took it," Grannie Mae said.

Iris didn't think he did either but didn't say anything.

"Oh, he did," Marj said. "All he could talk about on Monday night on the way home was Will's fiddle and how 'that woman' must have stolen it."

Iris winced. No wonder Judson was so unsettled when she ended up being his new teacher.

When they reached the barn, Grannie Mae said, "You two look up in the loft. I'll start in the tack room and then check in the goat pen."

The goats were bleating, although Iris couldn't see them. She followed Marj up the ladder to the loft. They checked behind and between hay bales and in each corner of the loft. By the time they came back down the ladder, they were covered with hay.

"Find anything?" Grannie Mae asked.

"No," Marj said, "but he could have wedged it down between two bales of hay where we couldn't see."

"Possibly," Grannie Mae said.

Fiddle music started up, faint but sure.

Grannie Mae sighed. "Judson must have found your pa's other fiddle. Sounds as if they're out on the porch." She motioned toward the barn door. "I'm going to go check the shed. You two go on."

Judson was playing "Wild Rose." Marj and Iris stood at the bottom of the steps until he finished and then joined Judson and Will at the table.

Judson extended the bow to Will. "Would you take a turn?"

Will shook his head. "I haven't played since I left for overseas. Well, except for a violin I found in a chateau in the Ardennes."

"Did you keep it?"

"Absolutely not. I played 'The Rose of Tralee' on it and then put it back in its case. I hope it made it through the war. The chateau was cold and wet—the owners had long ago fled." Will paused a moment and then said, "Thank you for the offer, Judson. I'm hoping to be finding my own fiddle soon."

Iris thought it was time to take their leave. "Thank you for answering my questions, Judson. If you remember anything from yesterday, please let me or Sheriff Whitaker or Grannie Mae know immediately."

He gave her a curt nod.

Grannie Mae came toward the house. "Judson and Marj—time to do the milking."

Marj groaned.

"I'm coming," Judson said. He went into the house and came right back out, without the fiddle. Marj headed down the stairs. Judson darted past her, slapping her on the shoulder as he did. "You're it." He took off at a sprint for the barn with Marj running after him.

"We'd better get going," Iris said to Will.

"Glad we had this time together," Grannie Mae said.

Iris started down the stairs. "So am I."

Will followed. "Do you mind if I ask you a personal question? About Judson and Marj's pa?"

Grannie Mae wrinkled her nose. "I'm guessing you want to know what happened to him?"

Will nodded. "If you don't mind."

"Normandy is what happened." Grannie Mae sighed. "Earl signed up in '42, even though he was thirty-two. He shipped out to England, then was part of D-Day." She shook her head. "That was it. He was killed coming ashore."

Iris took a deep breath. She knew her students would have losses from the war, but the story still shocked her.

"Marj acts as if it didn't happen," Grannie Mae said. "But Judson hasn't been the same since."

"How tragic," Iris said. "Especially after the children lost their mother too."

Grannie Mae shook her head. "Is that what Marj told you?"

"Yes. Isn't it true?"

"Well, they did lose their mother, but she didn't die. That's what Marj tells people, even though she knows the truth. Their mama took off after the twins were born. It's easier for Marj to comprehend a mother dying than abandoning her babies."

Iris put her hand to her chest. Marj seemed so confident and, in many ways, older than her fifteen years. But she was still a hurt child. And so was Judson.

Will drove on the way back into town, pleased to be behind the wheel of his Bantam convertible again. Obviously, Iris had taken good care of the engine. It felt so normal to be driving and have her sitting next to him, just like old times.

With her scarf tied over her long chestnut hair, her dark eyes appeared even larger than usual. As she stared straight ahead, her profile toward him, he could smell her rose-scented lotion even with the top down. It was the most comforting smell in the world to him.

He glanced down at her hands, folded in her lap. She hadn't put his ring back on her finger. No doubt, she didn't want a slew of questions. Besides, depending on the school board's reaction, it could mean losing her job—at least by the time they married. His heart lurched. He hoped she still wanted to marry him. But he didn't dare bring it up, not after he'd reacted so badly the day before.

He longed to reach over and take her hand. To feel the warmth of her skin against his. To be reassured of her love. Did she still love him? If only she'd married him before he left for the war.

His thoughts shifted, with a jerk, to the men in his squad who had died, both those on the battlefield and those in the POW camp. Then he thought of Judson and Marj Johnson and their deceased father. His heart hurt for the twins.

Iris interrupted his thoughts. "Do you think Judson took the fiddle?"

"No." Will struggled to focus on the stolen fiddle. Yes, it was the matter at hand, but its importance paled in comparison to the death of Earl Johnson, to the deaths of so many.

"Who do you think stole it?" Iris asked.

Will was beginning to wonder if perhaps Charlene had something to do with the disappearance of the fiddle—perhaps as a joke or out of spite—but he wouldn't say that out loud. She lived in Nashville, and he had no reason to believe she was back in town.

Iris shifted in her seat to face him. "Are you all right?"

"Yes." He glanced at her and gave her a quick smile. "Why?"

"Because I asked who you thought stole your fiddle and you didn't answer."

"Oh."

She exhaled. "So, who do you think stole the fiddle?"

"I don't know," he finally answered, staring straight ahead.

He wasn't sure he was fit to be around people yet, especially not Iris. Maybe it had been a mistake to find her so soon—especially when he hadn't received any letters from her.

Had she really sent letters, as she'd said?

Iris turned her head and stared at the fields to the right of the road. He sensed she was frustrated with him.

Will kept driving without saying anything for several minutes. Finally, he asked, "So who hired you for the job?"

Iris faced him. "The school board president."

"Bernie O'Reilly?"

"No. Scott Parker. Do you know him?"

"I don't know a Scott Parker from Nameless. But I knew one in Asheville. He used to come to my gigs. He worked at the college."

Iris shook her head. "I don't think it's the same Scott Parker. I've never seen him before."

Will shrugged. "You're probably right."

"Back to the fiddle," Iris said. "I found a piece of evidence yesterday when I returned to my cottage but before I drove to Gainesboro."

"What did you find?"

"A silver cuff link. I gave it to Sheriff Whitaker."

"No one around here wears cuff links."

Iris pointed at his wrist. "You do."

Will chuckled. "But I have both of mine."

They rode in silence again, but then Iris started to sing. "In the far fields of India, 'mid war's dreadful thunders, Her voice was a solace and comfort to me.... I'm lonely tonight for the Rose of Tralee.... Yet 'twas not her beauty alone that won me; Oh no, 'twas the truth in her eyes ever dawning, That made me love Mary, The Rose of Tralee."

When she finished the song, Will didn't respond.

"Who were you thinking of when you played the song in the Ardennes?" Iris asked.

When he didn't answer, Iris said, "I hope you were thinking of me."

Will stared straight ahead. "Of course I was thinking of you. Who else would I be thinking of?"

Iris knew she'd been his Rose of Tralee. He'd played the song for her many times. If she'd agreed to marry him then, would things be so awkward now?

Honestly, he hadn't truly understood why she wouldn't marry him before he left. And when her letters stopped, he questioned her commitment. In fact, he was still questioning her commitment.

When they reached town, Iris said, "You should keep your car. You're going to need it. I won't be going anywhere."

"No, you keep it for now," he said. "Drop me off at the store. I'll call my uncle and ask him when he needs his car back."

Iris shook her head. "I'll drop you and the car off. There's no reason for me to keep it."

"You might need it," he said. "To go visit another one of your students' homes. I'd like you to have it, for now. Until I return the Studebaker to my uncle."

"All right, if you insist," Iris said. She pointed at the store as he rounded the curve. "I need to pick up some groceries."

❧ Chapter Seven ❧

It took a minute for Iris's eyes to adjust after she stepped into the store. An older woman stood behind the counter. There was a post office area in the near corner, and an iron stove, a table, and several chairs straight down the middle, toward the back. The floor was worn oak. The whole place smelled of coal oil and baking bread.

She turned down an aisle to the right, looking for oats. Will asked at the counter if he could use the phone, and Iris tried to focus on her shopping. Why was Will acting so strangely? Perhaps he was more upset about the fiddle than he let on.

She grabbed oats, eggs, a small bag of potatoes, a cabbage, a loaf of day-old bread, coffee, sugar, buttermilk, and a tin of ham, and then juggled the items as she headed to the counter.

Will had finished his call and was buying a chocolate bar. Once he was done, he waited while Iris purchased her groceries.

"So, you're the new schoolteacher," the woman said.

"Yes, ma'am. I'm Iris Pitts."

"Nice to meet you," the woman said. "I'm Lela Wilson. If you need anything, let me know. Postage stamps. Your rationing coupons. To make a phone call. Advice." Lela smiled, showing a few gaps in her teeth. "I won't charge you for that."

Iris laughed. "Thank you, Miss Lela. I'm sure I'll take you up on all those things." She handed over her rationing coupons for the ham, sugar, and coffee, and a ten-dollar bill for the rest.

Miss Lela gave her change and then began bagging the groceries. "You have a couple of letters already." She scooted the bag and potatoes across the counter. "I'll go get them."

She returned with two envelopes. One was from Iris's mother and the other from her neighbor in Memphis. "Thank you," Iris said, slipping the letters into her purse.

Will stepped forward and grabbed her groceries before she could and then dropped the chocolate bar in her bag.

"What are you doing?" Iris asked.

"I know how much you like chocolate." He smiled.

As they turned to go, Miss Lela said, "Will, I was surprised to see Paul in town on Monday."

Will pivoted back to the counter. "Paul was in town?"

She nodded.

Will moved toward the exit as he waved goodbye to Lela. "See you soon," he said.

"Take care," she replied.

On the way out the door, Iris asked, "Who is Paul?"

"My cousin."

"You never mentioned you have a cousin."

"No, I didn't," Will answered.

He practically marched to the convertible, put the groceries in the front seat, and then tipped his hat and said, "See you around."

"See me around?" Iris asked. "That's it? You're not going to tell me anything about your mysterious cousin?"

Will shook his head. "Nope."

Iris watched him go, baffled. Will had seemed so simple and straightforward before he went off to war. Now she couldn't figure him out. He was moody and unpredictable.

"Lord," she prayed as she drove home, "Will McCrae is driving me crazy."

She parked the car, grabbed her groceries and purse, and headed into the cottage. After she'd put the groceries away and scrambled a couple of eggs, she sat at the table and opened her letters.

Her mother's was full of complaints. She wished Iris had come back to Charleston instead of moving to some 'nameless' town. She'd postponed her upcoming wedding, again. *We've rescheduled for Christmastime*, she wrote, *when you can be here.* Iris had no desire to go to Charleston for Christmas. But what would she do? Stay in Nameless? She wouldn't have a car by then.

Have you heard from Will McCrae? If he shows up, don't trust him. Some men can deal with war, but most can't.

Iris folded the letter and slipped it back into the envelope. Her mother wasn't right about much, but perhaps she was right about men and war. Iris wasn't sure what the story was between her parents. Just that her father had come home in 1919 from Europe, she was born in 1920, and her parents divorced in 1921.

And that her mother had never once said anything positive about her father. According to her mother, he'd lived in Washington, DC, ever since he left Charleston after the divorce. Her mother seldom talked about her first marriage—she'd had one more since then, and now, at the age of forty-five, she would soon marry for the third time—but she did say once that she'd married rashly the first time. Iris was pretty sure she'd married rashly the second time too, and she had no idea about the third.

She opened the letter from her neighbor, Betty.

Just a short note to get this in the mail right away so it will get to you as soon as possible. You might know by now that Will McCrae showed up looking for you on Monday, soon after you left. I can't help but wonder what's going on. First my sister contacts me to let me know there's a teaching position in Nameless in case I know of anyone interested. Then Will McCrae appears, looking for you, and when I say you've left for Nameless, he says that's where his mother's family lived. He'd spent quite a bit of time there growing up. He seemed suspicious about you getting a job there—is he paranoid? Or is there something going on? I have to say it all seems a little suspicious to me too. Anyway, I hope you're doing all right. Write when you can and let me know. I hope everything's okay. Your friend, Betty

Iris read the letter a second time. What exactly did Betty's observations mean?

What was going on with Will? Why had he told Betty about his family in Nameless but not her? And why hadn't he ever mentioned his cousin?

Iris had followed him to Memphis when he voluntarily joined the army and was sent to Fort Pickering. She didn't bother looking for a teaching position but applied for a job at the ordnance plant. She hadn't hesitated in following Will. He was her everything—and yet although she said yes to his proposal, she refused to marry him before he left. The story of her parents' marriage haunted her. Her father's disappearance. Her mother's bitterness. She didn't want that to be her story.

She'd never shared her parents' story nor her own fears with Will. They'd both kept secrets from the other.

Her eyes fell on the chocolate bar in the middle of the table. *Dear Lord,* she prayed, *will we ever be honest with each other?*

Thursday morning, Judson didn't come to school again. Iris didn't bother to read his name. When she made eye contact with Marj, the girl simply shrugged. The day went smoothly—the students listened and did their lessons. During the lunch hour, BJ and Marj got into an argument about whether Marj slid into home safely. Not surprisingly, Marj won the argument, and her team—which included first-grader Hannah—won the game.

Iris read another chapter of *Five on a Treasure Island* after lunch. Several students fell asleep again, but Iris didn't mind. She knew most of them got up before dawn to do chores before they headed to school.

At the end of the day, the students cleaned their desks and swept. A few minutes after the last child left, there was a knock on the schoolhouse door, even though it was still open.

"Miss Pitts?" someone called out. "Are you here?"

"Yes, sir," she called back and headed toward the cloakroom. Before she reached it, Mr. Parker stepped into the schoolroom.

"Well, hello," she said.

He held his hat in his hands. "Two days late, I'm afraid."

"I was getting worried about you. I thought you'd at least stop by yesterday."

"I intended to. Tuesday, I was out in the north part of the county, checking in with a few of my clients. I was delayed, and it was dark by the time I finally got home. Then yesterday, the rain came through a leak in my office ceiling, and I had to move my files and paperwork. Thankfully a roofer was able to see to it today." He glanced around the room. "Are you off to a good start for the school year?"

"Mostly," Iris said. "Except for Judson Johnson. He skipped school yesterday. I went out to his house with Marj and thought we had an understanding. But he was absent again today."

"Did Marj say why?"

"No," Iris said. "She left before I had a chance to ask her."

"Well, Judson Johnson is a handful. He's a big kid. It's probably time for him to go to work, if Mae would only face reality and let him do it. It's better all around, for you and the other students, if he stops coming and gets on with his life."

"But he's smart and capable," Iris said. "If he stops now, he won't go on to high school."

"There are plenty of kids in these parts who don't go to high school. How many eighth graders do you have?"

"Five. Judson, BJ, Marj, Temperance, and Erasmus."

"Marj and BJ will go to high school for sure," Mr. Parker said. "I'd be shocked if any of the others do. And that's fine. There's no need for them too. Mae needs help on the farm. Judson can help her and another nearby farmer too. Temperance will likely be married by the time she's sixteen. Erasmus will probably go to Michigan where his brother is and get a job." He shifted his hat from his right hand to his left. "It'll all work out."

Iris didn't respond. Wasn't the goal to get them all to high school and then for them to graduate? That's what she thought she was working for, starting with the first graders.

"Well," Mr. Parker said, "I should get going."

"I'll walk you out." Iris tried to think of exactly what she wanted to ask him.

As they reached the cloakroom, she said, "I've been wondering. Was it purely a coincidence that I found out about the job, or is there more to it than that?"

Mr. Parker stepped aside so Iris could step through the front door. "Why do you—"

A man was walking across the schoolyard. It was Will.

"Will McCrae?" Mr. Parker hesitated a moment, glanced at Iris, and then hurried down the steps.

Iris stayed on the top step.

"I heard you were in town," Mr. Parker said. "So good to see you back in the States, safe and sound."

"Scott." Will increased his stride. "I had no idea back in Asheville that you had a connection to Nameless."

The two shook hands, and then Mr. Parker said, "I grew up here. Moved back a couple of years ago. I had no idea you had a connection here either, until our new schoolteacher stepped onto the stage at the grange hall with your fiddle."

Will sighed. "Was it that obvious it was my fiddle?"

"Absolutely. All around me people were saying, 'That's Will's fiddle. Is he back?' That's when I found out your grandparents were Colin and Maude Little."

"Well, isn't that something." Will glanced up at Iris. "Do you realize that Iris was in Asheville when we were both there?"

"No." Mr. Parker turned to Iris. "You were in Asheville?"

"Yes." She started down the steps. "As a student at the teachers college. That's where I met Will. He gave me fiddle lessons."

Mr. Parker smiled at Will. "Well, you're certainly a good music instructor. Iris gave quite a performance at the grange hall."

"She'd had years of violin lessons—she was already quite skilled. I just taught her to enjoy our music." Will smiled broadly, his old smile that used to make Iris's heart melt. Now it made her heart ache as she remembered how he used to be.

"So," Mr. Parker said to Will, "now that you're back, do you have the fiddle?"

"No." Iris joined the two men.

Mr. Parker addressed Will. "You gave it to Miss Pitts?"

"Not exactly." Will paused a moment and then said, "The fiddle is missing. Someone took it from Iris's cottage."

"How awful." Mr. Parker turned to Iris. "Have you reported it as a theft?"

"Yes. I drove to Gainesboro and spoke with Sheriff Whitaker on Tuesday, late afternoon."

"Any suspects?"

"Not really," Iris answered.

"If you see the fiddle around, would you let one of us know?" Will asked. "I'll be leaving soon, but I'm staying at the boarding-house for a few more days."

"Absolutely," Mr. Parker said. "I hope to hear you play it again."

"I would like that too," Will answered.

Iris stared at Mr. Parker. He knew Will. He saw the fiddle Monday evening. He'd hired her. Maybe all of that was coincidental. But he hadn't stopped by the school like he said he would. What exactly was Mr. Parker doing on Tuesday afternoon when the fiddle was stolen?

"I'd best get going," Mr. Parker said. "I hope to see both of you soon. Miss Pitts, be sure to let me know if you need anything." He put his hat on. "Good day."

"Goodbye," Iris said to Mr. Parker as Will tipped his hat.

Mr. Parker walked toward his Oldsmobile, and Will said to Iris, "I wanted to let you know that Olly fixed the Studebaker and can look at the damage to the convertible tomorrow. I thought I'd drive it over there now, if that's all right. If you need to go anywhere, come over to the boardinghouse. I'm in the upstairs room with the view of the school. I'll give you a ride."

"Of course it's all right," Iris sputtered. "It's your car. I'll pay for the repair."

"There's no need for that."

"Yes, there is. It was in my possession when it was hit."

Will exhaled. "We'll talk about it later."

Both Iris and Will watched as Mr. Parker started his car. They waved at him, and he smiled and waved back.

Iris turned to Will, her back to the highway. "Don't you think," she said, "that Mr. Parker would have remembered I went to the teachers college in Asheville? I sent him my credentials."

"Maybe he didn't read them."

"Then why did he hire me?"

"It does seem odd," Will said.

"You know what else is odd?"

It was Will's turn to sputter, "No, I don't."

Iris crossed her arms. "That you never told me anything about your grandparents, Colin and Maude Little, or your time here in Nameless."

"Like I said before, I never had any reason to. My mother grew up here but married my father and moved to Nashville, where I was born. We came to visit my grandparents in Nameless a few times a year. I've played my fiddle enough at the Fall Fiddle Festival and events like that, so people have come to know me."

"And know your fiddle?"

"Oh, they knew the fiddle long before I owned it."

"How's that?"

"It belonged to my grandpappy. He's the one who made it, who carved the hummingbirds and irises into the back, when he was a young man. He made a lot of the fiddles that people in these parts own, but nothing like his," Will said. "Now, will you get the key? I need to get the car over to Olly so he can get started on it."

"All right." Iris started toward her cottage. She'd never known anyone as well as she'd known Will before he went off to the war, and she'd never trusted anyone the way she'd trusted him. Now she wondered if she'd ever truly known him. Why hadn't he told her about his family and about Nameless?

Chapter Eight

Iris spent the evening grading papers and adjusting the lessons for the next day—and thinking about Will, as much as she didn't want to. Then she thought about Mr. Parker. She needed answers from him. But how could she ask the questions without sounding accusatory? Maybe she should get Will to question him.

The next morning, Judson came to school and behaved. He followed directions. He didn't poke BJ or Marj. When she split the students into groups to study the state capitals, Judson led his group with patience, teaching the younger children. Obviously, he knew the material and seemed to enjoy sharing it. But at noon, when the other children grabbed their lunch buckets, Judson headed out the door and through the schoolyard toward the road.

Iris watched him go until Marj stepped to her side. "My brother is such a drip. He didn't used to be this way. He used to be reliable and kind." She took a step down the stairs. "Oh well." She ran the rest of the way down, the baseball bat held over her head.

At the end of the day, after the children left, a wave of loneliness swept over Iris. She enjoyed the students—the learning and the laughter. But once they were gone, all she had to look forward to was an evening alone.

Except today, she needed to go talk to Mr. Parker at his insurance office in town.

She couldn't rely on Will to question Mr. Parker. She needed to bite the bullet and do it herself.

The afternoon was hot and humid, with darkening clouds above. She walked to the road. Before long she came to Olly's shed next to the store. The convertible was parked outside, and Will stood next to it.

She crossed the road to the insurance office and tried the door. It was locked. She knocked, but no one answered. As she turned to leave, Mr. Parker drove up and parked his Oldsmobile in the driveway next to the building. He waved and climbed from the car. "Miss Pitts," he called out. "Is everything all right?"

"Yes, sir. I just have a few questions for you."

"All right. Let me unlock the door, and we can sit down to chat."

A few minutes later they were seated in two comfortable chairs beside his desk. The office was small but appealing with artwork on the walls and certificates above the desk.

"Before you ask me your question, I need to apologize," Mr. Parker said.

Iris cocked her head. "Oh?"

"Yes, ma'am. I knew that you'd graduated from the Asheville Teachers College, but I'd forgotten. I've had a lot on my mind the last month, between my work, running the school board, and some other volunteer work I'm doing."

Iris smiled. "I understand. It's been a crazy time, hasn't it?"

"Yes, indeed. A crazy four years, for certain."

"What other volunteer work do you do?" Iris asked.

"I'm on a board that sees to the needs of Great War veterans—World War I, I mean. I have a hard time getting used to the term."

"Why are you on the board?"

"I'm a veteran," he said. "I'm concerned about my fellow soldiers who haven't fared as well as I have."

"Interesting…" She thought of her father.

"How is Will doing?" Mr. Parker asked. "I heard he was captured before the war ended."

"He was, although he hasn't talked about it much. He said the camp wasn't too bad."

Mr. Parker's eyes filled with concern. "Does he seem different? On edge?"

Iris paused for a moment. "He definitely seems different. I'm not quite sure he's the same man he was."

Mr. Parker tilted his head. "I've heard others say that too. His being in a POW camp will have affected him in ways we can't imagine. And I would think that his fiddle being missing isn't helping."

"We do need to find that fiddle," she said.

"I agree." Mr. Parker smiled.

"Speaking of finding the fiddle, do you mind if I ask you a few questions?"

He paused a moment and then laughed. "Am I on your list of suspects?"

"It's more about your connection to Will," Iris said. "You knew him and his music from Asheville. You recognized his fiddle on Monday evening. But I can't figure out if you hiring me was coincidental or orchestrated."

He chuckled again. "I told several people I know we needed a new teacher. Someone in Memphis heard about it and then told you, right?"

She nodded.

Clearly, he wasn't feeling defensive—or if he was, he managed to hide it. "Ask me whatever else you'd like."

"Where were you on Tuesday afternoon?"

"I was out near Bloomington Springs at the Lambert farm. I planned to leave by two, to arrive in Nameless by the time school ended. But Old Mister Lambert was having chest pains, so I loaded him into my car and drove him to Gainesboro to the doctor. I called the store and asked Lela to get a message to you, but obviously she didn't. She probably got busy and forgot."

Iris paused a moment and then asked, "Then why didn't you stop by on Wednesday after school?"

"I already had a meeting planned in Nashville that day, all day."

Iris didn't respond.

"It was another veterans' meeting," Mr. Parker said. "We're trying to think ahead to the needs of soldiers coming home from Europe and soon from the South Pacific, and not just the ones who are hospitalized. Sometimes the injuries aren't obvious."

"You're a busy man," Iris said.

"I am. But it's all work I want to do." He stood, went to his desk, wrote on a piece of paper, and extended it to her. "Go talk with Mr. Lambert. Hugh Lambert. He'll tell you I was with him. Call the doctor in Gainesboro if you'd like. I wrote down his name. And you can call the last name on the list. It's one of the board members of the organization we're trying to get started in Nashville."

Iris took the piece of paper. "Thank you."

"I don't resent you asking questions," Mr. Parker said. "In fact, I credit your inquisitiveness. It pleases me to have a teacher with the confidence and thinking skills that you have. I'll keep my eye out for the fiddle, of course."

Iris stood. "I think it's wonderful that you want to help men like Will."

"I hope you can give him some grace," Mr. Parker said. "We have no idea what he went through during the war, nor do we know what other factors may have influenced him. Give this some time. Hopefully he'll come around, whether or not the fiddle is found." He clasped his hands together. "Anything else I can help you with?"

"If you did somehow target me for the job, did it have something to do with Will?"

"Absolutely not." For the first time, Mr. Parker seemed agitated with her questions. He lowered his voice, "I enjoyed Will's music when I lived in Asheville. But I had no idea he had connections to Nameless, I can assure you."

Will stood in front of Olly's garage under the sign that read, Automotive Repair, Horseshoeing, and Wagon Repair and watched Iris cross the road from the insurance company office.

"Good afternoon," she called out.

"Hello." Will tipped his hat and then introduced Iris to Olly, who held a mallet in his hands. The convertible was parked to his left, in front of Olly's ramshackle shop.

"Pleased to meet you." Olly gestured to the car with his mallet. "Good news. The frame of the car wasn't damaged—and the metal wasn't creased too badly. I think I can pound the dent out and then repaint."

"That is good news," Iris said. "Can you tell what color the vehicle that hit the convertible was?"

Will crossed his arms. Why hadn't he thought to ask about that? Or look himself.

"Another shade of blue," Olly answered. "Pretty close in color to the Bantam."

"Do you know of any vehicles around painted that color?" Iris asked.

He shook his head. "Nothing comes to mind."

Will nodded toward the insurance office. "Any luck talking with Scott?"

"Yes. That's why I stopped by. Do you have time to drive me out to Hugh Lambert's place, out by Bloomington Springs?"

"I could do that," Will answered, pleased for a reason to spend time with Iris. "Now?"

"Yes, please."

They walked the half block to where the Studebaker was parked and then drove east, past the grange hall and then up and down hill after hill after hill. "Some people call this area the Switzerland of Tennessee," Will said.

"I can see why," Iris said. "Although I've never been to Switzerland."

"I haven't been to Switzerland either," Will said, "but I saw the Alps."

"You did?"

"Yes, in Eastern France, after I was released. It was a sort of roundabout way back to England."

"What were they like?"

"Really big. Enormous." He glanced out the window. "Much, much bigger than these hills."

"Do you want to go back?"

He winced. "To Europe?"

"I'm sorry."

"No need to be sorry. Ask me in a few years. I can't imagine going back now." He tried to think of something else to talk about, but his mind seemed to be blank.

Finally, he said, "What reason would Scott Parker have had to take the fiddle? Certainly not a financial one."

Iris nodded. "I agree he wouldn't have taken it to sell it. If he did take it, I'm guessing it would be as a collector's item, since he wouldn't be able to show it to anyone else, at least not around here."

Will was pretty sure Scott Parker hadn't taken the fiddle, but he understood that Iris wanted to know—for sure—what he was up to on Tuesday afternoon.

They rode in silence until Iris said, "These are Mr. Parker's directions." She read, "Turn left on Shady Grove Road, right before Flynn Creek. It's the last farm on the left."

"All right. We're almost there."

Will knew exactly where to turn, although the road was more deeply rutted than he remembered from when he was a teenager driving the back roads in Grandpappy's old truck. Iris braced herself with her feet, trying not to bounce around.

"Sorry," he said.

She laughed. "I've never been on a road like this before."

He smiled. "At least there's a road and we don't have to go by boat."

She laughed again. "That would have been fun too." He'd forgotten how easygoing she was—how much she liked a new experience. That was how she'd been with his music, with both learning to play it and to love it.

Ahead was a house that had once been painted white. Now it was gray. The barn was a dull red. A mangy dog ran alongside the Studebaker. "Can these folks even afford insurance?" Iris asked.

"Maybe not. Mr. Parker was most likely making a social call, hoping if Mr. Lambert did choose to buy insurance at some point, he'd become a client." Will parked to the left of the house. A middle-aged man came out on the porch. He pushed his hat higher on his head and squinted.

Will opened his door as the man called the dog. Then Will came around and opened Iris's door.

"Howdy," the man called out. "What do you need?"

"We're looking for Mr. Lambert," Will called back.

"That would be me." The man shaded his eyes. "What do you want?"

"Mr. Scott Parker sent us," Iris told him.

"To check on me? Wasn't that kind. He saved my life the other day. I'd be feeding the worms by now if it wasn't for him. The doc said I have angina and gave me nitroglycerin."

"Is that right?" Will asked as he reached the bottom of the stairs.

"Well, I'll be," Mr. Lambert said. "Are you Colin Little's grandson? Will...? Oh, there I've gone and lost your last name. I blame it on almost dying Tuesday afternoon."

Will grinned. Either Mr. Parker really had saved Mr. Lambert's life or they were both incredible liars. "I'm Will McCrae. And yes, I'm Colin and Maude Little's grandson." He reached the porch and extended his hand. "It's a delight to meet you, Mr. Lambert. This is my friend, Miss Iris Pitts. She's the new schoolteacher in Nameless."

"McCrae. That's the name I was looking for. I used to listen to you play when you were a boy." He nodded to Iris. "Nice to meet you, young lady. Scott Parker had nothing but good things to say about you."

"Thank you," Iris said. "I imagine you need to rest after being ill on Tuesday. We don't want to keep you."

Mr. Lambert rubbed the back of his neck. "But you needed something from me."

"Just confirmation that Mr. Parker was out this way on Tuesday," Will said. "He sent us on a sort of treasure hunt."

"Oh."

"Thank you," Iris said. "We appreciate your help."

"I hope to hear you play sometime soon," Mr. Lambert said as he stepped back to the door of the house.

"I hope for that too," Will replied. He put his hand on Iris's back as they headed down the steps, relieved—but not surprised—that Scott Parker's alibi was legitimate.

When they reached the car, Iris said, "If neither Judson nor Mr. Parker took the fiddle, who did?"

Will pulled onto the dirt road. "I'm not sure, but I'll put more thought into it."

"Do you have an idea?"

Will accelerated. "I'm not sure."

"Is there something you're not telling me?"

Will stared straight ahead and didn't answer. He didn't want to keep thinking about Charlene, not when Iris was beside him. Was he thinking about Charlene because she had something to do with his missing fiddle? Or was he thinking about her because Iris was in the process of dumping him too?

Finally, Iris said, "Thank you for taking me out to see Mr. Lambert. I'll cross Mr. Parker off my list of suspects."

Will simply nodded his head, afraid if he spoke his voice would give away his fear—and she'd prod him for an answer to her question.

The next morning, Iris felt lonelier than she had in years, since before she'd met Will in Asheville. Even when he was overseas, she didn't feel like this. Yes, Will was gone then, but she looked forward to him coming home. Then when the letters stopped, she still hoped he would come home. But here he was, home, and she'd never felt lonelier.

The rift between them was unbearable. Iris thought of what Mr. Parker said about giving Will grace—about not knowing what he went through during the war or what else might contribute to his doubt of her. But what if his experience had truly changed him? Could their relationship survive?

First, she needed to find the fiddle. Then she would figure out what to do next. She spent the morning grading papers and writing lesson plans for the next week. She had expected teaching multiple grades would be difficult, but she was enjoying it more than she thought she would. The older students were a help with the younger ones, and it was a benefit that she enjoyed arithmetic. Her music education, she was sure, helped inspire her love of math. Whole notes, half notes, quarter notes, and eighth notes all gave her an early understanding of fractions. The rest of it, including geometry and algebra, came easily too.

After lunch she decided to go for a walk down by the creek. The day was cool, and the mountain mist still hung in the treetops. She thought more about what Mr. Parker said about Will, which made her think of her father. Her mother always made it sound as if her father had been no good, but what if his problems, as unspecified as her mother had been about them, were because of his experiences as a soldier and not a character defect, as her mother had always implied?

Iris reached the creek and found a boulder to sit on under a willow tree. She heard a rustling and leaned forward. Downstream was a figure, casting a line into the creek. It was Judson, whistling "Medley of Reels." He seemed settled as he fished. Not fidgety or restless as he was in school. She wondered if he used to fish with his father.

Empathy filled her. Her father hadn't passed away, but she'd lost him before she ever had a chance to know him. What had been his story? What was Will's story?

She climbed down from the boulder and walked back into town and then to the store. Lela was at the counter. "What do you need, hon?" she asked.

"To make a collect call."

Lela nodded to the telephone on the wall. "Help yourself."

Iris dialed the operator and gave her the Charleston number and then waited, thinking of the call placed to probably Knoxville, and then Charleston. Finally, the operator called her back. "The charges have been accepted."

"Mama?" Iris said.

"I'm here, darlin'. Everything all right?"

"Yes, I'm fine."

"You gave me a fright."

"I'm sorry. School is going well. I got your letter and will write you back this afternoon. I just have a question I want to ask you."

"All right."

"It's about Daddy."

Her mother didn't respond, which felt icy over the phone.

"Was he really very changed when he came back from Europe after the Great War?"

Instead of answering, she asked, "Has Will come home yet?"

"Yes."

"Is he a broken man?"

"No."

"Then why are you calling?"

"Because he's…different."

"What a relief you didn't marry him." Mama sighed. "At least you can start fresh."

Iris bristled. She shouldn't have expected her mother to be helpful. "Tell me about Daddy when he came home."

"The problem with your father was that I didn't know him well enough when I agreed to marry him. He had a few character flaws that I knew nothing about."

"Like what?"

"He was quick to anger. He worried about everything. He couldn't hold a job."

"Did he have shell shock?"

"You sound like his mother," Mama said. "She used that as an excuse for him."

"The anger, worry, and unsettledness—those could all be because of shell shock."

"Even if they were, a stronger man would have overcome those things."

Iris hesitated. It wouldn't do any good to argue about her father. "Do you have an address for him?"

"Don't tell me you want to see him."

"Yes, I do. I want to see him."

"After he abandoned you? After he treated me so badly?"

"Wanting to see him has nothing to do with all of that. I never had the chance to know him. I've been thinking about him a lot."

"No," Mama said. "I have no idea where he's living now. He kept in touch with your grandmother, and she'd give me updates—unsolicited ones—periodically. Since she passed, I have no idea."

"All right. Thank you for the information."

"I hated the idea that you were in that town without a name, but now I'm rather relieved. At least you won't have Will close by to try to win you back."

"He is close by—he's in Nameless right now too."

Someone clearing their throat caught Iris's attention, and she turned away from the wall.

Will stood a few feet away.

"I've got to go, Mama. Thank you for accepting my call. I'll send you some money to cover it."

"Wait. Iris—"

"Bye."

Iris hung up as her face grew warm. "I was talking to my mother."

Will nodded.

Iris gave him a little wave, ducked around the corner and out the front door of the store, and headed to the school.

"Iris!"

She turned.

Will jogged after her.

"Wait!"

Chapter Nine

Iris kept walking as she swiped away one tear and then another. As footsteps fell behind her, she began to run. She didn't want to speak with Will, not while she was crying.

"Iris!"

She could hear his footsteps right behind her. She stopped, swiping both index fingers under her eyes.

"I won't keep following you," Will said. "I just have one question. Would you go to church with me tomorrow?"

Without hesitating, she answered, "Yes."

"I'll stop by your place at nine forty-five. See you then. There's a potluck afterward, but we don't need to go to that. I just want to go to church."

"We can go. I'll make apple stack cake." It was Will's favorite.

Maybe it wasn't anymore, because he simply said, "All right." He turned and headed back to the store. His pants and shirt hung loose on him, even though they were new.

As she entered the schoolyard, she wondered what it would be like to sit by Will in church again. They'd gone to the same church in both Asheville and Memphis and never missed a Sunday. She loved hearing the mix of his baritone with her alto. And although Will never held her hand or even put his arm around her while they were in church, having him next to her was a combination of comfort and anticipation.

Her mother had never been a warm person. Iris received far more hugs from her paternal grandmother than Mama, and losing Nana when she was a sophomore in high school had been devastating. Nana was the one who had taken her to church. Nana was the one who taught her to pray.

Sadly, Nana never talked much about Iris's father, and Iris had been afraid to ask about him, fearing it would make Mama angry if she found out.

Oh, how she wished she could call Nana now and ask her about Daddy, about the impact the war had on him. Now Iris had no connection at all to her father. Too much time had passed.

Iris opened the door to her cottage and started the fire in the stove. Then she pulled out the ingredients for the cake and put them on the table. Flour, sugar, salt, butter, baking soda and powder, shortening, eggs, buttermilk, and dried apples. First, she chopped the dried apples and started them boiling in her Dutch oven. Then she mixed the cake batter. Once it was done, she poured half into her three cake pans and baked the cakes for ten minutes. Then she emptied the pans and repeated the process. While the cakes baked, she made the filling, adding sugar, cinnamon, and nutmeg to the cooked apples.

She thought about Will and his fiddle as she worked. She hadn't heard from Sheriff Whitaker. Wouldn't he have contacted her if he had found anything? She imagined the more time that passed, the less likely the fiddle would be found. She needed to call him.

There was no evidence Judson took the fiddle. Nor any evidence that Mr. Parker took it. Who else who'd seen the fiddle on Monday evening might be a suspect?

When everything had cooled, Iris spread the apple filling on the first layer of cake and then the next and the next and the next. When she finished, she sifted confectioners' sugar over the top and sides.

Perhaps tomorrow at church and the potluck she could pinpoint people she recognized from Monday night. Perhaps she could come up with a few more leads.

The next morning Will arrived at nine forty-five on the dot, announcing his arrival with a knock on the door. Iris wore her navy-blue Kitty Foyle dress again. She held her cake carrier in one hand and in the other a church fan her grandmother had given her on an especially hot Sunday in Charleston. The morning was already warm.

"It's not far." Will took the cake carrier from her. "I thought we could walk."

"All right," Iris said.

After they started out Will asked, "How are you doing today?"

"Fine. How about you?"

"Good," Will said. They walked in silence until he said, "I overheard part of your conversation with your mother yesterday. I wasn't eavesdropping, not intentionally."

"I shouldn't have been talking about private things in a public place."

Will smiled. "That's hard to do around here."

They walked in silence the rest of the way.

Fifteen minutes later, they'd found seats inside the simple church. The first hymn they sang was "Farther Along." "Farther along we'll know all about it, Farther along we'll understand why, Cheer up, my brother, live in the sunshine, We'll understand it all by and by."

Iris wondered who chose the music for the day. Was the song to mark the end of the war, the surrender document having just been signed the week before? Or to mark all the people who'd been lost?

She thought of her relationship with Will. She stole a glance at him. Would she ever understand why he was acting so strangely? His lips were moving, but she could hardly hear him. He wasn't singing with the gusto he used to. She wondered if his fiddle playing would suffer also.

Her mind wandered during the sermon. The closing hymn, "Rock of Ages," brought her back to the present. "Rock of Ages, cleft for, let me hide myself in thee…"

Nana used to say that life was both beautiful and tragic and that the only place you could put your trust was in the Lord. Iris had tried to do that over and over throughout her childhood and throughout the war too. She vowed to continue trusting the Lord as best she could.

When the service ended an older woman approached them. "Will McCrae! You're home."

He gave her a hug. "Miss Shirley," he said. "It's good to see you."

"Are you coming to the potluck? We can catch up then."

"Yes," Will said, holding up the cake carrier.

"Oh good," Miss Shirley said. "Did you bring plates and silverware?"

Iris's face grew even warmer than it had been. She'd forgotten. "I'll go back to my place and get some."

"Don't bother," Miss Shirley said. "I have extras."

"Thank you." Iris smiled at her. "We've been looking forward to it." She was anxious to get a closer look at the townspeople.

Will and Iris walked with Miss Shirley to her car. Then Iris carried the cake and Will carried Miss Shirley's basket to the churchyard, where several tables were set up for the food. Once Miss Shirley had unloaded her dish of scalloped potatoes, a pan of ham slices, and a pan of greens, she handed a blanket to Iris and said, "Go spread that on the ground under the maple tree. We'll join you in just a minute."

Iris did as the woman said and then glanced around. She saw Grannie Mae, Judson, and Marj and gave them a wave. Grannie Mae and Marj waved back while Judson stared right through her. She saw BJ talking with a girl who appeared to be a couple of years older than he was.

She spotted a couple of her younger students, including Hannah, who ran over and gave her a hug.

All the while, Miss Shirley and Will were deep in conversation. Clearly, they knew each other well. A couple of minutes later the two joined her. A moment later a woman came toward them. She wore her auburn hair in a twist at the nape of her neck, red lipstick, and a bright yellow dress. She looked like a glamorous model. Or an actress.

Wait. She was the woman dancing with the man who reminded Iris of Will last Monday evening.

"Oh my!" the woman shouted. "If it isn't Will McCrae. I didn't know if you were dead or alive."

"Hello, Charlene." His voice was guarded. "I'm very much alive." He turned to Iris. "I'd like you to meet Iris Pitts. Iris, this is Charlene."

"Pleased to meet you," Iris said to Charlene.

"Likewise." Charlene looked Iris up and down. She didn't acknowledge that she recognized Iris, nor did Iris indicate she remembered Charlene.

Charlene reached over and tapped Will's arm. "Looks as if Mother roped you into the church potluck."

"Are you staying?" Will asked.

"No. I'm on my way to Nashville for a couple of days. I need Mother's car."

"How will I get home?" Miss Shirley asked.

"I'll give you a ride," Will said. "My car is just over at the boardinghouse." He turned back to Charlene. "Are you living here now?"

"Oh no," she said, "I'm just here helping Mother pack. She's selling the place and moving to Nashville with me."

Miss Shirley shook her head. "And I'm not happy about it. Charlene seems to think I'm not capable of caring for myself."

Charlene patted her mother on the shoulder. "You know that's not true. I just hate to have you all the way out here on your own." She stuck out her hand. "I need your car key. And I'll see you by Tuesday afternoon. I'll bring more boxes."

Miss Shirley opened her purse, pulled out the key, and handed it to Charlene.

Charlene took it as she said, "Goodbye!" to Will and Iris.

A minute later, the pastor said a blessing for the food. After everyone called out "Amen," Miss Shirley handed a plate to Will and one to Iris.

After Will and Iris dished up their food and were back on the blanket, Iris searched for Miss Shirley. She was talking with Grannie Mae by the far table.

"So," Iris asked, "who exactly are Charlene and Miss Shirley?"

"Mother and daughter," Will answered.

"I gathered that. Who are they, exactly, to you?"

"People I used to know."

"It seems you knew—know—them very well."

"I did."

"And yet you never mentioned them to me."

When he didn't answer her, she added, "Reminds me of you never mentioning Nameless before either. Would there be a connection?"

"Could be." Will concentrated on eating.

Iris glanced around as she ate, taking note of the people she saw who were at the grange hall on Monday. She noticed a few more but not as many as she'd anticipated. Perhaps her memory wasn't as good as she'd hoped it was. Except Charlene and the man she was with had certainly made an impression.

"Is Charlene married?" Iris asked Will.

"I don't think so."

"Dating?"

"I have no idea."

"She was with someone at the grange hall when I played your fiddle."

Will finally looked up at her. "She was at the grange hall?"

Iris nodded.

Will groaned, stood, and headed to the dessert table. A few minutes later he returned with a slice of the apple stack cake on his plate. He sat back down and took a bite. After he swallowed, he said, "This is your best cake yet."

Iris simply said, "Thank you." She was pretty sure Will wasn't telling her something, probably about Charlene, but she wasn't sure how to get him to talk.

Fifteen minutes later, Iris told Will goodbye and then thanked Miss Shirley and excused herself, saying, "I'm going to go rest up for tomorrow."

She gathered up her cake plate and carrier—the cake itself was completely gone—and started toward the road. She could feel Will's eyes on her, but he didn't follow.

Being away from Will was achingly lonely, but being with him was almost as bad. Nameless, Tennessee, offered her no companionship. Except when she was with her students or praying. At least she had those two things to counter her loneliness.

Monday morning, Judson wasn't in school again. Iris imagined him down by the creek fishing. She broached the topic of the fiddle with her students, telling them she'd had it in her possession and played it at the grange hall on Labor Day. "But then it was stolen from my home, behind the school, last Tuesday. It has hummingbirds and irises carved on the back."

"Is one of the hummingbirds named Iris?" Hannah asked.

"No," Iris answered.

"Is it named Miss Pitts?"

"No," Iris answered again.

"I also heard Will McCrae was going to marry you but he decided not to because—" BJ had a smirk on his face. "You know, because his fiddle is gone."

Marj elbowed BJ. "Knock it off." Iris turned to the chalkboard, stifling a laugh at Marj coming to her defense.

After school, Iris stopped by the store and called Sheriff Whitaker. When he came to the telephone, he asked, "Have you found the fiddle?"

"No," Iris answered. "Have you?"

"I keep looking for a man with one cuff link," he joked. "But haven't found him. I'll leave a message with Lela if I do."

Iris left the store, feeling discouraged. Next, she stopped by the café and asked everyone inside if they knew anything about the fiddle. All of them had heard the fiddle was missing, but no one had any information about it, although a couple of them said they'd heard she'd sold it.

Judson didn't show up for school on either Tuesday or Wednesday. Both days after school Iris returned to the café and quizzed people on whether they knew anything about the fiddle. No one did. Will wasn't in the café on any of the three late afternoons. She didn't see the Studebaker at the boardinghouse. Perhaps he'd gone back to his uncle's place in Nashville. No doubt he'd be back to claim his convertible and Iris would be carless in Nameless. She would have laughed at her word play if not for the pain she felt.

On Thursday Judson did show up for school. And early, before any other students had arrived. Even Marj.

"Miss Pitts." He stood at the back of the room. "I need to tell you something."

Her heart raced, sure he was going to confess.

"I've been thinking about this ever since the sermon on Sunday when the preacher read the verse from John 16 about telling the truth."

She didn't remember the pastor talking about telling the truth.

"I memorized it," Judson said. "It's verse thirteen. 'Howbeit when he, the Spirit of truth, is come, he will guide you into all truth: for he shall not speak of himself; but whatsoever he shall hear, that shall he speak: and he will shew you things to come.'" He bowed his head. "I need to tell you something."

Iris stood. "Yes?"

"I saw something last Tuesday afternoon after I left the school. At the time, I didn't trust you, so I didn't say anything. But I should have."

He wasn't confessing. "You saw something?"

"I saw a pickup hit Will McCrae's convertible. An old blue pickup."

"Did you see who was driving?"

"No," he said. "But I recognized the vehicle. It belonged to Mr. Morrison, but he's dead now. No one drives the pickup—it's been parked inside a shed for years. So I guess it belongs to Mrs. Morrison now."

"Mrs. Morrison? Do you know where she lives?"

"Past the grange hall. On the right-hand side. It's a big brick house with a wide porch. Three stories tall. You can't miss it."

"Thank you, Judson. I appreciate the information. Are you going to stick around today?"

"Yes, ma'am. I've been playing some basketball with Will this week. He said he'd help me get ready for the season. And give me fiddle lessons. Plus, he was able to fix my fiddle."

"Fix it?"

"Yes, ma'am. He had a special glue."

So, Will *was* in town. And it sounded as if he planned to stay for a while.

Iris managed to smile at Judson. "I'm happy to hear about the fiddle lessons and the basketball games, all of it."

The day seemed to crawl by, but finally the students were cleaning the schoolhouse, led by Judson, and at three, Iris dismissed everyone. As they left, she quietly thanked Judson for his help.

He waved and hurried down the steps. Iris locked the door and then walked briskly down the road. A few cars drove by, but no one stopped. The day grew warmer and warmer. Finally, she saw a group of trees. She hoped a house was in the middle. Not until she was right in front of a long driveway did she see the house at its end. Three stories, wide porch, and brick. She quickened her pace.

CHAPTER TEN

Iris didn't see a pickup anywhere as she reached the house, but there was a shed. She hurried up the steps. There was a screen door, but it was too dim to see inside the house. Iris knocked. No one answered. She knocked again. Finally, someone yelled, "Charlene, is that you? Come on in."

Charlene?

Iris knocked again and said, "It's Iris Pitts. The new schoolteacher."

An older woman wearing a housedress appeared. "Iris? Goodness, what are you doing here?"

"Miss Shirley! I was looking for Mrs. Morrison."

"Well, darlin', that's me. Shirley Morrison. Why were you looking for me, not knowing it was me you were looking for?" Miss Shirley held up a hand. "Wait. Don't tell me yet. I've forgotten my manners. Come on in."

"Thank you."

"Sit down," Miss Shirley said once Iris was inside. "I just made a pitcher of sweet tea. I'll go fetch two glasses."

Iris sat down in a chair with its back to the fireplace. She glanced around as she waited. There was a stack of boxes by a bookcase along the far wall. A sheet covered what looked like a sofa. A painting on the wall beside the bookcase was of a brick house—this house. Although the trees around it were shorter and there was no shed.

Miss Shirley returned with two glasses of tea. As she sat down in the chair next to Iris's, she seemed to forget her previous question and asked, "Are you and Will serious?"

"I'm not sure." She didn't want to discuss her personal life.

"Oh." She took a sip of tea and then said, "When I saw you at church, I thought you might be."

When Iris didn't respond, Miss Shirley said, "Well, give it time." She took another drink of tea and then asked, "How is teaching going?"

"Good. I'm enjoying the students."

Miss Shirley lowered her voice. "I wanted Charlene to get that job. In fact, I was surprised she didn't. Scott Parker indicated to me that he planned to hire her, but then he went to Washington, DC, on business after he went to Charleston for his reunion at the Citadel."

Iris stammered, "Wh-a-at?"

Miss Shirley gave her a puzzled look.

"Mr. Parker went to the Citadel?"

"Yes, ma'am. He graduated from there, oh it must have been thirty years ago."

Iris's father had graduated from the Citadel. In 1915? Maybe 1916? She wasn't sure, but had her father and Mr. Parker been there at the same time?"

"What was Mr. Parker doing in Washington, DC?"

"Oh, he seems to go there a lot. Some sort of business he's involved with."

Was it a coincidence that her father was in Washington, DC, and Mr. Parker had gone there during the summer? She stopped herself.

Lots of men in the south graduated from the Citadel, and Washington, DC, was a big city. Many people had business there.

"Anyway," Miss Shirley said, "when Scott returned, he said he had another applicant he was looking into."

"How odd," Iris said.

"Isn't it?" Miss Shirley shrugged. "Charlene's not disappointed. She didn't want to move back to Nameless. She's much happier packing me up and moving me to Nashville."

"Do you want to go?"

Miss Shirley's eyes teared up. "No, I don't. But I'm tired of bumping around in this big house by myself." She held up her empty glass. "I'm going to get more tea. Would you like another glass?"

Iris lifted hers. It was still half full. "No, thank you." She'd ask about the blue pickup when Miss Shirley returned.

After Miss Shirley left, Iris looked at the mantel. It was covered with photographs. She stood to get a closer look. There was a photo of Miss Shirley and a man, presumably her husband, that looked to be a couple of decades old. A photo of Charlene—a high school graduation photo most likely. Behind it was a photo of Charlene with—Iris took a step to the left to get a better view. Charlene with two men. One was Will, who looked much like he had when Iris first met him five years ago. The other was the man Charlene had been dancing with at the grange hall.

Footsteps came from down the hall. Iris turned to ask Miss Shirley who was in the photo with Charlene and Will just as other footsteps fell on the porch.

"Mother! I'm home."

Charlene flew through the front door and gaped at Iris. "What in the world are you doing here?"

Caught off guard, Iris said, "I stopped by because I have a few questions for your mother. But now I have a question for you too."

"What is it, Iris?" Miss Shirley asked.

Iris hesitated. "Well, first, one of my students said your blue pickup hit Will's convertible, which was parked at my place last Tuesday."

"Oh, I don't drive that pickup," Miss Shirley said. "Not at all. It had to be someone else's pickup."

"What about you?" Iris asked Charlene. "Do you drive the pickup?"

"No," she answered. "I don't. I drive Mother's car."

Iris pointed at the mantel. "Who's in the photo with you and Will? You were dancing with him Labor Day evening."

"Charlene?" Miss Shirley asked. "Who were you dancing with?"

"She's mistaken. I was in Nashville. She has me confused with someone else." Charlene turned her attention to Iris. "You need to go."

"I'd like to look at the pickup."

Charlene put her hand on her hip. "Did Will tell you about him and me? That I broke his heart and he left here for Asheville, a shell of a man?"

Iris didn't answer her.

She smiled a little. "And then he fell for you. But after all this time, you're no longer together, right? Maybe he never really got over me."

Iris wouldn't dignify her insults with an answer.

"I heard he's heading back to Asheville again. That seems to be where he goes when he can't face the music." She pointed to the door. "Go."

"I'd like to stop by the shed and look at the pickup."

"If you go close to that shed you'll be sorry." Charlene smiled.

Miss Shirley yelped, "Charlene. Don't talk like that."

Charlene opened the screen door. "Leave. I'll stand here and watch you walk to the road. And don't come back."

Will dropped his suitcase into the trunk of the Studebaker and then let the lid slam. The Bantam convertible was parked beside it, the crease in the driver's side completely repaired.

He was a coward to leave—he knew it. But he wasn't fit to be around Iris now, not when he wasn't sure she wanted him back. He'd go to Asheville and find work teaching music again and try to clear his head.

"Will!"

He turned and saw Iris headed his way. "There you are. I was just at the school looking for you."

Breathless, she asked, "Where are you going?"

"Asheville, by way of my uncle's house in Nashville. But I'm leaving the Bantam for you."

"What about Judson?" Iris swiped the back of her hand across her forehead. "He said you're giving him fiddle lessons. That you've been playing basketball with him."

Will shrugged. "Plans change, right?"

"Will McCrae, don't you dare. What's happened to you? That boy is hurting. Don't walk out on him—at least tell him in person."

Will paused a moment and then said, "I suppose you're right."

"And you need to talk to me too. I've just come from Miss Shirley's place. Her daughter had some interesting things to say. If nothing else, you owe me an explanation."

He shook his head. Why had she gone to the Morrison place? "There's nothing I want to talk about that has to do with Charlene Morrison."

"If you won't do it for me, do it for yourself. I'm afraid there are things from your past you've never worked through."

"Oh, I've worked through them." Hadn't he?

"No," Iris said. "You never mentioned her to me."

"It wasn't relevant."

"Are you sure? Did whatever Charlene do to you make you doubt me, make you think that I stopped writing to you? Stopped loving you?"

He raised his head and lifted his eyes to the treetops. Would he have thought that Iris stopped writing him if he hadn't been hurt by Charlene? Perhaps he would have come to that conclusion regardless. He shuddered. No, he wouldn't have. He met her gaze. "I'll meet you in the café in a few minutes. I'll answer your questions then."

Will watched Iris walk away and then glanced upward again, to the tops of the fir trees swaying in the warm breeze above his head. He had no idea what to say to Iris. Or why he'd suggested the café. They'd have no privacy there. Was that his intention? To get out of having to speak honestly?

As he began shuffling toward the café, he prayed, "Lord, give me courage to be the man Iris deserves. Honest. Willing to be hurt again, if that's what's best for her."

Best for her. Having Charlene dump him had turned out to be the best thing in the world for him—except for the residual fear that had apparently been left behind.

He stepped into the café. The usual afternoon coffee group said hello to him, but none of them stopped him. In the far back corner of the café sat Iris, at the only table in the place that offered any privacy.

"Are you hungry?" he asked as he sat down.

"Starving," Iris answered.

He smiled. He'd always liked her unabashed honesty. "Let's have an early dinner," he said. "My treat."

"That sounds wonderful," Iris said. "Thank you."

The waitress came to take their order—the fried chicken dinner for both of them. When the waitress left, Iris asked, "How much time did you spend here in Nameless as a child?"

"Every holiday. And a month or two every summer. My grandparents' farm was just past the Morrison place." Will exhaled at the thought of his grandparents. They were always so good to him. "I grew up playing the fiddle with Grandpappy. He left me his fiddle when he died, which caused a rift in the family."

"How so?"

"My uncle wanted the fiddle for his son. He thought it should be passed down from son to son, not to me, the son of his sister."

"Was the rift bad enough that your uncle would have tried to steal it?"

"No." Will shook his head as he spoke. "Uncle Teddy is a good guy. He was upset, but he wouldn't do anything like that." He pointed out the window. "Besides, I have his car, and his wife, my aunt Carrie, is ill. He wouldn't be able to get up here anyway."

"Why did he loan you his car?"

"Because he's a good guy, like I said. I didn't ask. I arrived in Nashville on the train. I was going to call you to come get me, but Uncle Teddy said I should just take his car and surprise you."

"Anyone else in the family who might want the fiddle? Anyone up here in Nameless?"

"No. Everyone's gone now."

The waitress brought sweet tea for each of them, and then Will asked Iris, "Why did you go out to the Morrison place?"

"Judson said he saw someone driving an old blue pickup that belongs to Mrs. Morrison hit your car that afternoon the fiddle was stolen," Iris answered. "I didn't realize Mrs. Morrison was Miss Shirley until I arrived at the house."

"Oh." He paused a moment and then said, "Do they still have that old truck?"

"Apparently, although Charlene wouldn't let me look at it."

"The paint on the Bantam was blue," Will said. "A lighter color."

"I remember Olly saying that," Iris responded.

He hadn't thought of the Morrison truck, but it certainly was blue. "I'll talk to Miss Shirley," he said, "but I'm sure it wasn't her. She loved my convertible. She would have told me if she hit it."

Iris wrinkled her nose and said, "I didn't see the pickup today, but I did see something else of possible interest."

"Oh?"

"A photograph of you and Charlene with another man. A man who was dancing with her at the grange hall the night I played your fiddle."

His eyes narrowed. "What did he look like?"

"Well, kind of like you. Tall, not as thin though, brown hair. A square chin. I'm not sure what color of eyes."

Will didn't respond.

She leaned toward him. "William Colin McCrae, I know you once loved me. You asked me to marry you. Technically, we're still engaged."

"You said no to marrying me."

"I didn't say no. I said I would when you got back. After that, you wrote me love letters. There was no indication you didn't love me in a single letter. In fact…" She pulled a packet of letters from her purse. "Quite the opposite. What changed?"

"What changed? I didn't get one single letter from you after I was captured. Others got letters through the Red Cross. I got nothing."

"I wrote to you. I wrote to the Department of Defense. I tried to track down your uncle, but I didn't have the right last name. Remember? I had no idea his surname was Little. You told me nothing."

Will stared into her dark eyes. Could he really believe her? He didn't respond.

"I'm telling you the truth. I thought you dumped me. Then I decided, when you didn't come back for your fiddle and car, that you must be dead."

Will looked down at the tabletop.

"So, who is the man in the photo?"

He raised his head. "Most likely my cousin Paul." He leaned back in his chair. "I wouldn't be surprised if she dumped me for him. He got a deferment from the war because he was studying engineering at Vanderbilt."

It was starting to make sense. "Lela said that your cousin was in Nameless, and now we know Charlene was with him at the grange hall that night, although she denies being there. Couldn't your uncle also confirm that Paul was in Nameless that day?"

Will shook his head. "He and Paul had a falling out over some business issues. Paul started a recording business on the side and borrowed money from Uncle Teddy, supposedly for just a few months, but now it's been a few years. Paul still hasn't paid him back. Like I said, my aunt has been ill, and they need the money for treatments."

"What about you and Paul? Were you close?"

"No. He's four years younger than I am. Charlene and Paul were closer to the same age. He enjoyed music—sounds as if he still does, but mostly the producing part of it. We didn't have a lot in common."

"So, who exactly is Charlene to you?"

"Who *was* Charlene to me?"

Iris nodded.

Will took a sip of water. "She was my fiancée."

Iris pursed her lips together. "And she broke up with you before you left for Asheville?"

"That's right. She hated me being up on the stage and not dancing with her. Being gone in the evenings. Traveling. When I went on a tour, she stopped writing—although she claimed her letters were lost in the mail." He shrugged. "Then she left for Nashville. Soon after she made it very clear she was no longer interested in me. So, I moved to Asheville."

Iris felt as if she'd been kicked in the stomach. "And then you met me?"

Will nodded, wishing he'd told Iris about Charlene five years ago. "My second day in Asheville. I held my fiddle—my grandpappy's fiddle—with the irises carved in the back as you said, 'Hello, I'm Iris.' At that moment, I felt as if it was meant to be."

Iris tossed and turned all night. Why hadn't Will been honest with her? True, he hadn't out-and-out lied, but he'd omitted the truth.

If only Will had told her the story of his fiddle and that his uncle Teddy wanted it and that his cousin Paul was dating his ex-fiancée. All of that would have been good information to have the day the fiddle disappeared.

"What now, Lord?" Iris asked as she climbed out of bed early the next morning before the sun rose. She heated the water she'd pumped the evening before, washed, dressed, put on her jacket against the morning chill, and then headed to Will's boardinghouse. She wasn't sure if she believed him or not.

They'd stopped talking the afternoon before when the waitress brought their food. Then, after they'd finished eating, Will said he would wait until this morning to leave. He didn't want to have car trouble and be stuck on the side of the road overnight. And besides, he needed to see Judson before he left.

Both the Studebaker and the convertible were parked in the same spots as the day before. Iris bent down and scooped up a handful of gravel. Will's room was on the right-hand side in the back—with the view of the school and her cottage. She threw a piece of gravel at the window. Then another. Finally, he raised the window.

"It's me," she said. "I have a question for you."

"I'm asleep," he answered.

"Not anymore. Come down and talk to me before I need to unlock the school."

He yawned and closed the window. A few minutes later he came down with his hair uncombed, wearing his jacket over a white T-shirt.

"Let's sit in the Studebaker," Iris suggested.

Will stepped ahead of her and opened the passenger door for her. Then he rounded the car and climbed in behind the steering wheel.

"I'm really sorry none of my letters reached you," she said.

"So am I," Will said. "Every day I prayed for a letter from you."

"And every day I prayed for a letter from you too. I didn't know if you'd been killed, captured, or had dumped me."

He exhaled. "Well, I knew you hadn't been killed or captured, so I became certain you'd dumped me."

"Because of the way Charlene had broken up with you?"

"I'm embarrassed to say it, but yes. You're right." He shook his head. "I didn't make the connection at the time. I didn't make it until yesterday, in fact."

"And now she's dating your cousin."

He nodded. "And has been for years."

"Do you still care about her?"

"No," he said. "All along, I've been better off without her."

"And you've never regretted it?"

He shook his head. "In essence, she wanted me to choose her over my music. But choosing my music was like choosing oxygen. I couldn't *not* choose my music."

"I know." Iris paused a moment as she tapped her temple. "Help me think this through. The fiddle was stolen on Tuesday. Paul and Charlene both saw it on Monday evening. Paul needed more money to support his recording studio." Iris shifted in her seat to face him. "And Judson saw the Morrison pickup hit your car the day the fiddle went missing."

Will stared straight ahead. "I've wondered since the first I heard it went missing if Charlene took it out of spite."

"Why didn't you say something?"

"Because when I asked Miss Shirley if Charlene was in town, she said she wasn't. I believed her."

"Was Miss Shirley at the grange hall that evening?"

Will shook his head. "She was in Gainesboro visiting her sister. She didn't come back until Thursday, after the fiddle was taken." He turned to Iris. "I believe you that you saw Charlene and Paul at the grange hall."

Iris smiled. "Let's go to Nashville this afternoon," she said, "and talk to Paul. Let's see what his reaction is when we show up asking about the fiddle."

"All right. How soon can you leave?"

"Noon. I'll need to find a substitute. I'll talk with Mr. Parker. I need to ask him about something else too. I'll see who he recommends as a substitute, but I'm thinking Charlene." Iris cocked her head and smiled. "It would be good to keep her busy this afternoon, don't you think?"

CHAPTER ELEVEN

Iris walked down the road hoping Mr. Parker was in his office already, but as she approached the café, a man came around the side of the building. It was Mr. Parker.

"Good morning," she called out.

"Iris? Is that you? What are you doing out so early?"

"Looking for you."

"Come on in," he said. "I'll buy you breakfast."

Iris followed him. She'd gladly accept another meal.

After they ordered coffee and eggs and ham, Mr. Parker said, "What can I help you with?"

"Two very unrelated things," Iris said. "First, I need to take the afternoon off to go into Nashville with Will. We have someone we need to question about the fiddle."

"Oh? Anything you can share with me?"

"I'd rather not," Iris said. "Right now, it's entirely circumstantial evidence."

"All right." He thought a moment and then said, "I could take over the classroom this afternoon."

"That's kind of you," Iris said. "But what about Charlene Morrison? I can pay her from my salary—but I'd rather not ask her."

The waitress brought their coffee, and they both took a sip.

"I can ask her," Mr. Parker said. "What time?"

"Noon. I'll leave the lesson plans on my desk. I read aloud in the afternoon, and then the students will do a class-wide geography lesson on Virginia."

"All right," Mr. Parker said. "If Charlene can't do it, then I will."

"Thank you."

"What's your other question?"

"Do you know my father, Thomas Pitts?"

Mr. Parker leaned back in his chair. "What makes you ask that?"

"You graduated from the Citadel around the same time he did. You fought in France during World War I. You traveled to Washington, DC, this summer. I grew up thinking my father was a weak man, that he had character flaws. But now I'm wondering if he came home shell-shocked and never recovered."

Mr. Parker sat up straight. "Your father is not a weak man. Nor does he have any character flaws. He's a good, courageous, and brave man."

Iris's brows shot up. "I take it that you know him, then?"

He smiled. "Yes, I know your father. I've known him since 1915. I was a year ahead of him at the Citadel. I was at your parents' wedding. Your father and I shipped out together. And—" His voice caught. "Your father saved my life only to lose most of his own."

"What do you mean?"

"He was in the trench, watching a group of us advance, when I was struck and knocked unconscious. He ran out after me, threw me over his shoulder, and carried me back to the trench as artillery rained down. Then he did the same thing for three other men. One man died on his back. The other three of us survived. He was, miraculously, unhit. Or so we thought. He was never the same after that. He tried to pretend he was. A year after our return, you were born. He wanted so badly to be happy, but he couldn't sleep. He couldn't stop shaking. He couldn't hold a job. People thought he was a drunk. Your mother thought he was a failure. His own mother tried to help him, but after the divorce, he thought it would be better if he left Charleston. Tom didn't want you to be embarrassed by him."

Iris felt ill. "What?"

"I'm sorry," Mr. Parker said.

"He left because of me? But stayed in touch with you?"

"It's not that simple." Mr. Parker's voice grew quieter. "It's rather complicated, actually."

The waitress arrived with their breakfasts. After she left, Mr. Parker said, "I'm sorry about all of this. It's rather difficult to explain."

"You were in Asheville when I was there. And then you hired me to work here. Why?"

"Because your father asked me to keep an eye on you. In Asheville, once I saw you and Will together, I befriended him. He told me that the both of you were going to Memphis. I didn't follow you there. But when no one had heard from Will for months, I feared he was dead. I visited your father this summer, and he asked me to offer you the teaching job here, thinking it would be a good place for you. I did too."

Iris shook her head. "I'm dumbfounded." She supposed she should be angry to have Mr. Parker following her and meddling in her life, but she wasn't. She felt relieved to know that someone was looking out for her. And that her father cared.

"Do you have a phone number for my father?"

He nodded. "I do. But let me talk to him first. Stop by before you go to Nashville. You can call him on my phone."

They were quiet for a moment as they ate, but then Mr. Parker said, "Don't be too hard on your mother. War can change everything. She was young. She expected your father to come home and meet her needs. She didn't expect him to have any of his own."

"Is that why you suggested I give Will grace? Because you thought I'd react like my mother?"

"No," Mr. Parker said. "You're nothing like your mother. And anyone coming home from war needs an extra dose of grace. We've all gone through a run of hard years. We all need a measure of grace, don't you agree?"

Iris agreed. Will. Judson. Maybe even Charlene and Paul. Certainly her father.

When Iris arrived at the school to unlock the front door, Marj was waiting for her. "I have something I need to tell you, Miss Pitts."

"All right. Let's go inside."

Once they were in the room, Iris said, "What is it?"

Marj went to her desk, sat down, and brushed her curls away from her face. "I've been thinking about the sermon from last Sunday all week, the one about being truthful."

"Oh?"

"I wasn't truthful with you, about our mama. She didn't die. She left us."

"I'm sorry," Iris said.

"I really like you, Miss Pitts," Marj said. "And I don't want to deceive you. I always tell myself that story because it makes me feel better. It's pretty awful to have your mother leave because of you."

Iris stepped down the row and sat in Judson's chair. She put her arm around Marj. "It wasn't because of you," she said. "As children, we can't understand what our parents are going through. Your mother might have left for a dozen different reasons. Yes, she might have been exhausted and had the blues from pregnancy and her confinement, but she didn't leave because of you. Not because of Marjorie Johnson. She must have been going through something dreadful to let it pull her away from her newborn babies."

"Do you think so?"

"I do." Iris hesitated to tell her what little she knew of her own story when she hadn't even spoken to her father yet. But then she decided to tell Marj what she knew, ending with, "What I thought I knew all those years isn't what happened at all."

"Thank you," Marj said. "I'm going to hold on to that. And try to be more honest."

Iris gave her a smile. Here she was smiling at a student, and it wasn't even Halloween. Oh, who was she fooling? She'd been smiling at her students since the first day.

She pulled Marj close and gave her a hug.

At noon, Iris released her students for lunch and waited on the front steps. No one appeared—not Charlene nor Mr. Parker. Will walked into the schoolyard and up the steps to where Iris stood. "Are you ready to go?"

"I'm waiting for someone—Charlene or Mr. Parker—to relieve me." Iris stepped to the side of the porch and glanced to the road. Then she turned back to Will. "Do you want to go ask Mr. Parker if he arranged for Charlene to come?"

"Sure," Will said. "But give her another minute."

Several of the children finished eating. Judson yelled, "Mr. McCrae, come play ball with us."

Will waved. "Next time, I promise."

Would there be a next time? "Don't let Charlene see you," Iris said. "If she figures out we're headed to Nashville, she might call Paul."

"Good thinking."

"Meet me at Mr. Parker's office."

Right after Will left, a car—Miss Shirley's—turned into the schoolyard and parked by Iris's shack. Charlene climbed out, dressed to the nines.

Relieved, Iris started down the steps. "Children," she called out, "Miss Morrison will be taking over for me this afternoon. Please be of help to her. I'll see you on Monday morning." Several of the younger children came and gave her hugs. "Judson and Marj, would you please assist Miss Morrison with anything she needs?"

"Yes, ma'am," they said in unison.

When Charlene reached her, Iris explained that the instructions were on her desk. Then she said, "Thank you."

"I'm doing it for Mr. Parker," Charlene said. "He feels bad for not hiring me."

Iris smiled, not believing a word of what she said, not sure if she should trust Charlene with the students. She'd ask Mr. Parker to check on them in a little while.

As she hurried to Mr. Parker's office, Will waved. He was waiting for her. When she reached him, she said, "I need to make a phone call."

"Who to?"

"My father."

"Your father," Will said. "I didn't think you knew where he was."

"I just found out this morning."

Mr. Parker met them at the door. "Come in, come in," he said. "Tom's expecting you to call."

For a moment, Iris feared speaking with her father. Her last memory of seeing him was at Nana's house when she was five. He'd seemed angry at the time. But now, as an adult, she knew that other emotions masqueraded as anger. Frustration. Grief. Loss. Back then her father would have been close to the age she was now.

"I'll put the call through for you." Mr. Parker stepped to his desk, picked up the receiver, and gave the operator the city and the phone number. A minute later, he said, "Thank you, ma'am." And then, after a pause, "Hello, Tom. I have Iris here." He handed the phone to her.

As she stepped to the desk, Will stepped with her.

"I'm okay," she said to him. And she was. She took the receiver and said, "Hello, Daddy. How are you?"

The conversation was a blur, but Iris treasured every minute of it. Finally, aware of the cost, she said, "I should go. But I'd like to come visit you sometime. How about in the summer when school lets out?"

"Let me give it some thought," he said. Then he added, "I've prayed for you every day of your life. I won't stop."

"Thank you," she said.

"And I'm sorry—" He began to cry.

"It's all right," Iris said. "I'll write to you. We'll figure this out. I promise."

"Thank you," he said.

"And I'll be praying for you too," she said. "Every day."

Mr. Parker reached for the phone and said, "Tom, I'll call you back this evening. After you've had your supper. Goodbye for now."

After Iris thanked Mr. Parker, she turned to Will. "Let's be on our way to Nashville and see about your fiddle. If we can find it, that would make this day perfect."

CHAPTER TWELVE

As Will drove down the windy mountain road, the windows of the Studebaker opened to the hot early September air, Iris basked in the breeze. As soon as they were on the outskirts of Nameless, he said, "Tell me what happened with your parents."

Iris leaned back against the seat. "The truth is," she said, speaking loudly above the wind, "I had my own secret, my own lie of omission that I didn't tell you." She thought of Judson confessing that he'd been convicted by the sermon about not telling the truth. Iris was upset Will hadn't been honest with her—but she also had to confess she hadn't been honest either.

"My parents married before my father left for the Great War, a few weeks before. He came home shell-shocked, although no one—except Mr. Parker and maybe Nana—recognized it as such. My mother just thought he was a lazy drunkard. I grew up thinking he was a bad person—and I was too embarrassed to tell you that."

Iris paused a moment. "I should have told you all of this a long time ago instead of just saying my father left when I was a girl." She took a deep breath. "They divorced when I was one. The only time I remember seeing him, I was five. Mama made it sound as if he left us, but I think she's the one who asked for the divorce—and maybe with good reason. I don't know. She told me he took a job in Washington, DC, but he's been in a home there all these years."

"And what's Scott Parker's connection?"

"They were in the war together. Daddy saved Mr. Parker's life and the lives of two other men. Daddy asked Mr. Parker, when I left for college, to look out for me." Iris exhaled and then took a raggedy breath.

"Were you afraid I'd come home damaged too? Is that why you wouldn't marry me before I left?"

"I don't think I realized I was afraid of that, but I think Mama's words about Daddy scared me more than I realized," Iris said. "However, I was afraid you'd change your mind about me once you came home because that's what Mama always implied about Daddy. That he was the one who left." That lie had cost her father Iris's respect and her empathy all these years. But Mama had been young and in a difficult relationship, with a baby. None of it was easy for her either. Perhaps, in time, Iris could find healing with her too.

Will was silent. Finally, he said, "Those past hurts tend to stay with us, don't they?"

"Yes," Iris said, "they certainly do. Especially if we don't talk about them. Especially when we don't even realize how they affect us."

"I'm glad we're talking now," Will said. "Mr. Parker is a good man. As is your father."

"It seems so." Iris turned to Will. "And so are you, Will McCrae."

"If I am," he said as he reached for her hand, "it's because of God's grace and your help. Which makes me realize there's something else I need to be honest about."

She squeezed his hand and swallowed the lump in her throat, grateful they were finally talking. "What's that?"

"You asked me if it was horrible in the camp, and I said it wasn't too bad. But it was horrible. I just don't think I'm ready to talk about it yet—and I can sympathize with your father. I don't know how damaged I am, but I know I'm changed. I know my scars run deeper than my skin."

She squeezed his hand. "We'll figure this out, together. Maybe it would help you to talk to Scott Parker."

In a voice that was low and deep, he said, "That might be a good idea."

When they arrived in Nashville, Will drove straight downtown. Several soldiers in uniform, with women on their arms, strode down Broadway. Smoke billowed out of barbecue joints. And music poured out of the bars.

"Uncle Teddy said Paul's studio is just off of Broadway." Will found a place to park. "Let's go there first and then find something to eat."

The studio was located only a block away from the Grand Ole Opry, now located in the Ryman Auditorium. "It's a good location for a recording studio," Will said.

When they arrived at the studio, the door was locked. Will knocked and knocked. Finally, a man wearing slacks and a short-sleeved shirt opened the door. "The studio is closed today," he said.

"I'm looking for Paul Little," Will said.

"I'm not sure where he is," the man said. "He let me use the studio for the day, to practice for a recording session next week, and told me to lock up when I leave."

"I'm mainly looking for my fiddle," Will said. "There's a possibility Paul might have it."

"And who are you?" the man asked.

"Paul's cousin. Will McCrae."

"Will McCrae!" The man shook Will's hand. "I'm so happy to meet you. Paul mentioned you were his cousin."

Iris nudged Will. "That's your case." She pointed to a case on the desk behind the counter.

"Mind if I take a look?" Will asked the man.

"Go ahead."

Will slipped past the counter and opened the case. "It's empty," he said. "He probably put the fiddle in another case."

"Look around," the man said. "See if you can find it."

Will and Iris headed into the studio. There weren't any fiddles, in cases or otherwise. Will thanked the man and took the case with them as they left. Once they reached the street, Will said, "We'll go by Uncle Teddy's and see if he's heard from Paul. I need to pay him for the Studebaker."

"Pay him?"

"I'm buying it from him."

"Why? You have a car."

"I'm going to loan the Studebaker—it's better on the mountain roads in the winter—to you for as long as you need it. Cars are impossible to get now and will be for a while. I don't want you stuck in Nameless without a car."

"You don't need to do that," Iris said.

"I want to," Will said. "When you no longer need it, I'll give it back to Uncle Teddy. He says he doesn't use it—but I'm afraid he just needs the money more."

After stopping for hot dogs from a street vendor on their way back to the car, Will drove across the Cumberland River into East Nashville and then turned right onto Holly Street. He pulled over in front of a bungalow. After he shut off the engine, he climbed out of the car and then opened Iris's door as she pulled her scarf from her head and tucked it in her purse.

"Come on in," he said. "And meet my uncle Teddy."

Will led the way up the steps and knocked on the door.

"Coming!" Uncle Teddy called out. He opened the door. "Will! Come in!"

Will motioned for Iris to enter the house first. As he did, he said, "Uncle Teddy, I'd like you to meet Iris Pitts."

"Pleased to meet you," Uncle Teddy said to Iris. He took her hand.

She smiled that endearing smile that put everyone she met at ease. "I'm so happy to meet you," she said.

Will pulled an envelope from the inside pocket of his jacket and handed it to his uncle. "Here's the money for the car."

"Thank you," Uncle Teddy said. "This is a big help. We don't need the car anymore. We can take a taxi to Carrie's appointments."

"Thank you for selling the Studebaker to me," Will said. "It's a good car."

"Do you plan to sell your convertible?"

Will shrugged. "We'll see."

Uncle Teddy motioned to the sofa. "You two sit down. I'll get some lemonade." He glanced toward the kitchen. "Carrie's resting."

"Don't wake her," Will said. "But tell her I said hello when she gets up."

"I will." Uncle Teddy headed to the kitchen.

Iris glanced around the room. There weren't any photographs, and there was only one painting, of a deer in a meadow.

When Uncle Teddy returned with three glasses of lemonade, he said, "So you're on your way to Asheville?"

Will stood, took two of the glasses from his uncle, and handed one to Iris. "No, I've postponed my trip. I'll take Iris back to Nameless first."

"Oh, you didn't need to come all this way today to give me the money. It could have waited."

"I came to see Paul," Will said. "But he wasn't at his studio. Any idea where he might be?"

Uncle Teddy shook his head. "You're not going to believe this, but he called Carrie and told her he was going up to Nameless this week for the Fall Fiddle Festival."

Will exhaled. "You're kidding. Any chance she told him I was going to Asheville?"

Uncle Teddy shrugged. "Probably. I told her. She wouldn't have any reason not to tell him."

Grasping the cold glass, Will leaned forward a little. "Have you seen my fiddle anywhere?"

"Pappy's fiddle?"

Will nodded. "Iris had it while I was overseas and took it to Nameless with her. It disappeared last Tuesday."

"That's a shame."

"Is there any chance Paul was in Nameless on Labor Day?"

"If he was, he didn't tell me. But he doesn't tell me much, not since we had our falling out over the money he borrowed."

"I'm sure he was in Nameless that Monday evening," Iris said. "I saw him dancing with Charlene Morrison at the grange hall."

"That's no surprise. He and Charlene have been dating for a—" Uncle Teddy shrugged and then said, "—a few years. He asked me not to tell you."

"That doesn't surprise me," Will said. It stung that Charlene had left him for Paul, but it certainly explained Paul's distance through the years.

"Charlene's been helping her mother get ready to move here," Uncle Teddy said. "At least that's what Carrie said. Paul calls every couple of weeks to talk with her." He looked so sad. It pained Will to think of the two of them having problems. "I hope Paul and I can patch things up soon," Uncle Teddy said. "I doubt I'll ever see the money I loaned him. I need to let it go."

Will felt sorry for his uncle. Paul had taken advantage of his own father and mother, at an especially hard time in their lives. Will took another sip of lemonade and then said, "The case for my fiddle was in Paul's studio, on his desk."

Uncle Teddy grimaced. "I'm sorry." He put his glass on the end table beside him. "I need to be honest about something. I insisted Pappy should have given the fiddle to Paul, but it was Paul who was hurt and asked me to stand up for him. Initially, I was fine with the fiddle going to you, especially since Paul never learned to play."

Paul had wanted the fiddle. He'd been in Nameless the evening before it went missing. The fiddle case was in his studio. "Thank you for telling me that." Will put his lemonade on the table too. "Well, it looks as if we'd better head back to Nameless." He stood. "I forgot all about the Fall Fiddle Festival. I have a lot of fond memories of it."

Uncle Teddy stood too. "Don't we all." He cleared his throat and said, "You have a God-given gift, even more than Pappy did. The fiddle was meant to be yours."

"Thank you," Will said. "If I'd known all the trouble this would cause, I—"

Uncle Teddy held up his hand. "You did nothing wrong. I hope you get the fiddle back tonight. If not, let me know, and I'll see what I can do."

Iris and Will didn't talk much on the way back to Nameless. The air was heavy and the drive hot. The wind whipped at Iris's scarf and hair. She kept her sunglasses on and stared at the landscape. Her eyes stung. From the wind?

Maybe not. She felt emotional enough to cry.

When they arrived in Nameless, Will slowed and drove through town straight to the grange hall. There was an even larger crowd than on Labor Day. Will parked along the side of the road, past the hall. He grabbed his fiddle case as he climbed out of the car. As they walked, he pointed to an Oldsmobile in the parking lot along the row of poplar trees. "That's Paul's car, over there."

Will led the way into the hall through the open doors. The light inside was dim, and it took a moment for Iris's eyes to adjust. The guitarist and banjo player who played on Labor Day were playing "Cheek to Cheek."

She searched the crowd.

Paul and Charlene were dancing. He wore a white shirt with the sleeves rolled to his elbows.

"Funny, he has his sleeves rolled up," Will whispered. "Maybe he's missing a cuff link."

Judson stood along the far wall of the grange hall by Marj and motioned for Will and Iris to join them. As they approached, Will asked Judson, "Have you seen my fiddle today?"

"No," Judson said.

Before the musicians finished the song, Paul locked eyes on Iris—and then his gaze shifted to Will, who motioned to Iris to follow him. As she did, she noticed Judson and Marj both headed toward the exit.

Paul, with an expression of shock on his face, let go of Charlene's hands and dashed up the stairs to the stage as Will held up his case and called out, "Hey, cousin! What did you do with my fiddle?"

When Paul dashed behind the curtain, Will took off after him, followed by Mr. Parker, who must have realized what was going on. Iris bolted for the exit after Judson and Marj, guessing Paul was headed to his car.

Once outside, she came to a quick stop. Will and Mr. Parker had Paul cornered at the back of his car.

As she approached, Will said to Paul, "You're going to stay here while I search your car."

"I'll do it," Iris said. She opened the back door first, but the seat was empty. Then she looked up front, but there was no fiddle. However, there was a lone cuff link on the dash. She snatched it up.

"We need to check the trunk," she said, just as Judson, with Marj beside him, stepped out of the trees, holding up a fiddle.

"Looking for this?" Judson called out. "I took it out of the trunk, thinking Paul might drive away."

"I didn't take your fiddle." Paul glared at Will and then pointed at the twins. "Judson Johnson did."

Iris held up the cuff link. "Is this yours, Paul?"

He laughed. "What does my cuff link have to do with anything?"

A man's voice boomed, "Quite a bit."

Iris looked beyond Paul, Will, and Mr. Parker. Sheriff Whitaker stood in the middle of the parking lot, his shoulders squared. "Paul Little, you're under arrest for stealing Will McCrae's fiddle."

A half hour later, Sheriff Whitaker hauled Paul along with Charlene—to question her about the Morrisons' pickup being seen at the scene of the crime—off to Gainesville. But he left the fiddle with Will, saying, "Soldier, you've been without this long enough."

Will took it and tuned it in the middle of the parking lot and then said to Iris, "I think I'd like to play tonight."

She motioned to the door of the grange hall. "I think there's a whole town in there who would love to hear you play."

When they stepped through the doors, with Judson and Marj on either side, the audience began to clap. As Will headed for the stage, they began to cheer.

He held up the fiddle, showing the carving of the two hummingbirds and the irises. Iris thought he might say something, but he didn't. He pulled the fiddle to his chest and began to play "Haste to the Wedding."

This time, Iris couldn't stop the tears.

The crowd surrounding them sang, "Come haste to the wedding ye friends and ye neighbors, The lovers their bliss can no longer delay. Forget all your sorrows, your cares, and your labors, And let every heart beat with rapture today."

Will played on, his eyes closed, his body swaying. This was the Will she knew. Iris began to sway too. Judson and Marj clapped to the rhythm.

As the music filled her soul, Iris sent up a prayer of thanks. She had found both Will and herself again, in this nameless town.

"Then come at our bidding to this happy wedding," the crowd sang as the song came to an end.

Will pulled the final note from the strings and then raised his bow with a flourish. He opened his eyes and called out, "Iris Pitts, will you marry me? As soon as possible?"

Iris called out, "Yes!" And then she flew up the stairs to the stage and into Will's arms—into a hug filled with love. And music.

WORTHY TO BE NAMED

by

ELIZABETH LUDWIG

To my Pops. I miss you.

"Again, the kingdom of heaven is like a merchant looking for fine pearls. When he found one of great value, he went away and sold everything he had and bought it."

—Matthew 13:45-46 (niv)

✒ CHAPTER ONE ❧

Nameless, Tennessee
Present Day

Dust floated on the humid air…a fog so thick Maggie almost couldn't see. Slowly, the motes filtered like snowflakes to settle on her lashes.

The Realtor at her side waved his arm, disturbing the dirty cloud even more. "Sorry about this. If I'd known you wanted to see the place today, I'd have aired it out some. Thursdays are usually pretty slow around the office."

Fighting a sneeze, Maggie shook her head and skirted piles of rotted wood and broken plaster to move toward the door. "It's okay. I knew I'd have some work ahead of me."

"Yeah. Well…" He lifted his eyebrows and glanced around the room skeptically. "This is it. What do you think? Want to see more?"

His tone suggested he didn't see the need.

Maggie touched the wall at her shoulder where a piece of black slate poked from behind fragments of jagged shiplap. At one time, the room had probably smelled of chalk and books. Now, it smelled mostly of dirt and damp wood. "You say this used to be a schoolhouse?"

His gaze ran the length of the ceiling and returned to her. "That's the story, anyway. People from the town built it back in the

1800s. It closed in 1965. You'd probably have to talk to a local to get more information."

"You're not from around here?"

He pushed his glasses higher on his nose and shrugged. "Nope. I live a few miles east, in Cookeville." A spider scurried over his arm. He shuddered and flicked it away, his feet nervously dancing in the rubble. "Hey, I'm gonna—"

Maggie nodded. She couldn't blame him. Spiders creeped her out too.

He clapped his hands together, sending more critters scurrying to the corners. "Okay. Feel free to look around. Everything downstairs is relatively safe. Upstairs is a little trickier."

"There's an upstairs?"

He nodded. "There were several changes made over the years. The old cabin was torn down, and an upstairs added, things like that. That section is newer than the rest of the place, but it's still pretty old. Maybe don't go there until you've had a contractor check it out?"

"Thanks. Will do."

"Okay." He hesitated, and for a second, Maggie thought he intended to talk her out of staying, but then he spun and high-stepped out the door.

Left to herself, Maggie blew out a breath and turned a slow circle. What was she doing? This place wasn't what she'd had in mind when she said she wanted a fixer-upper. This was more like a tear-it-down-and-start-over. And yet…

She bent toward the tiny bit of black slate visible behind the shiplap. Apparently, whoever had last lived in this place hadn't bothered tearing the old chalkboard out. It was unusual. Cool, even. But was it reason enough to take on a project of this size? She ran her finger across the shiplap, cringing when she caught a sliver. She paused to pluck it out.

Then again, what else did she have to do? She brushed the sliver away. It wasn't like she had big-name musicians pounding down her door, begging her to join their tour.

The reminder of her failure hit hard. She blinked against a sudden burning in her eyes and yanked on a loose piece of shiplap. It gave easily. As did the next. And the next, until a large section of the chalkboard was exposed. To her surprise, there was writing on it.

Her heart skipped a beat. A message from the previous owner, or was the writing older than even that? Maybe the remnant of a lesson from the last schoolteacher?

Her curiosity fully piqued, Maggie grabbed her phone and turned on the flashlight. In the dim light caused by the grime-caked windows, she needed it to see.

The cursive letters were beautiful in their swirling perfection— like something off a chart, or from the cards she used to see in classroom pictures from the seventies and eighties.

"Jeremiah."

The name was partially obscured, but she could read enough to be sure of the word. One of the students? She shined her phone against the blackboard, angling it to see behind the remaining shiplap.

"Two…nine…"

She jerked back. She didn't need to see the rest. She knew it by heart.

"For I know the thoughts that I think toward you," saith the Lord…

She snipped the thought before it could fully form. She didn't believe those words. Not anymore.

"Miss Lange?" The Realtor's voice warbled through a broken window. "Everything all right in there?"

"Everything's fine." Lifting her chin, Maggie crossed over piles of rubble and trekked out the front door. Expecting only Sherby, she was surprised to see a middle-aged woman waiting next to him. With a scowl creasing her flushed face and dark hair sticking to the sweat at her temples, she looked more than a little unhappy to be standing in knee-high grass with the sun beating down on her head.

Sherby pressed a black binder to his chest and extended his hand toward Maggie. "Miss Lange, this is—"

The woman cut in before he could finish. "Betty Rutherford. Mind if I ask what you plan on doing with the schoolhouse?"

Caught off guard by her directness, Maggie glanced at Sherby. He was no help. His gaze was fixed firmly on his shoes.

"I don't suppose I have any plans, yet," Maggie said carefully, returning her gaze to Ms. Rutherford. "Mr. Dixon was just showing me around." The frown lifted from Ms. Rutherford's face, only to snap firmly back in place when Maggie added, "Though I am looking to purchase a property here in Nameless."

Crossing her arms over her chest, Ms. Rutherford narrowed her eyes. "I see. You do realize the schoolhouse is over a hundred years old. As such, it qualifies as a historical landmark."

"Really?" Maggie raised her eyebrows and turned to survey the property. "I didn't see a marker."

"Well…" She pulled a tissue from her pocket and used it to dab her forehead. "There isn't one yet, but I'm working on it. Me and a lot of other people in this community would hate to see the character of this place altered."

Maggie threw a meaningful glance at the broken windows and sagging doors of the schoolhouse. "But surely some alterations would be all right?"

Ms. Rutherford's mouth clamped shut, and she spun to train her heated gaze on Sherby. "This is your fault."

"I don't know what you want me to do, Betty. The property has been up for sale for months, and the town council is insisting I show it."

"Then maybe it's time I spoke with a few of those council members." Whirling, she stomped back to a silver sedan and drove off without another word.

His head still bowed, Sherby peeked at Maggie. "Sorry about that. Betty is the self-appointed head of the Nameless Historical Society, and she's pretty rabid about the schoolhouse."

"I didn't realize Nameless had a historical society," Maggie said.

"It doesn't, but that doesn't stop Betty. I'm sure she'd buy the schoolhouse herself if she could afford it, but between the taxes and cost of the repairs?" Sherby flipped his black binder open and thumbed through the pages. "Anyway, I have several more listings we can look at today—"

Maggie held up her hand. "No need. I've seen everything I need to."

"I'm sorry?" He jerked his head up to stare at her through the thick lenses of his glasses. "You've seen..." His gaze slid over her shoulder to the crumbling brick walls of the schoolhouse.

"I've seen enough," she reiterated, then reached into the back pocket of her blue jeans for her checkbook. "I assume the seller is willing to negotiate on the price given the state of the building?"

He snapped his mouth closed and mimicked the motion with the binder. "Like I said, the town owns the place. They're definitely eager to sell, but Miss Lange, I really feel I should make you aware of the amount of work it would take to bring this place up to code."

"New plumbing and electrical?"

He nodded. "To start. There's also the well and septic, and the foundation will have to be inspected."

"I'm aware of the job ahead of me," Maggie said firmly, holding up the checkbook. "When can we close if I pay cash?"

He pulled his glasses off, dabbed a drop of sweat from his forehead with his sleeve, then replaced his glasses solemnly. "There's no need for a title search, because like I said, the town owns the building, but the inspections will take time. If everything goes smoothly, you're probably looking at a couple of weeks. But Miss Lange—"

Maggie stopped listening. Two weeks to put the past behind her and start life afresh. It seemed almost too good to be true.

Another part of her brain argued she was crazy. The schoolhouse was in shambles. Even if she got the property for a decent price, it would probably take more than she had in her bank account to make it livable. Why did she want the old place anyway? Except for the chalkboard, it wasn't like it was full of charm just waiting to be restored.

She shifted her focus to a small green sign some distance down the road. Though it was too far away to make out the letters, she knew what they said.

Nameless.

Like her. Though she would probably add "forgettable" and possibly "failure."

"I'd like to make an offer," she said, interrupting the Realtor midsentence. Seeing the affronted look that crossed his face, she added, "But I am grateful for your concern. And you're probably right on several counts. Still, I'm confident this is the place for me, so if we could move on to the details of the contract, I would really appreciate your help."

After a long moment, the frown slipped from his face, and he motioned to the car parked at the end of the overgrown drive. "I have everything we need. Just give me a moment to put it all together."

Maggie nodded and watched as he picked his way through the tall grass, his head swiveling from side to side.

He's checking for snakes. She shivered as the realization struck. Snakes creeped her out even more than spiders.

The sun glinted against the window as he swung the door open. A few minutes later, Sherby returned with the paperwork in hand.

"Okay, I have everything." He shot a glance over her shoulder at the huddled shell of the schoolhouse. "You're sure about this?"

She followed the direction of his gaze and shrugged. The truth was, she was hiding. From herself. From her failed music career. From the shadowy figures of a mother and father who'd abandoned her.

And what better place to do that than a town with no name?

"It's as good a place as any," Maggie said, reaching for the pen Sherby Dixon held toward her.

As good a place as any.

Even as she said them, she had the feeling the words would come back to haunt her. But for now, she had a house to call her own.

And that was all that mattered.

CHAPTER TWO

Maggie clutched the cold iron keys to the schoolhouse tightly in her palm. A little over two weeks ago, she'd put a bid on the place. Today, it was officially hers.

As is.

The words spider-crawled up her spine. For all her claims that she knew what she was getting into, the reality of her purchase settled over her like shackles. Broken windows. Stairs that tilted to one side. Doors that leaned inward and barely closed. What had she done?

Down the road, a noisy pickup rattled closer, finally coming to a stop at the end of the driveway. Could this be the contractor the Realtor recommended? Shading her eyes, she turned to watch a muscled figure climb out, the truck groaning and squeaking in relief as though glad to be rid of his weight. The man was clad in blue jeans and a plaid shirt rolled to the elbows. Blond hair curled around the edges of a baseball cap with a smudged brim.

"Mr. Weber?" When he didn't answer, she stiffened, eyeing him warily as he walked toward her, his long legs gobbling the yards of overgrown grass and weeds. "Are you the contractor Mr. Dixon told me about?"

He stopped a couple feet shy of her and extended his hand. "That's me. And Ian is fine. You must be Maggie Lange."

She blew out a breath and shook his hand. "Yes. Thank you so much for coming."

"No problem. I always set aside Monday mornings to check out possible jobs." He scratched his cheek and eyed the schoolhouse behind her. "I'm surprised somebody finally bought this old place. What are you planning to do, raze it and build on the land?"

If she was smart, she'd probably do just that. Still, it was rather rude of him to suggest as much. She stretched a little taller and crossed her arms. "Actually, I'm going to renovate it and turn it into a home. I believe the place has good bones."

Good bones. That was a phrase she'd heard on several home reno shows.

He snickered, his lips curving in the charming kind of grin Maggie had learned to distrust. "Beggin' your pardon, but the only bones you're likely to find in there are from the rats."

She didn't smile. "Do you have a clipboard or something to take notes on? I'd like to get started going over the work that needs to be done so I know what I'm looking at, cost-wise."

One eyebrow arched, but at least he quit grinning. Reaching into his back pocket, he pulled out his phone and waved it at her. "Ready whenever you are."

He took notes on his phone? Wasn't a clipboard standard equipment for these guys? Granted, he didn't look anything like a run-of-the-mill contractor. With those piercing blue eyes and the tanned skin visible at his neck, he looked more like a country music star.

And she hated country music stars, especially good-looking ones.

"This way." She skirted the leaning front doors and wound to the back of the schoolhouse, toward the entrance the Realtor had used when he first showed her the place.

Inside, the air was only slightly cooler than outside, thanks to the cross-breeze flowing from one broken window to the other.

Glass crunched under her feet as she eased farther into the room. "I'd like to start with the windows and doors. I'll be staying here while the work is being completed, and I want to feel safe."

"Safe." His mouth dropped incredulously. "Ma'am, you do realize—"

"Maggie. Not ma'am."

He tipped his head in agreement. "Maggie, you do realize there's no water hooked up."

"There's a well."

"Which won't run without a pump."

"Fine. Then we'll start with electrical. When do you think you could get me an estimate?"

Pressing his thumb to his eyebrow, he thought a second, then studied her quietly and held up both hands. "Ma'am—"

"Maggie."

"Maggie, there's a whole lot of work that needs to happen before this place will be even close to livable."

"Are you saying you can't do it?"

His jaw hardened. Typical. Hit a man's pride, and he'll agree to all sorts of things.

"The work isn't the problem. It's the permits. Inspections. Ordering materials. Lining up a crew. All those things take time."

"Which I have plenty of." She angled her head, hoping for a confidence she didn't quite feel. "As far as a crew, you should know I plan on doing some of the work myself."

He crossed his arms and peered at her. She could almost hear him appraising her ability. Her chin lifted. She was small, her hands calloused. Okay, so not from holding a hammer, but still... She wasn't afraid to get dirty, and if he gave her a job, she'd work on it until it was done.

"Okay."

She blinked. "What?"

He shrugged. "I can always use an extra pair of hands." He tapped something into his phone before shoving it back into his pocket. "Mind if I take a look around?"

Her phone buzzed against her hip. It was probably Gwen, calling to check on her. She motioned around the room. "Go right ahead. Careful on the stairs. The Realtor said the upstairs probably isn't stable."

Jerking her phone out, she hit the answer button then stepped outside. As expected, her agent's voice immediately flooded her ear.

"Serena, where are you? I've been calling and texting for days. Do you have any idea how worried I've been?"

"No need to use my stage name, Gwen. Right now, I'm just Maggie."

"Whatever." She could almost hear Gwen rolling her eyes. "When are you coming back to Nashville?"

For a moment, hope flickered in Maggie's chest. "Has there been an offer?"

Gwen hesitated. Not long, but enough to make the muscles in Maggie's middle tense. "Not for a tour, but I have gotten some nibbles on a few local gigs." Her long sigh grated on the other end of the phone. "Maggie, you need to be here. Fiddle players are a dime a dozen in Nashville. I need to be able to tell people you're available immediately when they call."

Local gigs. Maggie knew what that meant—downtown bars, honky-tonks, maybe even a few art festivals. She was done with that. She'd paid her dues. Not that she wasn't grateful. At least Gwen was trying.

She tightened her grip on the phone. "Sorry, Gwen, I'm not going to be able to do that, at least for a while. I'm busy here."

"Busy doing what? And where is 'here'?"

Exasperation made her voice sharp, but Maggie didn't mind. Gwen had been her friend a lot longer than she'd been her agent.

Maggie eyed a loose brick in the schoolhouse wall. If she pulled it out, would the whole thing come crashing down? "I'll tell you about it…soon. For now, I promise I'll do better about staying in touch, okay?"

"Okay." She paused, the tension on the line building. "Have you talked to Doug and Marlene? They're worried too, you know. They've called me twice."

Of course her adoptive parents would be worried. It had been almost a month since Maggie had spoken to them, and she used to check in every day when she was on tour. She fingered a belt loop on her jeans. "No. I should call, but…"

They had looked so hurt when Maggie told them she needed time and space to look for her biological family.

"Call them, Mags." Gwen's voice took on the warmth Maggie remembered from before she'd become a client. "They need to know you're okay."

She wiped a bead of sweat from her eyebrow and nodded. "I know. You're right."

There was another pause, longer this time, and then Gwen said, "Okay. We'll talk soon, right?"

"Yeah."

"Thanks. Bye, Mags."

As usual, Gwen disconnected without waiting for Maggie's reply. Gwen lived her life at a hundred miles per hour. For a while, Maggie had too. It was what she wanted, or thought she wanted. She wasn't so sure now. That life was risky. And it hurt, especially when it all came grinding to a halt.

"Everything okay?"

Maggie whirled around. Ian leaned in the entrance to the schoolhouse, filling the space, one hand shoved into the pocket of his jeans.

"Everything's fine." She tucked her phone away. "What did you find?"

He straightened and crossed his arms. "Well, it's like you said. It has good bones."

"Really?" The word popped out before she could stop it.

He nodded. "You have a good eye. Still, it's gonna take some time to make it livable. You sure you wanna stay here? There's a perfectly good hotel a few miles down the road, and they have running water."

Maggie shook her head. She'd done the calculations. Right now, a hotel was a luxury she couldn't afford. "I'll be fine. It'll be like camping."

His jaw worked, like he was chewing over a thought that never quite reached his lips. "Right." He shifted and motioned with his hand. "So, I'll work on your estimate and send something over to you this afternoon. Would you prefer email or text?"

"Text is fine."

"All right. Want me to use the number you gave me when you called?"

"That's the one."

"Okay. I'll be in touch."

He moved past her, and though the yard was big, Maggie still felt it necessary to keep a good distance. She stumbled back a step then sighed when he disappeared around the corner.

She really needed to chill if she was going to be working with this guy. Besides, her contractor was the least of her worries. Doug and Marlene topped that list, right along with her vanishing career and dwindling bank account. And then there was the mystery of the parents who'd abandoned her, leaving her with only the name Margareta for a clue to her heritage. All told, Ian Weber was probably fifth—she eyed the schoolhouse—make that *sixth* in the order of things that mattered to her. Except…

He didn't look the type to settle for sixth in anything. So maybe she'd be smart to keep her distance. Because the last thing she needed was one more complication in her life. And if her reaction to his looks told her anything, it was that he could be a complication.

A bad one. The kind she'd already decided she didn't need. Yet, here she was, still thinking about him five minutes after he'd left.

That fact filled her with irritation as she stomped back into the schoolhouse. She'd told Gwen she would call her parents, and she would, once she'd had a chance to work off the tension building between her shoulder blades. And while the process would take some time, it was fine, because she had a mountain of work in front of her.

Grimacing, she reached for a bucket and began scooping rubble into it. The schoolhouse meant sweat and blisters, but that was a pain she could handle. The other would have to wait. Her parents would understand. At least, that's what she told herself. Over and over again. Until it became a rhythm that matched the scraping of her shovel. Until her hands were raw and her feet ached. Until the sun dropped below the horizon and dusk made it impossible to see.

Then Maggie climbed into her SUV, turned the A/C to full blast, and tilted her seat back. She was hot and hungry, but at least she was too tired to think, which was good because she'd already lain awake too many nights mulling over things she couldn't change. She was done with that. At least for now.

Rocking onto her side, she locked the doors and let sleep claim her.

CHAPTER THREE

Maggie startled awake Tuesday morning to tapping on her window, followed by a muffled, "Rise and shine, sleepyhead."

Ian was here? What time was it? She blinked against the warm sunlight streaming through her windshield and glanced at her watch. Just after six. Of all the nerve—

Ian's hand lifted. He held a paper coffee cup. Ducking to look at her through the driver's door window, he grinned and brought the cup ever so slowly to his mouth.

"Stop." She hit the window button, but she'd turned off the engine during the night. It didn't budge. She turned the key in the ignition and rolled down the window, raising her seat to a sitting position at the same time. "Is that coffee for me?"

He nodded and handed her the cup through the window. "I don't know how you drink it, so…hope you like it black."

"Today, black is perfect." She took a sip, let the coffee soak her tongue, then nodded at him over the cup. "Thanks."

"No problem." He eased forward to rest against the hood of her SUV. "Looks like you got a lot done after I left."

"You've been inside?" How long had he been here?

"Just for a second." He motioned to the back of the schoolhouse. "I set you up with a full rain barrel. That should tide you over until we can get the wiring done and the electrical approved. Did you see the bid I sent you?"

She set her coffee in the drink holder and fumbled for her phone. She hadn't checked it, hadn't even bothered to plug it in. Luckily, it was still at thirty percent. She grabbed the car charger and inserted it into the bottom. "No, I fell asleep and—"

"No problem. We can go over it later."

She hid a grimace behind another sip of coffee. Was anything ever a "problem" for this guy?

"If you don't mind, I'm gonna go inside and start getting a few measurements while you finish up." He nodded to the cup.

"Oh, I can help." She reached for the door handle.

Ian straightened to look at her. "Are you sure?"

Of course she was sure. What did he think…she couldn't handle a tape measure? And then her full bladder hit her, and she realized what he was asking.

She settled against her seat. "Actually, I could probably use a couple of minutes."

"No problem." He grinned, and she knew this time, he'd said it on purpose. Was she that easy to read? He angled his head toward the schoolhouse. "Meet you inside."

"Yep."

Maggie waited until he disappeared around the corner before scrambling out of the SUV. When she got back, she grabbed a couple of bottled waters and used them to wash up and brush her teeth. Feeling slightly more presentable, she swept her long brown hair into a ponytail, grabbed her coffee and a breakfast bar, then followed Ian inside.

By the light of day, Maggie was clearly able to see what she'd accomplished the night before. Though there were still piles of rubble to be removed, she was able to cross the large, open space without having glass crunch under her feet.

Ian glanced at her over his shoulder. "Hey."

"Hey." She found a clean spot on the floor to set her cup then rubbed her hands down her jeans. "How's it going?"

"Actually…" He punched a few more keys on his phone and turned to her. "All done."

"Done… Wait, what?" She looked around for a tape measure and didn't see one. "How?"

When she glanced back at him, he held up his phone. "I used an app."

"Oh." She took a moment to process the difference in what she'd imagined and the man standing in front of her. "You're full of surprises, aren't you?"

"That depends." He pocketed the phone and crossed his arms.

Okay, she'd bite. "On what?" She fought to keep the snarky edge out of her voice.

He met her gaze steadily. "On what you expected."

She sucked in a breath. Something told her he knew exactly what had been going on in her head. No sense trying to hide it. "Fine. I admit, I sort of expected somebody a little less tech savvy. Is that what you want to hear?"

"It'll do."

She dropped her shoulders a little.

"For now."

Aargh! Infuriating man. She spun to look for her shovel. Spotting it leaning in a corner, she started that way, surprised when Ian clasped her by the elbow and pulled her to a stop.

"Careful, there's a weak spot in the floor." He nodded to a bright orange *X* he'd marked with spray paint. "I'll need to pull up some of the hardwood to see what's going on with the subfloor, but for now, you might just want to work around it."

She managed a nod. "Okay. Thanks."

He dropped his hold, and Maggie fought the urge to rub the spot where his fingers had been. He, on the other hand, looked completely unfazed.

He took out his phone and swiped through several screens then tapped on one. "Wanna look through this estimate?"

Yes, and since her phone was still in the car...

Maggie retrieved her coffee and the breakfast bar—mainly just so she had something to hold—and wolfed down the food while he went over the specifics. Basically, it was everything she'd thought as far as the construction and labor were concerned, slightly higher on the plumbing and electrical. Still, she could make adjustments, maybe tackle the painting herself to lower costs, even handle part of the demo. Of course, that wouldn't leave a whole lot of time for tracking down her family tree.

"You all right?"

Realizing he'd fallen silent for a while before he spoke, she wiped the crumbs from her fingers and glanced up at him with a shrug. "Fine. Just thinking all this through."

"Well, if you have any questions, I'd be happy to go over them with you. In the meantime, I just need your okay to start on the work before I call in a crew—"

"Okay."

"Sorry?"

"You have my okay." She drained the last of the coffee from her cup then shoved the wrapper from her breakfast bar inside and added both to a pile of rubble. "I'd like to get your guys in here as soon as possible."

"All right then." He eyed her as though she were a curiosity to be figured out then hitched his thumb toward the door. "I'll make some calls."

"Thanks." Skirting the *X* on the floor, she retrieved her shovel while Ian went outside. He was right. In the light of day, she could see the floorboards sagged inward. She was lucky she hadn't stumbled over the spot last night. Lucky, or blessed, as her mother would say.

Thinking of Marlene made her pause. She'd put off the call long enough. Outside, in her SUV, she dialed the number then listened as it went straight to voice mail. She'd forgotten it was Tuesday. Her mother would be with her Bible study group. She left an apologetic message with a promise to call later that night and hung up.

Much as she'd dreaded that call, she was a little disappointed her mother hadn't picked up. She missed hearing her voice, missed the snippets of wisdom she sprinkled into her words like salt. Missed…

Her gaze traveled down the road that wound like a gray ribbon through the trees and fields of blowing grass. In the distance sat a car—white or possibly silver—it was hard to tell with the sun glaring in her eyes. What was it doing there? Her thoughts instantly sped to Betty Rutherford and the displeasure on her face the first time Maggie had looked at the place.

She grabbed the steering wheel and pulled up straighter, squinting to see. The car was too far away for her to make out if it was a man or a woman inside. She could walk over there. If it was Betty, she could talk to her, maybe let her know what she planned to do with the schoolhouse.

But then the sun glinted on the windshield, and Maggie realized the car was turning around. Driving away from her instead of toward her. It could be someone who'd gotten lost. And yet, she had the weirdest feeling that they'd been watching her. Which was crazy and probably just what came of sleeping in the car and waking up with a crick in her neck. Because really... Why would Betty or anyone else be out here, in the middle of nowhere, watching her muddle through the wreck of a building she'd just bought instead of talking to her?

She shook off the feeling of apprehension and climbed out to stand next to her SUV, watching until the car winked from sight over a hill. Slamming the door closed, she grimaced. She really ought to rethink that whole "camping out" thing, especially if she was jittery after just one night. What would she be like after a week? Or two, if Ian's projections were correct?

Dragging in a deep breath, she headed for the schoolhouse. Over the years, she'd learned that work wasn't always the answer, but in this case, it was better than the alternative—wondering and worrying what the future held. Fortunately, she had plenty of work ahead of her, at least a week's worth.

Her lips curved in a wry grin. Maybe two.

CHAPTER FOUR

By Wednesday night, Maggie was seriously second-guessing her idea to live and work out of her SUV while the preliminary work on the schoolhouse was finished. Her back and shoulders ached, her feet felt swollen, and that crick in her neck might just be permanent. And bathing…

Well, the rain barrel helped, but the thought of a hot shower had tempted her more than once to reconsider checking into a hotel.

Swatting a mosquito from her arm, she eyed the SUV. If she pulled her clothes and belongings out of the back, she could fold the rear seat down and actually lie semi-prone. Semi, because at five foot eight, she was a little long in the leg to stretch out completely. She lifted her hand to the back of her neck. Folding the seats would mean hauling everything inside before the sun set—and doing it against the protest of her already sore muscles. But wouldn't another hour or so of work be worth it for a good night's sleep?

Down the road, the rattle of an approaching vehicle caught her attention. She squinted to see against the glare of the evening sun. The grumbling muffler sounded like Ian's work truck, a thought that was confirmed when he slowly turned into the driveway, a beat-up travel trailer bumping along behind him. Maggie glanced at her watch. It was after eight. He'd left over an hour ago. What was he doing back?

She circled around to the front of her SUV and waited while he pulled to a stop. A second later, the driver's door squealed open, and Ian climbed out. Maggie pointed to the travel trailer. "What's going on?"

He jabbed the cap off his forehead with his thumb. "Welcome to my office. We use the trailer on-site when a job is going to take us a while to finish. I figured I'd go ahead and bring it over so the guys could have coffee in the morning." He paused, dug in his pocket, and then held out a key. "Plus, I thought maybe you could sleep in it until we get the schoolhouse livable."

"Live…" Her mouth dropped, and she turned to stare in disbelief at the boon of a rattletrap trailer.

He pulled the key back sheepishly. "I know it doesn't look like much. And it…uh…doesn't really have a bedroom. We took it out so we'd have someplace to store our tools. But there's a fold-out couch. I figured that would be better than the seat of your car. It also has a built-in generator, so you can store things in the fridge if you want to. Oh, and probably most importantly, it has a small water tank so you can shower."

She didn't answer. She couldn't. All of a sudden, her eyes burned, and she knew if she tried to say a word, she'd get weepy and emotional and break down like a complete idiot because she was overtired and stressed and thinking maybe she'd made a horrible decision to come to Nameless at all—

"Maggie?"

She blinked and focused on Ian, who dangled the key in front of her face.

One side of his mouth lifted a smidge, like he might smile at any moment. "So, trailer going once…"

She snatched the key from his hand. "I'll take it."

This time, he did smile.

Maggie cleared her throat. "What I mean is, I'll take it, and thank you."

"You're welcome." He pushed his hands into his pockets. "It'll only take me a second to get it set up. I figured I'd park it under the big oak next to the schoolhouse? The shade oughta help keep it cool during the day."

"Yeah, that'd be perfect."

"Good."

For a long moment, they looked at each other. Maggie was thinking she might have been wrong about that whole handsome-country-music-star thing. Right now, standing next to the trailer with the sun turning his hair golden, Ian looked more like a knight in shining armor. But what was *he* thinking?

He backed up a step, looked at her, then backed up another step. "Okay. I'll just…"

He sucked in a breath then spun and headed to his truck. Maggie helped him back the trailer into place then watched as he set the stabilizing jacks. When he finished, he followed her to the SUV.

"Wow." He eyed the things crammed into the crannies. "You've got a lot of stuff in here."

Maggie reached for the first suitcase and yanked it out. "Yeah, well, I let go of my apartment, so everything I own is right here. Luckily, I never accumulated much, being on the road."

"The road?" Ian grabbed a bag and followed her to the trailer.

Maggie glanced at him over her shoulder as she unlocked the door. Had she not told him of her past? He'd figure it out soon enough when he saw the fiddle. She shrugged and pulled the door open. "I used to perform on tour with a couple of musicians out of Nashville."

"You what?" He followed her up the steps and set the bag down next to her suitcase with a thump.

Maggie eyed the bag and then him curiously. "I don't anymore. That's all in the past."

He slid his hands slowly into the pockets of his jeans. "Why'd you quit?"

He didn't look impressed, or starstruck. Just interested.

She shrugged. "Not my choice."

Maggie avoided his gaze and looked around the trailer. It was sparse. Except for a small kitchen and bathroom, a built-in table, and the couch Ian mentioned, it was empty. But it was four walls, and that alone had never felt so good. She had to be tired, because all of a sudden, her throat felt tight.

She sucked in a breath then lifted her chin and crossed to rest her hand on the grimy, two-burner stove. "Listen, Ian, I'm really grateful for you letting me use this place. I, um, thought I could handle it, but turns out, I'm not really that enthused about camping out."

Though she tried to make light of it, the words were bitter on her tongue. It wasn't the camping that bothered her, it was the situation that made it necessary. Of course, her parents would argue that she could have come home to live, but something about moving into her childhood bedroom felt worse than living out of her SUV.

Ian's gaze drifted to the spot where her hand rested. "It's no problem. Like I said, we haul it around on long jobs. I...uh..." He squirmed a bit, and his jaw worked. "I suppose I could have cleaned it up a little. I just, well, my main concern was making sure there was fuel for the generator."

"And I appreciate that very much."

Quiet ticked by, and then Ian tipped his head toward the door. "Well, I suppose we should bring in the rest of your stuff before it gets too dark."

"Right." Maggie swallowed past a suddenly dry throat. At the SUV, she pulled out a cardboard box of the few mementos she'd allowed herself to keep. Suddenly shy, she glanced at Ian then down at the box. "You really don't have to help."

He took the box from her with a chuckle. "That may be true in Nashville, but out here, a man can't call himself a man if he walks away from a lady in distress."

In spite of herself, Maggie smiled at the note of teasing in his voice and reached for another box stuffed with some of her clothes. "Oh, I'm distressed, am I?"

"After three days working on that?" He nodded to the schoolhouse. "I sure would be."

"Oh, that's comforting coming from my contractor. Thanks."

"No problem. And speaking of the schoolhouse, did I tell you the guys found an old chalkboard behind some of the shiplap in the living room? I guess that must have been where they taught the kids."

"I already knew about it. It's one of the reasons I decided to buy the place." Inside the trailer once again, Maggie put her box down and pointed to the floor. "You can just leave that there." She waited while Ian deposited the box next to hers, then smoothed a lock of hair that had slipped loose from her ponytail behind her ear. "Listen, there was some writing on the chalkboard. Not sure if you noticed it."

Straightening, Ian nodded and braced his hands on his hips. "I saw it."

Maggie bit the inside of her cheek. She wasn't sure why it mattered all of a sudden, but it did. "I'd like to keep it, if we can. I mean, I know your guys will have to work around it, but it's kind of cool. You know. Thinking about the person who wrote it and stuff. So, if it's not too much trouble, I'd like to try."

She was babbling, and her face was growing hotter by the minute, but if he noticed, it didn't show.

"We can keep it. No—"

"Problem," she finished for him. "I know."

His mouth lifted in a grin…one she was hard-pressed to admit she was starting to enjoy.

"So, what made you choose Nameless?" Ian asked as they began another trip to the SUV. This time, it was for a stack of clothes that Maggie hadn't bothered to remove from the hangers. They each grabbed an armload and headed toward the trailer.

Should she tell him about the biological mother she knew only from a photo tucked into her baby things? She squelched the idea as quickly as it rose, and shrugged. "I needed to get away from Nashville for a while. Nameless seemed as good a place as any."

Inside the trailer, Ian skirted the kitchen and moved to a closet across from the bathroom. "I'm assuming you want to hang this stuff? My guys and I left the bar up. It should still be…yep."

He nudged the sliding door open with his foot then stepped back to give her a glimpse. The closet was spacious, more than enough room for her clothes and shoes.

"Oh, good. Yes, that'll be perfect."

She eased past Ian, which in the confines of the trailer was not an easy task. And even with the armfuls of clothing between them, the air around him seemed charged. Maggie held her breath and only let it out when she was at the closet. She hung her load first and then turned for Ian's.

"I'll take that now."

"I'll help." He handed his stack to her a few items at a time. When they finished, he nodded to the last of the hangers, most of which consisted of brightly colored, western-style dresses complete with fringe. "Nice."

"They were my performing clothes." Maggie reached into the closet and hung those things in the back then slid the door closed. "Okay, that should be most of it. There's just a couple of things left, and I can get those in the morning. Oh, except…" She scanned the boxes and bags on the floor and frowned. "I left my fiddle on the back seat."

"I'll get it," Ian offered quickly.

"No, that's okay. I can do it." Feeling like she needed to say more, she added, "Thanks again for your help."

Instead of the "no problem" she expected, he surprised her with, "I was glad to do it."

It wasn't the words that touched her, it was the sincerity with which he said them. Or was it just that she'd come to doubt there was any sincerity left in the world? The people she'd met on tour often said one thing and meant another.

Maggie moved out of the hall into the tiny kitchen and gestured to the banged-up fridge. "I'd offer you something to drink, except I haven't had a chance to stock anything."

Ian ducked his head. "Actually, I put a few things in there I thought you might need. It's not much," he added as she crossed to look.

Not much included a half-gallon of milk, some bottled water, a carton of eggs, some cheese, and a loaf of bread. There was also a small tub of butter and plastic bottle of grape jelly.

"You'll find some cereal in the cupboard. Hope you like shredded wheat. It's all they had at the Quick Mart. Oh, and coffee, of course, for the guys."

So, he'd picked up supplies when he stopped to gas up the generator? Maggie closed the door slowly, unsure whether to feel grateful for his thoughtfulness or suspicious. It had been her experience since going into the entertainment business that people very rarely gave something for nothing.

"Thank you." She forced the words out through stiff lips and crossed her arms. "Just let me know what I owe you."

Surprisingly, he didn't argue. He gestured to a row of cupboards above the couch. "There's blankets and pillows up there. If you get warm, the windows all have screens. And if you have any trouble, give me a call. Otherwise, I'll see you in the morning."

"Okay. Thank you."

Suddenly all business, Ian gave a brief nod and then let himself out. Left to herself, Maggie turned a slow circle, taking in her new surroundings. Cobwebs swayed in every corner, riffled by the slightest breeze, and under the table, a very large and very scary-looking cockroach had gone belly up.

Maggie sighed. The trailer would need scrubbing, certainly, but that was a small price to pay for the relief she felt crowding her chest. She didn't suppose…?

She crossed to the sink and checked underneath. Inside was a small bottle of dish soap and a scrub brush. And if she had running water…

She straightened and opened the tap, puffing out a happy gasp when a stream gurgled from it. But then she remembered that Ian had said the trailer had a "small" tank and quickly closed the tap.

Rolling up her sleeves, Maggie retrieved the soap and brush and set to work. In her task of scrubbing the floors and walls from top to bottom, she also uncovered an old broom and a dustpan tucked into a tiny cupboard next to the refrigerator. A couple of hours and plenty of elbow grease later, the trailer fairly sparkled, or felt like it did. This time, when Maggie turned a circle, she didn't shudder. And now that she was finished, she could shower.

Heaven!

She grabbed an old T-shirt and sweatpants from her suitcase and hurried to the bathroom. There were no towels in the cupboards, but she had a few packed into the boxes, so she ducked back out into the living room for one, pausing when a flicker through the window facing the schoolhouse caught her eye. At first, she thought it was a reflection on the glass, but then the beam of light arced from side to side, bouncing off the walls and illuminating the ladders and equipment the workers had left inside. A flashlight? Had Ian come back for something? And if so, why hadn't he knocked or texted to let her know?

She twisted her wrist to glance at her watch. Eleven thirty. Maybe he figured she was asleep? Still, it didn't make sense that he would be scrounging around inside the schoolhouse so late. But if it wasn't Ian, then who?

She tensed and reached for the broom she'd left leaning next to the stove. It wasn't much of a weapon, but it was better than nothing. She inched toward the door, pausing when her hand closed on the knob.

What if the person outside wasn't Ian? What if it was thieves, hoping to steal tools? That kind of stuff happened a lot around building sites. Or they could be after her SUV. Her fiddle was still inside, which was just about the only thing she owned that meant anything to her at all. She felt a moment of panic right before she threw the door open.

"Hey!" she yelled, the broom clutched tightly in both hands. "Who's out there?"

The beam of light stilled, frozen for a split second to a spot on the wall.

And then it clicked out.

CHAPTER FIVE

Despite her doubts, Maggie did manage to sleep. It was fitful, and she kept waking up to listen for sounds outside the door, but it was something. Combined with the coffee dripping through the filter she'd found in the cupboard, she might just make it through the day.

When at last the coffee maker gurgled to a stop, Maggie poured a cup and brought it to her lips. The sun was just starting to crest the trees. Ian would be pulling in any second. The crew would arrive shortly after, and then she could find out which one of them had been poking around in the middle of the night. At least, she hoped it was one of them. It was what she'd told herself all night in order to sleep.

As expected, Ian's truck rumbled into the drive a few minutes later. Maggie fetched a second cup of coffee and waited to hand it to him when he met her at the door.

"So you found all the stuff in the cupboards, huh?" He brought the cup to his mouth and took a drink. "Mmm. Thanks. I didn't have time to make a pot before I left the house."

Maggie walked down the steps and sat on the bottom one, her elbows braced on her knees, coffee cup balanced in both hands. "Yeah, I was up late last night giving the trailer a good scrub." She fingered the handle on her cup. "And speaking of being up late, did you happen to swing by here again after you left?"

"Swing by?" Ian lowered his cup to look at her. "No. Why?"

It wasn't the answer she'd hoped for, but it was what she'd expected. Still, she'd have felt a lot better if he'd said he forgot one of his tools or something. She shrugged. "I thought I saw someone poking around in the schoolhouse."

He sobered and set his cup carefully on the hood of his truck. "What time was that?"

"It was late. Eleven thirty or so." The nerves she'd felt when she first saw the glow of the flashlight returned. "I thought maybe it was one of your guys coming by to make sure everything was ready for this morning."

"Not that late. There have been several break-ins lately, people stealing tools and equipment, stuff like that. Or it could have been a homeless person wandering through, looking for a place to sleep." He yanked his truck door open with a squeal, reached in and grabbed a hammer, then turned to her. "Wait here. I'm going to have a look around."

And he needed a weapon? Maggie's heart slammed against her chest, driving her to her feet. "Ian, wait. Maybe we should call the police."

"If anything looks out of place, we will." He smiled at her, but she got the feeling that was just to help put her at ease, and then he circled the truck and disappeared behind the schoolhouse.

Seconds ticked by, with nothing but the hum of cicadas and the occasional warble of a bird to break the morning stillness. Finally, she could stand it no longer.

"Ian? Is everything okay?"

Relief made her legs weak when he reappeared from behind the schoolhouse. On his face, he wore a perplexed frown. "Everything looks normal in there. Nothing missing or out of place." He replaced the hammer on the seat of his truck and slammed the door. "You sure you saw someone?"

"Well, I didn't actually see the person." Realizing she still clutched her cup, she set it on the step then hugged her arms around herself. "I saw a flashlight beam swinging around, but when I yelled out the door to ask who was inside, it went out. I never saw it again, and I checked several times throughout the night."

"I wish you had called me." He stepped closer, one hand stretched out, but he quickly let it fall to his side. Was she imagining it, or did he look concerned for her? And not just the casual kind of concern people showed for a stranger. He looked genuinely worried. "I'll ask the guys when they get here, just to be sure, but I doubt any of them would have been out that late."

"Maybe it was kids?" Maggie voiced the thought that had occurred to her sometime between waking and sleeping. "This place has been abandoned a long time. If people don't know it's been sold, they might have just been hanging around for fun." She grinned wryly. "My friends and I used to find old, abandoned houses to walk through. We pretended they were haunted."

"Maybe." He matched her grin and reached for his cup, downing the contents quickly as another truck pulled up and several men climbed out. "There's the crew." He handed back the cup and nodded to the man closest, a tall, lean, Hispanic man Ian introduced as Cesar. "He's the foreman for this job," Ian explained. "If you have any questions, or if you see something that doesn't look quite right, he's the guy to ask."

"Nice to meet you," Maggie said, shaking Cesar's hand. Ian finished the introductions then pulled Cesar aside while the others returned to the truck to begin unloading tools and materials. While they talked, Maggie carried the cups inside and set them in the sink. When she went back outside, Cesar had joined the rest, and Ian walked toward Maggie with a slow shake of his head.

"I didn't figure it was him," he said, the note of worry still in his voice. "I'm sorry, Maggie. I hate that you spent all night scared. Were you able to get any rest?"

"Some." She smiled and motioned to the trailer. "But I sure am glad I was in there and not in my car."

"Me too." He dropped his gaze, his lips pressed into a hard line. "I know it's none of my business, but what are the odds you'd reconsider a hotel?" He looked up when Maggie didn't answer then gave a low grunt. "That's what I figured."

"Like I said, it was probably just kids." Maggie ran her hand through her hair and gestured toward the trailer. "I'm going to get cleaned up and make a phone call. I'll meet you all inside the schoolhouse when I'm finished."

Fine lines feathered the skin around Ian's eyes as he nodded, giving him a boyish Robert Redford look that made Maggie's heart thump. "Okay."

Back inside, Maggie sank onto a seat at the kitchen table. Her mother had tried calling twice since Maggie left her message, and both times, she'd been working on the schoolhouse. But this morning she really wanted to hear her mom's voice. She dialed the number then counted the rings until her mother picked up.

"Maggie, is that you?"

She sagged against the back of her chair. What was it about a mother's voice that instantly put the world to rights? "Hi, Mom. I'm so glad I caught you."

"Oh, sweetheart, I've been so worried about you. How are you doing? How's the house reno coming? I've been talking about it with your father. We'd both love to come help."

In her last message, Maggie had told them about the schoolhouse. Of course they'd want to help. They always did. "I appreciate that," she said carefully.

"But you don't want us to come," her mother replied. There was no anger or hurt in her voice, just understanding.

Maggie switched the phone to her other ear. "It's not that I don't want your help. This is just something I need to do by myself."

Her mother inhaled deeply. "Will you send us pictures?"

Maggie's eyes closed, and she smiled. "Yeah, Mom. I'll send pictures, but I may wait until it doesn't look quite so bad before I do. Otherwise, Dad will be on the next bus."

Her mother's light laughter echoed across the miles, warming Maggie's heart. They chatted a couple more minutes, and then her mother's voice sobered.

"So…what about the other thing? Have you had any luck tracking down your biological mother?"

For the first time, Maggie heard a note of pain in her mother's voice. From the moment she'd first told her parents of her plans to search for her bio mom, they'd been nothing but supportive. But now?

"To be honest, there hasn't been much time to do a lot of digging," Maggie said, squirming in her chair. "I've been too wrapped up in the schoolhouse."

"Mm-hmm. Well…if there's anything I can do, just ask."

Love swelled inside Maggie's chest. How much had it cost her mother to offer such a thing?

"Thanks, Mom. I'll let you know." Swallowing a sudden knot, she added, "I love you."

"Love you too, baby girl."

They talked a little longer, and then Maggie ended the call. She hadn't told her mother about the person hanging around last night because, biological or not, she was still a mom, and Maggie had caused her enough worry the past few months.

After her shower, Maggie tugged on a clean pair of jeans and a T-shirt, then twisted her long hair into a messy bun, poured the rest of the coffee into a thermos, gathered a stack of paper coffee cups, and went outside. Ian and another man were ripping out rotted shiplap. Maggie walked over to them.

"I thought your guys would want this," she said, holding out the thermos and cups.

Ian smiled. "Thanks."

He hollered over his shoulder for Cesar, and Maggie held up the thermos. One by one, the crew laid down their tools and wandered over to them.

"Just in time for our break," Cesar said, giving a nod of thanks to Maggie before twisting the lid off the thermos and pouring each of his guys a cup.

"So it's demo day, huh?" Maggie glanced at the growing pile of debris in the middle of the room. "What can I do?"

Ian handed her the crowbar from his toolbelt. "You can start behind the woodstove and work your way to the window. Since a lot of this wood is rotted and the whole place needs wiring, we'll go down to the studs. If you've got gloves, you'll want to use them."

The fact that he didn't question whether she could do the work instantly won him points, and that he didn't bother to explain in "simple" terms earned him more. Maggie grabbed the crowbar and a pair of gloves and set to work. Within hours, the entire room was finished and most of the debris carried to a dumpster that arrived shortly after lunch. By the end of the day, Maggie had a whole new appreciation for Ian and his crew. As a team, they worked cohesively, each one ready and willing to help the other.

"You guys have been together a long time," Maggie said to Ian as the crew wrapped up for the day.

He rubbed the sweat from his forehead with his sleeve. "Cesar's been with me the longest, almost ten years."

"It shows." She motioned around the room. "We got a lot done."

He nodded. "More than I hoped. I'll call the electrician tonight and see if he can get started in the morning."

Hope flared in Maggie's chest. "Really? Do you think I might have power this weekend?"

His upheld hand dashed her hopes. "It's already Thursday. I doubt we could get the inspection done that fast, but maybe by Monday or Tuesday of next week. Of course, we'll still have to wait on the power company."

"I've already called them and opened an account. I also requested a turn-on notice, so once we have all the paperwork from the inspection, we should be good to go."

He nodded in approval. "Good thinking. You sure you still need me?"

She smiled at the teasing in his voice. "I'm sure. What have you heard about windows?"

"They're supposed to be delivered tomorrow." His phone dinged, and he pulled it out to glance at the screen. "Just got the revised floor plan. Do you have a minute to go over it?"

Maggie's stomach rumbled, and she laid her hand over it self-consciously. "Can we do it over dinner? I'm starving." At his hesitation, her mouth fell open. "Oh, I didn't mean…that sounded like I was…"

He met her gaze steadily, no teasing smile, no embarrassed reluctance. "Give me thirty minutes to wash up, and then I'll meet you at Logan's. It's a little barbecue place on the outskirts of Granville, just a few miles from here. Want me to send you directions?"

She shook her head and willed the heat in her cheeks to subside. "I can map it on my phone."

"Okay. See you there."

He spun to head for his truck. Because Ian had warned the crew about the possibility of someone loitering about, they had locked all the tools that could be carried in the trailer. Cesar waved to her as they climbed into their truck and set off.

Thirty minutes. She rushed into the trailer to shower and dab on some makeup, although why she felt the need to bother with the latter was a mystery.

Maybe not altogether a mystery, she thought, as she wove around the booths at Logan's toward a seat near the back where Ian waited, dressed in faded jeans and a white shirt rolled at the sleeves. If that wasn't enough to steal her breath, he wore his damp hair slicked back, tendrils curling at his neck and above his ears—a fact she couldn't help but notice as he stood to help her into her seat.

"Thanks."

"You're welcome. You found the place without a problem?"

She wiggled her phone then set it on the table. "Yep, thanks to GPS. Not sure how anyone ever got around before without it."

The waitress arrived for their drink order, and when she brought it, Maggie took a quick sip of her sweet tea then pushed her glass aside. "So, the plans?"

She motioned to his phone. She'd made the mistake of making it sound like she was asking him on a date earlier. Best if she cleared that up now. This was work, nothing more. Well, maybe a little more. There were ribs. Her mouth watering, she eyed a plate balanced on a server's palm.

Ian grabbed both of their menus and gestured to their waitress. "How 'bout we eat first and look over the plans after?"

Maggie had to agree or risk passing out from hunger. They placed their orders, and she settled against the back of the booth with a sigh, happy to soak in the sights, smells, and air-conditioning.

Laughter echoed from a nearby table, and Maggie angled her head to look. Betty Rutherford? She was seated with a handful of other women, all about the same age. Obviously friends, they were talking and laughing over their food and drinks.

Maggie turned her attention away from them and glanced across the table at Ian. "So, you're a contractor, huh? You like building things?"

"Actually, I prefer restoring things." He slid his glass close and rubbed a drop of condensation from the side with his thumb. "There's just something about seeing a place come to life after it's been let go that makes me happy."

Happy? She envied how easily the word rolled off his tongue. She hadn't been truly happy since she left her folks to move to Nashville.

"What about you?" He braced his arms on the table and leaned closer, raising his voice a little to be heard over the din of the restaurant. "I don't think I ever asked what you do?"

The question caught her off guard. It was normal he should ask, of course, but when she'd decided to hide out in Nameless, Tennessee, she hadn't bothered to think what she would tell people when they questioned what she did for a living. She fingered the paper sleeve her straw had come in. "Well, uh, I told you I worked in Nashville for a while."

That was all she got out before he grimaced. She angled her head, curious.

"What, you don't like Nashville?"

He looked down at his glass of iced tea, his face a study in solemnity. "I knew a girl who was fascinated by it once. The music, the lights, the fame… She craved everything the city had to offer."

Maggie shifted in her seat uncomfortably. The same could have been said about her once. "Was that so bad?"

"Not bad, except we didn't want the same things."

Ah. They'd dated. Maggie matched his posture and leaned forward against the table. "What happened?"

His gaze met hers, and for a long moment, he didn't say anything. Still, his silence spoke volumes. "Let's just say it didn't end well."

If anything could sum up her stint in Nashville, it was that line. She dropped her gaze.

"Afterward, I decided I was done with anything to do with Nashville," he continued. "I moved back here, set up my construction business, and have kept busy ever since."

"So, you were from here, but moved away and came back. Do people here know what happened?" The question was out before she could stop it. She held up her hand. "You don't have to answer that."

At his grin, her heart flipped a little.

"It's no secret." He shot a glance at the crowded tables surrounding them. "People around here know everything about everybody, so you'd have heard about it soon enough."

His words stopped her, made her think. She bit her lip. "Ian, do you suppose people would recognize the picture of a woman from around here if I showed it to them?"

He frowned. "That's pretty vague. What have you got?"

Maggie sucked in a stabilizing breath and dug in her wallet for the picture she'd carried around since the day her parents told her she was adopted. After finding it, she stared at the face of the young woman looking back at her for a long moment before turning it to show Ian. "This is her. I believe her name is Sylvia. Does she look familiar?"

Several seconds ticked by while he examined the photo. Finally, he shook his head. "Sorry, no." His gaze lifted to hers. "Someone you know?"

"Someone I'd like to know." Maggie fought a tightening in her throat as she tucked the photo into the side pocket of her purse. The photo and the handwriting on the back that spelled out her name were all she possessed of the woman who'd given her life. "She's my biological mother. I'm the baby in her arms."

His eyes widened a bit. "She was from Nameless? I saw the sign in the background."

"I'm not really sure. I thought the sign might be a clue, but either way, Nameless was as good a place as any to start searching."

The waitress arrived with their food, and Maggie used the precious seconds to tamp the emotion tightening her chest. By the time they were alone again, she felt better, or thought she did, until Ian's hand closed around hers. She stared at him silently while he sat with his head bowed for a long moment. At last, he looked up and smiled.

"Hope it's okay. I thought you could use the prayer."

"It's fine." Maggie fumbled for her fork. Aside from her parents, who prayed for her every day, how long had it been since anyone else showed the same concern? It left her feeling warm and confused all at once.

"Did I tell you this place used to be one of Jaxon Birdwell's favorite haunts?" Ian sliced through a piece of brisket and stuffed it into his mouth.

Maggie picked up her knife and did the same. "The country music singer?"

"That's the one. People used to hang out here for hours hoping he'd come by."

Seeing the twinkle in his eyes, Maggie frowned. "Hold on. I thought Jaxon Birdwell was from Texas."

"Oh, yeah? Guess I was wrong." Ian's smirk grew as he handed her a bottle of homemade barbecue sauce. "Try some of this. It'll curl the hair on your legs."

"Um, I don't have hair on my legs, thank you very much."

Smiling, Maggie swiped the bottle from his hand. If he was trying to shake her out of her previous melancholy, it was working. And that wasn't the only thing working, she realized as she settled in to enjoy her meal. Suddenly, she'd forgotten all about her determination to keep Ian at a distance. In fact, she couldn't remember why she'd ever considered him a distraction.

Anyway, it didn't matter how many times she told herself to stay away. She was drawn to him like a kid to a cookie jar. And judging by the look in his eyes as he watched her, he felt exactly the same way. It was a thrilling thought, except for one thing—Ian said he was done with anything to do with Nashville.

She paused with her hand on a warm, buttered roll.

She'd come to Nameless to lick her wounds and find new purpose for her life. But no matter what she told herself, a music career in Nashville still tugged at her. So what would she do if Gwen called with news of a contract? Could anything Maggie found in Nameless be enough to make her stay?

CHAPTER SIX

The electrician arrived at the schoolhouse early Friday morning, just as Maggie was pulling out of the drive to head into nearby Granville. Since he'd be working on the wiring all day, and Ian and his crew planned on repairing the weak spots in the floor, Maggie had decided to spend the morning searching for clues to her birth mother.

Except, it wasn't the woman in the photo who occupied her thoughts.

Maggie flipped the vents toward her warm cheeks and turned the fan to high. There was something about Ian Weber that made her giddy inside. Something about the way his blue eyes sparkled that made her think he'd smile any second, yet always surprised her when he did. And last night, when she'd told him about looking for her birth mother, he hadn't scoffed or teased or asked a lot of questions. Instead, he'd offered to pray for her. Again.

Maggie's grip on the steering wheel tightened. Ian was a nice enough guy, the kind she'd dreamed of meeting at one point in her life. But now? The truth was, ten years ago, she'd traded everything she held dear for a shot at country music stardom. She couldn't honestly say she wouldn't do it again if the chance arose. And that meant that sweet guys like Ian were off-limits because the industry could be ruthless, and the people who chased after it had to be also. She'd learned that lesson the hard way.

Ahead, through the windshield, Maggie spotted a lazy cloud drifting slowly on the morning breeze. The sky behind it was a brilliant azure, unbroken save for that one puffy dot, and so clear she could imagine seeing all the way to heaven.

She swallowed hard and concentrated on the road ahead, except the car was too quiet. She turned on the radio, let it play for a minute, then shut it off again when a familiar song pulsed from the speakers. That was one of hers—she'd helped write it when she first got to Nashville. She'd never gotten credit for it though. That belonged to someone with a bigger name and deeper pockets. Still, she'd trusted God and believed her shot would come along eventually. When it did, she'd jumped on it.

"Was I not thankful enough?" she whispered to God through tight lips. "Did I not give You enough of the glory?"

She stared at the blue sky and willed an answer to come. When it didn't, she gritted her teeth and shifted her focus to her driving.

The small town of Granville was just over seven miles from the schoolhouse. Unlike Nameless, which was more of a community than a town, Granville boasted a general store, several restaurants and museums, and a park nestled along the banks of the Cumberland River. Surely someone there would recognize the woman in the photo.

As the morning wore on, Maggie's optimism dwindled. Two gas stations, a couple of restaurants, and one museum later and still no luck. Granted, everyone she'd spoken to was around thirty or younger. She guessed her mother to be in her late forties or fifties. If she'd moved away after the adoption, it could simply be that no one Maggie had spoken to that morning was even born when her mother lived here. At least, she hoped that was all it was, because with her birth records sealed, her only hope of finding her mother was stumbling across someone who might have known her.

With that thought weighing heavily on her mind, Maggie swung into a grocery store for a few supplies, then drove back to Nameless. The clear skies that had greeted her early that morning were gone, replaced by dark thunderclouds pushed in by a wind from the south. Already, heat lightning streaked the sky. It would only be a matter of time before rain pelted the pavement.

Thankfully, it held off while Maggie unloaded the groceries. The electrician's vehicle was gone, as was the work crew's, but Ian's battered truck was still parked in the drive. Maggie grabbed an umbrella from the back of her SUV and ducked into the schoolhouse just as the first few fat raindrops pattered the ground.

Inside, the gloom of the storm and boards over the holes where the new windows would go made it too dark to see. She stuck her hands out and steadied herself against the wall until her eyes adjusted. "Ian?"

"Hold on, I'm almost done."

Gradually, Maggie got her bearings. She skirted a stack of two-by-fours and drywall and headed for the sound of Ian's voice. Besides the new wiring, the crew had piled rolls of insulation against the walls, along with new windows, doors, and stacks of shingles that would go on the new roof. Even the fans she'd ordered for the living areas had arrived—which was surprising, since the original delivery date was slated for next week.

"You guys accomplished a lot," Maggie said, raising her voice to be heard above the rumbling storm outside. "Are you in the utility room?" She touched the wall and picked her way to the basement stairs. "I'll come there."

"Maggie, watch out for the—"

"Stuff on the floor? I saw it," she cut in before he could finish. "Hey, you were right about the windows coming today. That means we can start the framing—"

Ian's hard body pressed against hers stopped her from saying more. In the next second, he jerked her away from the wall and held her cradled to his chest.

"What…what are you…" Her breaths came as short and fast as his. Her senses returning, she struggled against his hold, which was rather futile, since his muscled arms felt like a vice. "Ian, let go!"

"The floor." He sucked in a deep breath and set her carefully away from him, positioning himself between her and the wall she'd been using to brace herself. Yanking his phone out of his pocket, he switched on the flashlight and shone it on a gaping hole in the floor.

Maggie's mouth fell open. "What is that? What happened?"

"Remember the weak spot I told you about?" He traced the light from his phone along the floor, to the wall, and finally to a dark stain leaching downward from the old windowsill. "Apparently, it had been leaking for a while. Everything was rotted. We had to rip out all the old subfloor from the window to this spot. Normally, we wouldn't have left it open like this, but the plywood didn't come on the delivery truck with the two-by-fours. I was digging around for something to cover it with when I heard you come in."

He'd saved her. Another step, and she'd probably have tumbled headfirst into the basement.

Remorse flooded his face, and he held out his hand to her. "I'm sorry, Maggie. I figured you'd be gone longer."

"I finished early. You couldn't have known."

Funny, now that the danger was past, she would begin to tremble. Or was it the danger and not...something else? She rubbed her hands over her arms and turned to leave, praying her shaking legs wouldn't give out before she reached the door. And then, Ian was beside her, supporting her with a light touch to her elbow and her back. This time, she didn't push him away.

"We should wait until the rain lets up," he said, his voice a low rumble, like the thunder outside.

This close, she realized something she hadn't before...he smelled wonderful. Like sawdust, sunshine, sweat, and a tiny bit of after-shave, all rolled into one. Swallowing hard, she let him lead her to a couple of five-gallon buckets.

"I see the paint came." She giggled nervously then clamped her lips shut and sank down on one of the buckets.

"And the doors." Ian gestured with the flashlight on his phone. "I figure we can get those installed in the next couple of days. Oh, and I heard back on the electrical inspection. Someone will be out Monday afternoon. Now that the house is wired, the only thing left is installing the new panel. Hopefully, that will be tomorrow."

For several minutes, Ian talked about the work on the school-house. Most of it was repetitive, but it filled the silent spaces between cracks of thunder and made Maggie feel better, which, of course, was what he intended. Finally, she gestured to his phone.

"The flashlight will run your battery down."

He smiled. "I have a charger in the truck." At her nod, he shifted forward to rest his elbows on his knees. "So, what happened in Granville?"

"Not much, unfortunately." A cold front had accompanied the rain. Maggie shivered and hugged her arms around her middle. "I asked around at several places, but nobody recognized my biological mother from the picture."

"We could try around Nameless. Maybe at church? A lot of the members have lived here all of their lives."

She perked up at the idea. "I did think maybe I was asking the wrong age group about her. Most of them were younger than what she would be."

He straightened. "That settles it then. I'll swing by on my way to church and pick you up."

"Oh, you don't need to do that," Maggie protested. "If you'll text me the address, I can always—"

"GPS it, I know." His smile broadened. "But wouldn't going to church with a friend be a lot better than showing up all by yourself? Besides, I know a great breakfast place. Best pancakes this side of the Cumberland."

She shot him an answering smile. "Well, I can't argue with that."

"Good. I'll pick you up around eight thirty."

"Okay, thanks."

He paused, a look on his face that said he wanted to ask her something. She braced for the inevitable questions about Nashville, what touring was like, where she'd performed and who with. It happened every time people learned she'd once been almost famous.

"Why now? I mean, what happened that made you want to search for your biological mother now?"

She blinked. Switched gears. "I…well, I've pretty much always known I was adopted," she began. "My parents thought it was important that I know so I wouldn't feel betrayed later because they'd not told me. Plus, they wanted me to know that they'd chosen me. That they"—she swallowed and looked down at the worn hem on her sleeve—"wanted me."

"And?" he prompted gently.

She sighed and met his gaze. "Finding her was always in the back of my mind, but for a long time, I was too busy to bother with it. And then I wasn't. I figured now was a good time."

He picked absentmindedly at a hangnail on his thumb, and she could see the wheels turning inside his brain. "What about your father?"

She shook her head. "I have no idea. I'm hoping when I find her, she'll be able to tell me something about him."

In a sudden flash of lightning, she saw him rub his chin.

"Have you thought about doing a DNA test? I've heard people have located relatives that way."

"I did it a couple of months ago, but I haven't heard back yet. And the people from the company I chose told me I would only get results if others in my family had done the same thing."

"That makes sense." He frowned. "Did you say your bio mom's name is Sylvia?"

She nodded. "At least, I think so. My parents had been trying to adopt for a while, and then a friend told them about an attorney who was setting up a private adoption for one of his clients. Mom overheard whispers about her during the adoption process. It struck her how hard it must be to give up a child, so she never forgot about her and prayed for her over the years."

"Your mom sounds like a good woman."

"She's the best." Maggie sniffed. "Anyway, I tried contacting the attorney who'd handled my adoption. He's the one who told me the papers were sealed. And that was that." She shrugged.

"But you decided to look for her anyway?" Ian asked.

Maggie clenched her jaw. "She may not want anything to do with me, but that doesn't mean my father won't, and she's the only link I have to him."

Once again, feelings of worthlessness welled up within her. Feelings of being less than enough. A voice from deep inside whispered that she was an outsider. An outcast. She'd struggled with it her whole life, and only standing on stage with the applause of the audience washing over her had ever been loud enough to drown it out.

"Maybe she didn't give you up because she wanted nothing to do with you. Maybe she did it because she knew you couldn't have anything to do with her."

Maggie lifted her eyes to meet his. Though she wanted to prompt him to keep going, the words wouldn't come.

He shifted to rest his arms on his knees, his gaze calming and steady. "Maggie, sometimes people choose adoption because they want a better life for their child. It doesn't have anything to do with not wanting them. It's wanting something better for them."

She licked her lips, taking time to frame her words so they didn't wobble when they came out. "My mom says the same thing. I just never quite believed her."

His jaw hardened, but his gaze stayed soft. Tender, even. She looked away then dragged her eyes back. If she read pity on his face...but she didn't. Not a trace.

She took in a long breath. So much for staying away from him. In the span of a few short minutes, she'd opened up to him. Revealed a vulnerable part of herself she normally fought to keep hidden. And suddenly, even the open space of the schoolhouse seemed too small. She stood. "I think the rain has let up some."

He rose too. "I can walk you to the trailer."

"There's no need." She held up her hand to stall him from coming closer. "Besides, you'll just end up getting drenched."

Though he didn't look pleased, he nodded and remained rooted where he stood.

She shoved her hands into her pockets. "Will the crew be out in the morning?"

He shook his head. "It's supposed to rain through the night, but it should let up after lunch. We'll come out then to patch that hole in the floor. Plus, I want to start framing the interior walls so the electrician can finish wiring the panel."

"Okay, then I'll see you tomorrow."

"Maggie?"

She paused at the door to glance back at him.

"I'm praying for you. I hope you find what you're looking for."

She gave one last nod before making a dash for the trailer. In the bathroom, she grabbed a towel and scrubbed it over her damp hair.

Why now? Why did she have to meet Ian now, when her life was in shambles? Was it coincidence, or just another cruel trick—allowing her to hope about something only to snatch it away?

She dropped her arms and stared at her reflection in the mirror. "That's what happened with my career. I got a few good contracts and then what?" She shifted her gaze to the ceiling. "You took it away. And I'm not supposed to ask why?"

She flung the towel onto the floor, bitterness making her feel angry and childish but helpless to fight it.

"It's not fair. You've blessed others, opened paths for them. Why not me?"

They were the same questions she'd asked a hundred times. Just like before, she didn't have any answers.

Deep down, she doubted they would ever come.

✤ Chapter Seven ✤

Saturday should have been a day for snuggling under the covers, especially with the rain drumming on the roof of the trailer to lull Maggie to sleep. But she couldn't. Not with a thousand thoughts whirling inside her head. After kicking back the blanket, she went into the kitchen, put on a pot of coffee, then perched on a chair at the table, staring out the window at the overcast sky.

Days like this, she used to enjoy reading from her Bible or playing worship music quietly on her fiddle. Those times were long gone.

Finished with her coffee, she rinsed out her cup then dressed and slid on a raincoat to head toward the schoolhouse. Ian had said the guys wouldn't be by until the rain let up, but that didn't mean she couldn't putter around doing odd jobs until they showed.

It was gloomy, but not quite so dark inside the schoolhouse as the night before. Skirting the wide hole in the floor, Maggie picked up a hammer and set to work removing nails from the hardwood. She loved the old floors, but they were too damaged to save. By the time she'd finished, she'd accumulated a pretty large pile of nails. She swept them into a bucket then pushed it against the wall. Other than sweeping up, there wasn't much more she could do.

From the corner, the door leading to the basement beckoned. She frowned. She'd been upstairs, where her new bedroom would be, but she hadn't yet been in the basement. Like most buildings of the era, the basement was fashioned from stones, had low ceilings, and was basically only good for storage. Still, she needed to check it out eventually.

The door squealed open with just a light tug. Peering down into the black stairwell yawning below her, Maggie couldn't quite suppress a shudder. She hated musty basements, and this one was the mustiest. Of course, the rain didn't help. It added a layer of dampness that made her shiver. But the weather already seemed to be letting up a little, and since she couldn't do anything more until the crew arrived…

She sucked in a breath and started down the stairs, or what constituted stairs. In this case, they were rough-hewn logs, sawed in two, and fastened to a crude riser. At least they felt stable underfoot. Judging by the size of the logs, the rest of the schoolhouse could fall down around her ears and the stairs would still be standing.

In the basement, dark shadows quickly reminded her that she'd left her phone sitting on the table in the trailer. But she remembered seeing a flashlight in one of the toolboxes upstairs. She retrieved it then headed back into the basement for a look around.

As expected, the ceilings were low and covered in cobwebs. Maggie shuddered thinking about the critters that had crafted them and swung her flashlight in a wide arc to take in the rest of the room. Boxes stacked three and four high huddled against one wall. She moved closer for a better look. Printed on the sides of the boxes were dates, the newest being on top. It read 1965, the year Sherby the Realtor told her the school had closed.

Student records, maybe? She tugged on the lid of the newest one, screeching when a large bug scurried out and across her hand.

"I guess I know why no one ever bothered moving the boxes," she grumbled, swiping her hand against her jeans. "Blech."

She ran the flashlight over the rest of the stack, the print on the paper fading as the dates grew older. Somewhere between 1945 and 1930, it hit her. If her mother was from Nameless, wouldn't her name be among the records? No, that wasn't right.

She squelched the idea as quickly as it came. Her mother would have gone to school in the seventies and eighties. At best, she might have had a grandparent who attended the school, but without a surname, she wouldn't know them even if she saw them. Still…

She ran her finger over the date on one of the boxes. It wouldn't hurt to look. What if one of the students was named Margareta? The spelling wasn't exactly common. Could she have been named after a grandmother? Another possibility was ethnicity. Maggie had always thought at least one of her parents was Hispanic, given her name and the color of her hair and eyes. Maybe she could find a student in one of these boxes whose name fit. Even a handful of names would give her someplace to start looking.

Over her head, a floorboard creaked, and Maggie crooked an ear to listen. A second later, she heard it again.

"Hello?" She swung the flashlight toward the stairs. "Ian, is that you? I'm in the basement."

Nothing. Maggie moved to the stairs then froze. What if the midnight visitor had returned? She'd told herself it was kids, but what if she'd been wrong? No, that was her nerves talking. They wouldn't come back in the middle of the day. It had to be the electrician. Or one of the crew.

She forced her feet to move, one step, and then another. Overhead, the footsteps seemed to be moving in the same direction. Faster. With purpose.

"Hey, uh, I'm down here," Maggie shouted, her voice cracking from a growing fear. "Can you hear me?"

Why didn't the person say something? Was the storm drowning out her words? Or was it something more sinister? She swung the flashlight around the room, but she already knew it was useless. The stairs were the only way out, so she'd either have to come face-to-face with whoever was in the schoolhouse or—

She didn't finish the thought. It was cut short by the slamming of the stairwell door.

ᘒ CHAPTER EIGHT ᘒ

"Hello?"

The word scraped from Maggie's throat in hardly more than a weak whisper. She licked her lips and tried again.

"Hello! Can you hear me?"

For a full second, there was nothing, but then an odd sound broke the stillness, followed by the scuffling of retreating feet.

Whoever was up there was leaving. Unsure whether to be happy about that fact or worried, Maggie eased toward the stairs. And then it hit her. The sound she heard…it couldn't be…

She hurried up the steps, slipping on one of them and slamming her shoulder into the stone wall. Regaining her balance, she scurried the rest of the way and nearly threw herself against the door. It didn't budge. The knob turned, but the door had been fastened shut.

The hook latch. She'd only subconsciously noticed it when she came downstairs, but the light scraping she'd heard was the sound of the hook being pushed into the ring. But why would anyone lock her in the basement and leave? Was it some sort of prank? What if she couldn't get out? She didn't have her phone, couldn't call for help. In a moment of panic, she almost dropped the flashlight.

"Stop," she whispered. "Ian and the crew will be here soon. Just relax."

Several deep breaths later, she felt calm enough to sit. Until she remembered the spiderweb canopy over her head and stood because she didn't want the spiders crawling over her. But wouldn't standing only bring her head closer to them? And what if spiders weren't the worst thing crawling around down here?

She pointed the flashlight at the stairs, which only served to freak her out more, because now there were shadows dancing *under* the stairs.

"Stop it, Maggie. You're not a child," she scolded. In fact, her present situation closely resembled the nightmares of her childhood. Then, as now, the words to a hymn her mother had taught her leapt to her lips.

Peace, peace, wonderful peace.

The first line rasped from her dry lips like a prayer. She swallowed and tried again.

Peace, peace, wonderful peace
Coming down from the Father above
Sweep over my spirit forever, I pray
In fathomless billows of love

Tears pricked her eyes with the last line. It had been a long time since she'd allowed herself to feel God's love. And why was that?

It was hard to avoid the answer in the stillness of the basement. Now, in Nashville—well, it was easy. All she had to do was bury herself in the noise and lights. But here? The truth was like a slap to the face.

"I'm disappointed in You, Lord."

There had been times since Maggie had left Nashville when she doubted her prayers had even reached the ceiling, much less heaven. But now, in this moment, Jesus felt so close, she wouldn't have been surprised to see Him standing at the foot of the stairs.

She closed her eyes against the hot tears she felt forming and let the words she'd kept pent up since she lost her contract come spilling out in an ugly, emotional rush. All of the hurt. All of the disappointment. Even the anger and jealousy she'd kept buried found voice in her heartbroken tirade. When it was finally over, she felt weary and spent. But she felt cleansed too. And surprisingly, she still felt the Lord's presence, closer even than before.

"I guess it's no secret to You that I've been feeling this way, huh, Lord? It just took getting stuck in a spooky old basement for me to admit it to myself."

How much time ticked by after that revelation, Maggie didn't know. It felt like hours, but it was probably more like minutes. Still, she nearly cried with relief when she heard voices echoing from the other side of the door.

"Hello! Hello, Ian? Cesar! Hello?" Jumping to her feet, she pounded the door with her fist and then nearly fell into a very surprised Cesar when the door sprang open.

Steadying her with both hands, Cesar frowned. "Miss, are you all right?" He glanced past her at the door. "What happened? What were you doing down there?"

"Maggie?" Ian stepped into the schoolhouse, his gaze bouncing from her to the foreman. "Cesar, what's going on?"

"I have no idea," he said, lifting both hands, palms up. "We came in, and she was—"

"Someone locked me in the basement," Maggie interrupted. "I was looking at some boxes and heard someone up here moving around, but when I called out to them, th-they locked me in."

The toolbox in Ian's hand plunked to the floor with a thud, and he crossed to stand in front of her—not touching, but worried. She could see it on his face.

"Are you okay? How long were you down there?"

She hugged her arms around herself and shook her head. "I don't know. It felt like forever."

"But you're all right?"

"Yes. Yes, I'm fine," she added quickly, then slapped her hand over her mouth when something over Ian's shoulder caught her eye.

"What?" Ian followed the direction of her gaze. One of the paint buckets had been upset. Paint spilled over a large section of the floor, and on the wall, someone had written two menacing words.

GO AWAY!

"Get the paint on the floor cleaned up, but don't touch anything else," Ian barked to the crew then turned to Cesar. "Take a picture of the wall for the police."

"Right, boss."

Maggie read sympathy in the fleeting gaze she locked with Cesar, and then he motioned to the crew and began giving orders.

Ian gently took the flashlight still clutched in Maggie's hand. "Come on. Let's go get you cleaned up."

"What? No, I…" She glanced down. Her clothes were covered in dirt and dust from sitting on the stairs. Her hands too were filthy. "Oh."

"The guys will probably want some coffee," Ian said. "Would you mind? They drink that stuff all day long."

She wasn't fooled. He was giving her something to do, to distract her. Warmth flooded through her at his thoughtfulness. "Yeah. Okay."

He held out his hand to steady her, and though she didn't need his help, she took it and let him lead her back to the trailer.

While she washed up, Ian put the coffee on to brew, then sat down across the table from her. "So, tell me everything that happened this morning. What time did you go out to the schoolhouse?"

"It was early. Probably around seven thirty," she clarified. "It was still raining, but I figured I could take care of a few odds and ends until the crew arrived." At his nod of encouragement, she pressed on. "I must have worked for a couple of hours, I guess, just pulling up some nails and sweeping. Then I remembered that I hadn't been down in the basement at all."

"That was around nine thirty or ten?"

"I think so. I didn't have my phone, so I can't be sure." She rubbed her hand over her face. "I don't know why I forgot it. I usually always have it on me."

She drew in a startled breath as Ian's fingers closed around hers, firm yet gentle. Somehow, that light touch was enough to stem the tension she felt rising. She dropped her shoulders a little and went on. "I found a bunch of old boxes down there. I think they're school records. Anyway, I was looking them over when I heard footsteps."

"Heavy? Light?" Ian's brows rose questioningly.

"I...I..." She shook her head.

He gave her fingers a squeeze. "It's okay. Then what happened?"

She tore her gaze away, thinking. "I thought maybe it was you or one of the crew, so I called out, but the person didn't answer. That made me nervous. I couldn't figure out why they weren't talking. But there wasn't any other way out of the basement, so I headed to the stairs."

Whether he realized it or not, his grip tightened as she talked. "Did you get a glimpse of them?" he asked, his words terse.

She shook her head silently, knowing if she tried to speak, she'd start crying. Ian must have realized it too, because he let go of her hand and touched her cheek.

"It's okay. We'll figure out who did this."

He didn't say how, but for some reason, she believed him. It calmed her enough to loosen her tongue.

"Thank you, Ian. I'm not sure that I could handle this by myself."

At her words, he drew in a deep breath through his nose and lifted his chin. "Okay, let's talk about the intruder. I think it's safe to say whoever was poking around the other night and again today are the same person."

"You think so?"

"It'd be too big a coincidence otherwise."

Maggie nodded in agreement. "What do you think they're after?"

He frowned and clasped his hands on the tabletop. "I was hoping you could tell me."

"I have no idea." Betty Rutherford's face took shape in Maggie's thoughts, and she shrugged. "I mean, I suppose it could be the schoolhouse. Or the land. Maybe someone else wanted it?"

"Why? The place is in shambles. And the land has been for sale as long as I can remember."

She explained what Sherby had told her about Betty being unable to afford the schoolhouse, and what she'd said about it being a landmark. "And what about the boxes in the basement? I assumed they were school records, but they could be something else."

"Could be." He looked and sounded doubtful.

"You don't think so?"

"Well, the boxes have been there a long time. If someone wanted them, why did they wait until now to go looking for them?"

He was right. She brushed her hair from her forehead in frustration.

He paused, and she could almost see him mulling his words. "Besides, I don't know Betty well, but it would make more sense that she had something to do with this than a random stranger after the boxes. Except…"

"Yes?" she prompted.

"The message on the wall makes me think this thing is personal," he said at last.

"But I don't have any enemies, that I know of," she said slowly, bracing for what she sensed was coming.

"No, but you did just recently start looking for your bio mom." He laid his hand over hers. "Now, I'm not saying it was her. It could be someone trying to protect her."

Maggie jumped to her feet to pace the length of the trailer. "Protect her from what? I'm not angry at her. I don't want anything from her, other than maybe the name of my father. Why is that so terrible?"

She stopped pacing and lifted her hands helplessly. Did her biological mother truly hate her so much?

"I'm sorry, Maggie," Ian said, crossing to stand next to her. He lifted his hand to rub small circles on her back. "I didn't mean to make this worse for you. I could be wrong. Whoever's behind this could be after something else. Something hidden in the schoolhouse. Or buried there."

"Like treasure?"

He stopped stroking to peer down at her. "What?"

"Like maybe pirate treasure? You did put a giant *X* on the floor. Maybe they thought it meant something other than a weak floorboard?"

He stared for a long moment, like he couldn't quite believe she could be joking. And then a chuckle burst from his lips, followed by another, until they were both laughing. Only, he was still touching her. And she liked it. Which scared her almost as much as being locked in the basement. Because falling for him would be way too easy.

And she couldn't risk that.

She stepped away, her laughter fading. Looked at the floor. The walls. Anything to avoid meeting his gaze.

She bit her lip and then said, "Um, did I hear you say something about contacting the police?"

Ian cleared his throat and combed his fingers through his hair. "Yeah. I don't know if they'll be able to do much. They may just chalk up the whole mess to vandals unless the message can be viewed as some sort of threat. And I'm not sure locking you in the basement will count for much either, but I still think it would be a good idea to let the authorities know what's going on in case—"

He didn't finish and didn't have to.

"In case something else happens," she said. "Something more serious."

Ian shifted his weight to one foot and scrubbed his hand over his cheek. "Maggie, look. I know you said you didn't want to stay in a hotel, but I wish you'd reconsider—just for a couple of nights until we can get the windows and doors installed."

She shook her head before he finished. "I can't do that, Ian. I can't let this person run me off. Besides, I'm perfectly safe inside the trailer."

"Are you sure about that?"

"As safe as I would be inside the schoolhouse, or any house." She lifted her chin stubbornly. "How is staying in the trailer any different than staying in my home?"

Setting his jaw, he dragged his fingers through his hair again. "You really should think about getting a dog. A big one."

She laughed and crossed to the cupboard to take out a thermos. "My dad tells me the same thing. All the time." She handed the thermos to him and nodded to the pot. "Mind filling that while I get the cream and sugar?"

"I bet your dad is proud of you," Ian said, unscrewing the thermos top and setting it on the counter. "Seeing how brave and independent you've become? It must make him blow up with pride."

"Yeah." Maggie's hands stilled over the creamer packets. She hadn't told her parents about losing her contract, just that she was "between" jobs. She didn't want to worry them. Eventually, though, she'd have to come clean, especially if Gwen didn't call soon with good news.

"He used to come to all of my shows, him and Mom both. Dad always said listening to me play was like helping himself to a little slice of heaven."

Her throat thickened, and she busied herself stuffing sugar packets into a Ziploc bag until the emotion passed.

"That's sweet." Ian's voice roughened a little. "Do you still play?"

"I haven't for a while." She avoided looking at the closet where her fiddle was stored, and held up the bags of condiments. "Ready?"

Was it her imagination, or did he look relieved by her answer? And if so, why should it matter to him? Too quickly, he turned away to pick up the thermos. When he turned back, his face was smoothed of emotion.

"All set."

Once outside, some of the nerves Maggie had felt locked in the basement returned. Was Ian right? Should she reconsider checking into a hotel?

"You okay?"

She hadn't realized her steps had slowed. Resuming her pace, Maggie continued to the schoolhouse. Cesar met her at the door.

"You probably shouldn't come in yet. We haven't finished cleaning up the paint."

A little deflated by his words, Maggie nodded. "Well, we brought you and the crew some coffee."

"Thank you," he said, taking the bag from her and motioning to the rest of the guys. "In the meantime, what would you like us to do with the boxes in the basement?"

Truthfully, she'd forgotten all about them. She glanced at Ian.

He nodded to the trailer. "Stack them in the old bedroom for now, until Maggie's had a chance to see what they are." Turning to her, he said, "If it turns out they're student records, we can contact the school district to see what should be done with them." He turned back to Cesar. "Did you contact the police?"

"I did. Matt Hooper down at the sheriff's office said the paint falls under criminal mischief. Whoever did it will probably be looking at a fine at most, and maybe the cost of removing the paint."

"And locking me in the basement?" Maggie asked, a bit of temper rising.

"I'm sorry." Cesar shrugged helplessly. "Matt said it sounded like a harmless prank."

"Harmless?" Ian growled

Maggie laid her hand on his arm. "Thank you, but he's right. I wasn't hurt, just a little freaked out." She turned to Cesar. "It's pretty dark in the basement, and the stairs can be tricky. Please tell your guys to be careful."

The sound of an engine curtailed further conversation. Ian crossed to the door to look out. "It's the electrician." He shot a troubled glance at Maggie. "The guys will need my help if we're going to get the interior framing up so he can finish the last of the wiring." Her heart thumped as he walked back to her, his blue eyes fixed on hers. "Will you be okay?"

Maggie squirmed a little under the interested stares of the crew. She nodded and headed for the door. "I'll be fine. Thanks, though."

The confidence in her voice wasn't real. It was practiced, as rehearsed as the music she played on her fiddle. She only hoped as she walked away, Ian's gaze prickling the skin on her spine, that he believed her. Because he couldn't know how heavily she was coming to depend on him. It wasn't good for him. It wasn't good for either of them. In the end, they'd both wind up with a broken heart. And while she didn't care about herself so much, she did care about Ian. More than she was ready to admit.

CHAPTER NINE

Maggie reached over her head and flicked on the light in the trailer. Though it was after eight, the last rays of the setting sun were still leaching from the sky. She had been so absorbed in sorting through the boxes that Cesar and his men had brought up from the basement, she hadn't realized that it was getting dark.

Startled by a knock on the trailer door, she stood, scattering a handful of papers she'd been studying.

"Maggie? It's Ian. I brought you some supper."

At the mention of food, her stomach rumbled. "Coming."

High-stepping through the maze of boxes, she hurried to turn on the outside light and opened the door. Ian held up two white paper bags, one in each hand. "You have your choice between a black bean burger and fries"—he gave one of the bags a shake—"or smoked turkey on rye."

"Black bean, yuck." She reached for the second bag then pushed the door open farther to invite him in. At the table, she pulled the edges of the bag apart and took a whiff. "Oh my goodness, this smells heavenly."

"I figured you'd be so wrapped up in going through those boxes that you'd forget to eat."

"Ha! That's exactly what happened." She went to the sink to wash her hands, then pulled a bottle of water out of the fridge and offered it to Ian. He took it with a grin then blessed the food so they could eat.

"I knew you wouldn't be able to stop once you got started," he said, unscrewing the cap on his water and taking a drink. "Did you find anything interesting?"

"To be honest, I haven't found what I'm looking for…yet," she clarified, lifting one finger, "but the names? My goodness, it's like reading through the 'begats' in Genesis." Pulling the paper wrapper down around her sandwich, she took a bite then reached for a napkin.

"How is it?" Ian tipped his head toward her food.

"Delicious. Thank you so much." She wiped her fingers then pulled one leg up on her chair. "Anyway, through the years, teachers wrote all these little notes on the records—brother of so-and-so, or sister of such-and-such. I bet someone who knows the history of this place would really get a kick out of reading through all of the records." Her mind jumped to Betty.

Ian reached for a fry.

"Oh, do you want some ketchup?" Maggie asked. "I bought a bottle while I was at the grocery store."

"I'll get it."

While he crossed to the fridge, Maggie continued talking. "Reading all those old names, I couldn't help thinking about the people, wondering if any of them were still alive, or if they still live around Nameless."

Ian retook his seat and held up the ketchup bottle. Almost without thinking, she moved to give him room to squirt a little of it on the paper package next to her fries. "There was a girl named

Temperance and a boy named Erasmus who went to school here. Aren't those names unusual? According to Erasmus's teacher, Miss Pitts, he was quite precocious." She looked at the ceiling. "Can't you just imagine teaching all those kids—all different ages—in one room?"

Ian smiled watching her, and soon, Maggie was smiling back—neither of them eating.

"What?" She touched her hair. "What are you looking at? Do I have ketchup on my face?"

"You really enjoyed going through those records."

He picked up a french fry and offered it to her. She took it self-consciously.

"Yeah, I did. More than I thought I would. It was interesting, seeing how the kids progressed through the grades and what they were learning."

"Have you ever thought about teaching?" He left the question dangling and lifted his burger for a bite.

"I thought about it once." She shook her head and dipped the fry in her ketchup. "But then I wouldn't have been able to pursue my music."

The truth of the matter was that the lure of Nashville had drowned out the call to teach, but she didn't tell him that.

"So, what were you looking for?" He wiped his mouth with a napkin and gestured to the boxes when she didn't answer. "You said you didn't find it."

She shifted and dropped her foot to the floor. "Well, like I said, I started thinking I might find something in the boxes that could lead me to my bio mom."

His brow puckered and then cleared. "Oh, right. Sylvia. You thought maybe you'd find a student with that name."

"Or possibly a student with a Hispanic-sounding name," she added.

"Why? Are you Hispanic?"

"I won't know for sure until I get the results of my DNA test back, but I always figured I might be, given my coloring and my name."

"Maggie?" Ian laughed. "Sounds more Irish than Hispanic."

"Actually, it's Margareta," she said, snapping his wrist with her napkin. "My bio mom wrote it on the back of the picture I showed you. I go by Maggie for short."

He held up his hands in surrender. "Okay, I give."

When she took another bite of her sandwich, he leaned toward her. "You know, Margareta could also be a German name."

She swallowed and looked up at him, a napkin clutched in her hand. "What are you talking about?"

Ian slipped the napkin from her fingers and touched it to the corner of her mouth. "Your name. Margareta is a German name and means 'pearl.' I took German in high school," he explained.

Finished wiping her mouth, he handed the napkin back to her and went back to eating as though he hadn't just dropped a bombshell.

"But…I always thought…"

"Well, I mean, it could be Hispanic," he said, gesturing with a fry. "I'm just saying, it *might* be German."

He wiped his hands on a napkin then balled up the empty wrapper his burger had come in and stuffed it into the bag. "How many boxes did you get through?"

"A few. There's still several to go through, but I made it to the fifties." She smiled.

"Do you want some help going through the rest of them?"

"It's nice of you to offer, but I'm sure you're tired after working all day," she said quickly, as Ian rose.

His grin widened as he leaned closer to tap her hand. "Actually, I only worked half a day. Do you mind?" He hitched his thumb over his shoulder and waited.

She knew what she *should* do. What she *wanted* was something else altogether, and that was to spend a little more time with him, even if it was just a few minutes.

She gave a slow nod and picked at a piece of bread. "Go ahead. I'm just gonna finish my sandwich."

He left and reappeared a moment later with the box she'd been working on in his arms. "So, what is all this stuff, anyway? Report cards?"

"There are a few of those," she said, "but mostly it's things like addresses and disciplinary referrals and homework assignments, all stuff they keep on computers now."

"Huh." He pulled out a folder, browned at the edges, and flipped it open. "Benjamin Hatmaker." He looked up. "I know some Hatmakers over in Granville. I wonder if they're related?"

"Possibly."

Maggie took a bite of her sandwich while Ian continued looking. After a bit, he tilted the box to look at the side. "What year did you say this was?"

Maggie frowned and wiped her mouth. "I think 1952. Why?"

Ian held up a folder. "See this name? Otis McBride."

Maggie gave a puzzled frown and sat back in her chair. "Do you know him?"

"I do. He's a deacon at our church."

"What?" Maggie sat straighter. "That's neat." She grinned mischievously. "Look and see if his teachers wrote any notes on his folder."

He sorted through several pages then gave a disappointed shake of his head, followed by a grin. "Nothing. Oh well. You can still talk to him tomorrow at church. Maybe he'll remember going to school with someone named Sylvia."

Maggie shook her head and stuffed her napkin and her sandwich wrapper in the bag with Ian's. "That would have been after his time."

"*Mmm.* Right. I keep forgetting." He took one last look at Otis's folder before sliding it back into the box. "Anyway, I guess we'll have to call the school on Monday to see what should be done with all this stuff."

"Yeah." Maggie slid off her chair to sit next to Ian on the floor. "Hey, look at this one."

She riffled through the folders until she found the one she was looking for and flipped it open for him. Ian leaned closer, his shoulder bumping hers.

"Viltris Caddel. That's some name."

"Uh-uh. Look at what he wrote." She pointed at a bit of scribble under a crayon depiction of a house.

Ian's eyes widened. "He said he moved from Mississippi because lightning killed the family's chickens?"

"That's funny, right?" Maggie giggled. "Poor kid. He must have hated thunderstorms."

"No kidding." Ian chuckled and reached for another folder. "Oh, how about this one? My name is Liz," he read. "It's short for Lizard."

"What?" Maggie laughed. "It doesn't say that."

He leaned over to show her. Above the words was a picture of a tiny green lizard. She couldn't help but laugh, and enjoyed the sound of his. And with the warmth of his arm pressed against hers, well, despite the warning bells ringing in her head, Maggie didn't want the night to end.

She clasped both knees and angled her head toward the tool room. "Should we grab one more box? The next one might be the lucky one."

"Agreed. If we stop now, we'll just lie awake all night wondering about it." He shoved to his feet. "I'll get it."

"I'll help." Maggie rose and followed him to the back. While he cleared a path, she finagled another box off the stack. Behind it, something slid to the floor with a thump.

Maggie froze. "What was that?"

"I don't know. Let me look." Ian took the box from her and set it aside, then bumped the stack away from the wall with his hip. "There's something back there." Grunting, he jammed his arm behind the boxes, rummaged around a bit, then yanked a black instrument case free.

"What in the world?" Maggie touched the rusted silver buckles reverently. "Is that a violin case?"

"Sure looks like it." Ian laid the case on top of the boxes and snapped the buckles open. Though still in good shape, the velvet inside was empty. "Huh. I thought the case felt too light."

Maggie sank back off her tiptoes in disappointment. "What a shame. I thought we might really have something there." She looked at the boxes strewn about the room. "Do you suppose that case was down in the basement with all the rest of this stuff?"

"Must have been," Ian said. Wetting his thumb, he rubbed a smudge of dirt away from a bit of embossing on the violin case lid. "Look at that."

"What is it?" She squinted and leaned in closer. "Is that…?"

"Hold on." Ian left and returned with his water bottle and a napkin. He unscrewed the cap and poured a bit of water on the napkin then handed the bottle to Maggie before wiping the lid clean.

When he finished, Maggie sighed with delight. "It's a hummingbird."

She glanced at Ian, who was staring at the violin case with a look of puzzlement on his face.

"What's wrong?" she asked.

"That mark… I think I've seen it before."

"Really?" Maggie traced the tiny bird with her finger. The detail work on the beak and the body was incredible. Even the feathers were elegantly tipped, each line adding beauty and depth. "You've seen another case like this one?"

"Not the case." He tapped the hummingbird. "This. It's on the back of a fiddle my grandpa left to my mom."

"You're kidding."

"Nope. I could swear it's almost exact."

"Does your mother still have it?"

"I'm sure she does somewhere, but no one in our family ever played, so she's probably just got it stored somewhere."

Excitement thrummed through Maggie, and her fingers itched for the vibration of her fiddle strings—something she hadn't felt for a long time. She touched the hummingbird again and wondered about its owner.

"I don't understand," she said. "Why would anyone take the fiddle and leave this beautiful case behind? And how did your grandfather come by it?"

"Mom always said it was a family heirloom," Ian said. "I could ask her about it, if you want. Better yet, why don't I take you by my parents' place tomorrow after church?"

"Oh, I wouldn't want to impose," Maggie began.

"You wouldn't be imposing. I invited you," Ian said. "Besides, it's not Sunday lunch at the Webers' if there aren't at least three guests at the table."

Though it sounded charming, still Maggie hesitated. "You're sure your mother won't mind?"

"Mom's gift is hospitality. Trust me," he said, his eyes twinkling, "she'll love having you."

The thought of a home-cooked meal and not something heated in the microwave was too tempting to resist.

"Okay," Maggie said, "but only if we swing by a store and pick up something for dessert on the way."

"Deal. And I know just what to get."

"Oh? You gonna give me a hint?"

"Not even a little one."

He grinned and touched the tip of her nose. It was then that Maggie realized he was close enough to touch the tip of her nose. Her mouth went dry as she looked up at him.

"Um…"

Ian seemed to have the same realization at exactly the same moment. He cleared his throat and retreated a step. "It's getting late. I should probably…"

"Get going? Yeah."

But he didn't move, and neither did she. In fact, she was pretty sure if she leaned toward him even a fraction, he'd kiss her. She'd already decided that wouldn't be fair to him. The way he was looking at her now, she was even more sure of it.

Her heart beating erratically inside her chest, she sucked in a deep breath and tore her gaze from his. "Thanks for your help today, Ian."

"Glad to do it." He circled the boxes and headed to the door. When he reached it, he paused with his hand on the knob. "See you in the morning?"

She smoothed a lock of hair behind her ear and nodded. "Eight thirty, right?"

"Right." He hesitated a second longer then pushed the door open. "Goodnight, Maggie."

"Night, Ian."

She sighed as he slipped through the door. The trailer felt a lot larger without Ian in it. It also felt quieter, and not in a good way. Growling in frustration, Maggie stomped to the closet to pull out a T-shirt and a clean pair of sweats. Ian had only been gone five minutes, and already she missed him.

"Might as well get comfortable," she grumbled, kicking off her shoes. "It's going to be a long night."

⮿ CHAPTER TEN ⮿

Maggie debated over what to wear Sunday morning and finally decided on a simple denim dress and a buff-colored pair of western-style ankle boots. A turquoise necklace and silver earrings completed the outfit.

Promptly at eight thirty a familiar rumble pulled into the driveway. After grabbing her purse and keys and the violin case, Maggie hurried out to meet Ian. Standing next to his truck, dressed in a pressed pair of khakis and a blue shirt that matched the color of his eyes, he nearly took her breath away.

Ian circled the truck toward the passenger side, a wide smile on his lips. "Wow. You look amazing."

Maggie touched her hair, which she had chosen to leave loose and flowing around her shoulders rather than her normal ponytail or messy bun. "Thanks." She dropped her hand and returned his smile. "I was about to say the same thing about you."

Grinning, Ian reached out to open the door for her. "Sorry about the work truck. Normally, I ride my motorcycle to church, but I didn't think you'd appreciate the helmet hair."

Maggie laughed and climbed up onto the seat. Once she was settled, Ian shut the door and went back around to climb in on the driver's side.

"I didn't realize you rode," Maggie said as he cranked the engine.

"Yep. Got a 2018 Harley-Davidson Softail. My dad and I ride every chance we get."

"*Mmm.*" Somehow, the image of him on a bike only enhanced his persona.

He pointed to the violin case lying across her lap. "So, you brought it, huh?"

"Well, I figured if it did match your mom's violin, the two belonged together. After all, neither one's good without the other."

His smile deepened. "So, are you hungry?"

"Oh yeah. I've been thinking about those pancakes you promised me all week."

"Good, because you're not going to believe the size of them. I'm talking as big as the plates and four to a stack."

"You've convinced me." She smacked his arm playfully. "Find the gas pedal, buddy."

Lucille's Place was an out-of-the-way diner with nothing but a small, hand-painted sign above the door to mark its existence. Maggie got out of the truck and eyed it critically.

"You're sure about this?" she asked as she joined Ian on the sidewalk.

"Trust me. This place will ruin you for pancakes." He swept his hand out invitingly.

"Okaaay," Maggie said, exaggerating her uncertainty with a lilt of her voice.

Inside, almost every table was occupied. Waitresses in black pants and white tops with red checked aprons around their waists hurried back and forth from the kitchen, plates stacked high with golden pancakes balanced in their hands.

Ian tilted his head to hers, his eyebrows lifting. "See?" he whispered. "If you want to find the best restaurants, eat where the locals do."

"I'm looking forward to it," she whispered back.

Angling his head, Ian gave her an appraising glance then motioned to the hostess. "Table for two, please."

In one smooth motion, the hostess snagged two menus and two bundles of silverware out of a tray. "Right this way."

Though Maggie had been teasing when she told Ian she was starving, the buttery scent of pancakes mixed with the savory smell of frying bacon made her mouth water. She didn't even glance at the menus the hostess laid on the table. "I'll have whatever you're having, so long as it's pancakes," she said to Ian.

"Every Sunday." He slapped his menu down on top of Maggie's and leaned forward to rest his arms on the table. They chatted until their breakfast came, and then Maggie took a bite and groaned in delight.

"Oh my goodness, you weren't kidding."

"I told you," Ian said, chuckling. He pulled a napkin from the dispenser and reached across the table to touch it to her chin. "Syrup."

"Thanks." She took the napkin from him, her breath catching in her throat when their fingers grazed, and finished the job herself. "So, I stayed up late going through the rest of the boxes last night."

Ian swallowed his own bite. "I figured you would. Find anything interesting?"

"A few Hispanic-sounding names I plan on researching later, but nothing concrete that I thought would help me locate my birth mother." She sighed and curled her fingers around her coffee cup. "I sure hope your friend Otis can tell me something about her. Otherwise, I'm no closer to finding her than I was a month ago."

"I hope so too, for your sake."

Maggie reached for her fork and took another bite. "Wow. I can't get over how good these are. I'm gonna have to ask the cook for her recipe."

"Ha! Good luck with that." Ian braced one elbow on the table and shook his head. "I've been asking Lucille for it for years, and she won't even give me a hint."

Maggie lowered her fork. "Wait, Lucille is a real person?"

"As real as they come, sweetheart." A portly woman with flaming red hair sashayed up to them and swatted Ian with her apron. "Who've you got with you?"

"Lucille, this is Maggie Lange. Maggie"—he nodded to the redhead—"Lucille."

"Lange. Lange." She tapped her chin a couple of times as she said Maggie's name and lifted her gaze to the ceiling.

Maggie tensed, unprepared to have someone recognize her and unsure what she would say if Lucille asked her about Nashville.

Lucille snapped her fingers and lowered her gaze to Maggie. "Are you the Lange that bought the old schoolhouse?"

Relief flooded through her. "I am. But how did you know?"

Lucille smiled and gave Ian a gentle shove, then sat down in the space he made for her. "Small town, honey. People talk, especially in here." She glanced at Ian and back at Maggie. "I hear some folks aren't too happy about you buying the old place."

Maggie frowned. "You mean Betty Rutherford?"

Lucille lifted one eyebrow. "Is it true, what she says? You're planning on tearing up the schoolhouse?"

"I wouldn't exactly say that," Maggie said, hesitantly. "I'm renovating it and turning it into a home. In fact, Ian is my contractor."

"Is that right?" Lucille's shifted her gaze to Ian. "Well, if I'd known that, I wouldn't have been so worried."

"You know how I feel about fixing up historical places," Ian said.

"I sure do, hon. I'm glad you're the one doing the work." She smiled at Maggie. "Not that I don't trust you. It's just, that old schoolhouse has been a part of Nameless as long as I can remember. I'd hate to see it disappear or be destroyed or turned into something modern."

"I understand," Maggie assured her. She leaned forward over the table. "So, what else did Betty say, if you don't mind me asking? And who did she say it to?"

"To be honest, not much," Lucille said. "Mostly, I just figured she wanted something to complain about, and seeing as you're not from around here, you were it. As for the other thing, well, she talked to just about anyone who would listen."

Maggie glanced at Ian. "It's funny that she would talk about the changes I'm making when she's never been inside."

She could see that he knew what she was hinting at. "Lucille, did Betty happen to mention how she knew about Maggie's plans?"

"Sugar, you know how rumors work. They don't have to be true. They're like butter, they just have to be churned." Lucille slid out of her seat and stood. "I'm gonna leave you two to your breakfast now, before it gets cold. Thanks for coming in, Ian. Pleasure to meet you, Maggie."

She gave Ian's shoulder a pat and shot a wink at Maggie before swaying to the next table.

"Does she chat with all her customers?" Maggie asked, picking up a slice of bacon.

"All the time. It's why people come in here—to catch up on all the gossip. That, and the pancakes." He saluted her with his fork then speared another large bite.

"Hmm." She didn't like it, but he was probably right. When it came to small towns, the grapevine was usually more reliable than the local news.

After breakfast, Maggie and Ian made the short drive to his church, a large brick and vinyl-sided building with wide windows and a plain, painted cross over the door. Two men dressed similarly in blue jeans and polo shirts with the church logo on the pocket greeted them as they approached.

"Morning, Ian. Who's your friend?" the taller of the two asked.

Ian made the introductions then spent a few minutes chatting with the two men before leading Maggie to the education wing of the church.

"Otis should be back here," he explained as they walked. "He and his wife, Norma, teach a Sunday school class together."

To Ian's surprise, and Maggie's disappointment, it wasn't Otis and Norma who waited in the classroom for students to arrive. It was another member of the church named Shane.

"I'm sorry, Ian," Shane said, tapping his watch. "Otis texted me this morning asking me to take over his class because Norma was sick. He stayed home to take care of her."

"Okay. Thanks for letting me know."

Shane withdrew into the classroom, and Ian shifted his gaze to Maggie.

"Sorry about that. They normally never miss, so she must be feeling pretty bad."

"It's no problem. I hope she feels better soon."

"Me too." Ian pointed to another class down the hall. "Let's go in there. Did you bring the picture of your bio mom with you? We can show it around, see if anybody recognizes her."

"Right here." Maggie pulled it out of a pocket of her purse. "You're sure no one will mind?"

Ian smiled and took her elbow. "They'll be glad to help."

As Ian predicted, the members of the class were eager to look at the picture after Maggie explained who she was searching for and why. Unfortunately, none of them were able to provide any insight, though many promised to be praying for her.

Afterward, the worship music in the sanctuary leading up to the sermon was much as she expected given the various ages of the congregation—a nice combination of contemporary songs and hymns. The band had just finished their third song when the worship leader stepped to the microphone and invited a young girl of about eleven or twelve onto the stage. Maggie was only mildly curious about her until the girl crossed to take a violin from a stand and pressed it to her shoulder. Taking a tremulous breath, she raised her bow and played the first timid notes of *Amazing Grace*.

Listening to her play, Maggie was instantly transported to her own first performance. It too took place in church, in front of friends and family. She'd been so nervous, standing up there all alone, but one glance at her mom and dad, and she'd found the courage to close her eyes and play. Afterward, she'd known the moment the applause started that she wanted the feeling to last.

"Hey...you okay?" Ian whispered.

Maggie jerked her eyes open. He held out a tissue, his face creased with concern.

Maggie took the tissue and pressed it to her cheek. She hadn't even realized she'd been crying, but now she couldn't make the tears stop. Only when the last note drifted from the violin and the girl stepped down from the stage did Maggie feel some semblance of control return.

"Sorry," she whispered to Ian. "It was just so beautiful."

Smiling, Ian patted her knee, and then they turned their attention to the pastor, who was just stepping to the podium to preach.

Later, after church was over and the two of them were back in the truck, Ian drew his seat belt across his chest and snapped it into place. "Well? What did you think?"

"I didn't realize how much I missed it," Maggie said. "Being around other believers, I mean. It's...been a long time. Too long." She looked out her window, afraid to see what Ian would make of her honesty.

Ian started the truck and drove slowly out of the parking lot. On the street, he said, "Maggie, I hope you don't mind me asking, but what happened back in Nashville? Why did you leave?"

She knew he'd get around to asking eventually. What surprised her was that she didn't mind. "I moved to Nashville right after college," she began, picking at the silver buckle on the violin case just to give her hands something to do. "My parents weren't too happy about it, but I think they both knew it was something I had to do. For a while, I played a lot of smaller gigs to get by, and then…"

She paused, remembering.

"And then?" Ian prompted gently.

She blinked and pulled her thoughts back to the present. "I met a guy named Rhett Smalley."

Ian's head jerked around to her, and she nodded.

"At the time, he was just breaking onto the music scene. He'd landed a major record label, and his first single was climbing the charts. One night, he happened to be in the audience and heard me play."

She rubbed her hand over her face and sighed. "I have to admit, I was flattered by the attention he showed me. His band needed another fiddle player, and he chose me. I thought I was set. It would only be a matter of time before my career took off."

"But it didn't?"

"Not the way I'd hoped. Rhett and I wrote a slew of hit songs together, but he kept telling me we needed to say he'd written them so that the label would produce them. Once the songs had been around a while, then we could tell people that I had helped write them."

"Let me guess. That day never came."

She blew out a sigh and stared at the trees rolling past. "Several months ago, I'd had enough. I went to Rhett and told him I wouldn't help him write any more songs unless he gave me credit for my work. Honestly, I thought he would agree. Instead, he canceled my contract and started spreading rumors about me causing problems for him on the tour. Next thing I knew, no one in Nashville would hire me."

Next to her, Ian sat stiff and silent. Then he scrubbed his knuckles over his jaw and gripped the steering wheel with both hands. "I'm sorry, Maggie. If it helps, I'll never listen to another one of the guy's songs."

She smiled, and they drove a while in silence.

"I've never seen you play, or even get out your fiddle. Is that why?" he asked. "Did this experience turn you off music?"

"It's not the music, or even Rhett," she explained quietly. "To be honest, I was more upset that God allowed it to happen, especially since—" She stopped and looked at Ian. "The verse on the chalkboard in the schoolhouse?"

"Yeah, Jeremiah 29:11. 'For I know the plans I have for you, declares the Lord, plans to prosper you and not to harm you—'"

She recited the last part of the verse with him. "'—plans to give you hope and a future.'"

Their eyes met, and then she quickly looked away from the compassion she read in his gaze.

"You stopped believing it."

"I thought so," she admitted, rubbing a small circle on the top of the violin case, "but today, hearing that girl play…" She shook her head. "I guess I'm still trying to work it all out."

When Ian didn't answer, she peeked over at him. What was he thinking? Was he disappointed in her for questioning God's plan? Was he sorry he'd bothered taking her to church or that he'd brought her to meet his family?

After turning off the main road and onto a winding gravel drive, Ian slowed and came to a stop in front of a picturesque country farmhouse. But instead of climbing out, he swiveled toward her on the seat and reached out to lay his hand over hers.

"I'm not going to pretend to know what you've been through," he began quietly. "I'm just going to say that the God I believe in is big enough to handle our doubts. And He's not done with you, Maggie. You're His child. Whatever He has planned, He's still working it out for your good."

Lifting her hand, he brought it to his mouth and placed a tender kiss on the inside of her wrist. Maggie couldn't speak, hardly dared breathe. Every word she'd told herself about keeping Ian at a distance went flying out the window—not that they'd have mattered anyway. Because whether she'd realized it or not, she'd already fallen head over heels for the sweet man sitting next to her.

And deep down, she knew her life would never be the same.

CHAPTER ELEVEN

Ian's father, Bennett, was an older, distinguished version of his son, with light flecks of gray highlighting the same blond hair and fine wrinkles, adding character to the same sparkling blue eyes. His wife, Rose, was also quite striking, with russet-colored hair that framed her heart-shaped face and a smile that instantly made Maggie feel warm and welcomed. After greeting Maggie, she turned to her son and wrapped him in a long hug.

"How was church?" With him towering at least a foot over her, she had to look up quite a ways. Somehow, that only made her adoration of him sweeter.

"It was good, except Otis McBride wasn't there. He stayed home to take care of Norma. Apparently, she's not feeling well."

"Oh? That's too bad. I'll have to give her a call." She turned to Maggie. "Ian's father and I used to attend that church, but we moved a few years back and started going to one a little closer."

Maggie smiled, and Rose continued. "Ian tells us you're searching for your biological mother. Have you had any luck?"

"Not yet," Maggie said. She took the picture out of her purse and handed it to Rose. "I showed this to a few people, but no one knew her."

Bennett eased to his wife's side to look over her shoulder. "Cute girl." To his wife he said, "Does she look familiar?"

"Dad's not from around here," Ian explained. "He and Mom met in college."

Maggie nodded in understanding and looked at Rose, who handed the photo back with a shake of her head. "I'm sorry, Maggie. I don't think I've ever seen this girl."

"No problem." She returned the photo to her purse and forced a smile. "I'm beginning to think she never existed."

Rose stepped forward to clasp Maggie's hands. "We'll be praying for you. Please let us know what God reveals to you."

Her face warming under Rose's direct gaze, Maggie stammered, "Th-thank you."

Letting go of Maggie's hands, Rose beckoned to her husband and Ian. "I've got lunch ready. Let's get something to eat, and then you two can tell us about the violin case you found."

Sitting at the table with Ian and his parents, two things struck Maggie—how close they were and how much Ian obviously respected them. He listened attentively when his father spoke and took every opportunity to smile at his mom affectionately.

Suddenly, longing for her own parents filled her. After lunch, she excused herself from the table and slipped onto the back porch to call them. This time, when her mother asked how things were going, she took time to explain, opening up about her feelings and talking about her disappointment. When her dad asked what they could do, she invited them down to help with the renovations on the schoolhouse. She ended the call filled with thanksgiving and more hope than she'd felt in months—not because her circumstances had changed but because she had.

Casting her eyes skyward, she whispered, "Thank You."

The back door slid open, and Ian poked his head out. "Everything okay?"

"Yep," Maggie said, swiping happy tears from her eyes.

"Good. Dad got the fiddle out. Wanna come see?"

"Absolutely."

Bennett and Rose waited for them in the living room. Like the rest of the house, this space was warm and comfortable, with overstuffed chairs and a sofa the couple occupied side by side.

"Ah, Maggie." Rose motioned to her. "Come and see. It appears the hummingbirds do match."

Everything else forgotten, Maggie crossed for a closer look. While she was fascinated by the birds, it was the craftsmanship of the fiddle itself that captured her attention. From chin rest to scroll, it was beautiful and elegant. Intertwined with the hummingbirds were beautiful, delicate carved irises.

"Oh my goodness." She held out her hand and glanced at Rose. "May I?"

"Of course." She motioned for her to pick it up.

Flipping the fiddle over, Maggie examined the pegs and strings, both still solid and taut, then moved on to the body, which had a deep patina that could only come with age.

"Do you play, Maggie?" Rose asked gently, watching her.

"I do, but I've never played an instrument like this. It's absolutely amazing."

Rose glanced at Bennett, who nodded and reached down to the floor to retrieve a bow from a modern violin case strikingly at odds with the vintage instrument that inhabited it.

"Would you mind?" Rose took the bow and held it out to her. "It's been so long since I heard it played."

"Oh." Maggie darted a glance at Ian, who smiled and nodded encouragingly.

"Go ahead," he said. "I never heard my grandfather play, so I'm curious to know what that thing sounds like."

Sucking in a breath, Maggie took the bow gingerly and stood, nerves making her knees shake. She gave the instrument a quick tuning.

"Sorry," she said, switching the bow and fiddle to one hand and swiping her free palm down her skirt. "I don't know why I'm so nervous."

Blowing out a breath, she brought the fiddle to her shoulder, the feel of it so familiar, she instantly relaxed. Then, closing her eyes, she touched the bow to the strings and played without thinking, lost in the full, warm sound.

At first, the songs were mournful, exactly the way Maggie felt in the deepest part of herself. Gradually, the songs changed, became lighter, as the hope of God's Word crowded out her doubts. The last notes were echoes of those she'd heard that morning, played by a young girl whose song had reminded everyone in the room of God's amazing grace.

Lowering the bow, Maggie opened her eyes to see both Ian and his father staring and Rose next to them dabbing her tears with a tissue.

Rose lifted her hands. "That was…"

"Heaven," Ian finished.

"Exactly. Like a little slice of heaven," Rose said. Rising, she skirted the coffee table and pulled Maggie into a hug. "Thank you so much. I had no idea the sound from that instrument could be so beautiful."

"It was my pleasure," Maggie said, and meant it. For the first time in a long time, she had enjoyed drawing the music out of herself and translating it to the instrument. Bending down, she placed the fiddle back in its original case, not the plastic one it had been stored in.

"So, tell me about the fiddle," she said. "Where did it come from, and who made it?"

"It belonged to my father, Will McCrae," Rose said. "His grandfather used to make fiddles, but this one was special to him."

"I can see why," Bennett said. "It's beautiful, of course, but the music you were able to make on it was just awesome, Maggie."

"That was mostly the instrument," Maggie said. "It really is an incredible piece of art." Switching her gaze to Rose, she asked, "What about the case? Do you know how it ended up in the basement of my schoolhouse?"

"Well, my mother used to teach there. Maybe it got left behind when they closed up the school?"

Maggie's heart skipped a beat. "Wait, your mother was a teacher?" She jerked her gaze to Ian. "Why didn't you tell me? Do you think maybe your grandmother might be able to tell me if one of my relatives was a student?"

Ian's face fell, and he reached out to clasp Maggie's hand. "Both of my grandparents passed away several years ago."

"Oh…" Maggie looked from Ian to Rose and back. "I'm so sorry."

"You couldn't have known," Rose said gently. "And anyway, they both loved the Lord, so when they passed, we all knew it would only be a matter of time before we saw them again."

She said it with such hope and conviction that any guilt Maggie felt for having brought it up faded. Reaching for the violin case, she closed the lid then laid it in Rose's lap.

"I don't know how the fiddle got separated from its case, but there's no doubt they belong together. Please, keep it."

Rose reached up to touch Maggie's cheek. "Maybe the case ended up exactly where it was supposed to in order to bring you into our lives."

Maggie covered Rose's hand with her own, and then straightened. "Thank you both so much for lunch, but I probably should get going."

Ian rose at her words and walked her to the door. After she said her goodbyes to the Webers, she and Ian walked out to his truck, but instead of opening the door for her, he stopped a few feet shy and reached for her hand.

"Mom's right, you know."

Maggie's heart rate sped at the look she read on his face. "About what?"

"The schoolhouse, the fiddle case…Maggie, I think God used them to bring you here. To bring us together."

Hearing the hoarseness in his voice, Maggie felt her knees go weak. "Ian…"

He stepped closer, cutting the words from her mouth with just a glance. "I have feelings for you, Maggie." His voice dropped a little. "Am I wrong thinking you feel the same?"

She couldn't lie to him. She closed her eyes and shook her head. "You're not wrong, but Ian, I'm not sure…that is, I don't know if…" She sighed and lifted her gaze to him. "I don't know what this is."

Or if she dared trust it.

"I don't either," he said, his lips curving in a small smile as he moved even closer to smooth her hair from her forehead. "But I know I want to find out, if you do."

"Yeah." She swallowed hard, loving the way his eyes flashed when she nodded, and even the way her insides melted when he dropped his hand to cup her cheek.

"I know it's hard for you to trust anyone right now," he whispered. "We'll take it as slow as you want, okay?"

Somehow, she managed to agree, and then Ian opened the truck door and helped her inside. This time, the ride to the schoolhouse seemed to fly by, and all too soon, they were at the trailer steps, neither one ready to part but neither one actually saying so.

"I enjoyed meeting your parents today," Maggie said, fighting a sudden wave of shyness. The wind had picked up and tossed the ends of her hair playfully. She grabbed her hair and smoothed it over one shoulder "They're really awesome."

"Thanks. I think so too." He grinned, pushing one hand into his pocket as he shifted to lean against the side of the trailer. "Mom really liked you."

"You think so?"

"I could tell by the way she talked to you."

"Oh, I think your mother is pretty much sweet to everyone she meets," Maggie protested, her face warming under his gaze.

"True, but you?" He shoved away from the trailer and moved close enough to rub one hand down her arm. "I think she knows you're special."

Maggie angled her head up at him with a smile. In response, Ian drew in a deep breath and closed the distance between them.

"I'd really like to kiss you, Maggie."

Her breath caught, and instead of answering, she closed her eyes and lifted her face to his. Ian's kiss was gentle but strong, much like him. Mostly, Maggie just wanted it to last, and was a little disappointed when he cut it short. But then he pulled her into his arms, and her heart tripped all over itself again.

"I should go," Ian said, but made no move to release her.

Finally, Maggie stirred in his arms and looked up at him. "Thank you for today, for helping me look for my bio mom. And for helping me with the schoolhouse." She smiled and stepped away from him reluctantly. "I'll see you tomorrow?"

"Yeah." He scrubbed his fingers through his hair, gave a wry laugh, and reached for the doorknob. When it turned in his hand, he froze and looked at Maggie. "Did you lock this when we left?"

Maggie stared at the door in confusion. "I thought I did."

Ian pushed Maggie behind him. "Wait here, okay? I'm gonna take a quick look."

"Ian."

"It's okay. I'll be right back."

Maggie retreated a step, her hands fluttering to her neck as she watched him mount the steps and open the door. He didn't go inside immediately. Instead, he looked at her over his shoulder, his face stony and eyes hard as ice.

"Maggie, do you have your phone?"

"Yes," she said, yanking it from her purse and holding it up. "It's right here."

"Good." He looked inside the trailer and then back at her. "Because you're going to need to call the police."

CHAPTER TWELVE

It didn't take the police long to get a statement from Maggie or for Ian to round up a couple of guys to help clean up the mess left behind by a determined intruder. Many of Maggie's clothes were torn and strewn about, the groceries pulled from the cupboards and scattered on the floor. But what hurt the worst was what had been done to her fiddle.

"Can it be fixed?" Ian asked, coming to stand at her shoulder.

Maggie stared at the splintered pieces in her hands, as broken and shattered as she felt inside. "No."

Striding to the door, she tossed it on top of the clothes and food piled in the trash bin outside, then yanked some soap out from under the sink. Armed with a roll of paper towels, she scrubbed the words LIAR and CHEAT from the kitchen window. Except she got madder as she worked, and tears collected in her eyes until she couldn't see.

"Here, let me help," Ian said. Taking the paper towel from her hands, he finished the job she was too upset to do.

Her strength ebbing, Maggie sank onto a chair. "It doesn't make any sense. What could I have done to make someone hate me enough to call me a...a..."

"Don't, Maggie. There's no point." Tearing off a sheet from the roll of paper towels, Ian pressed it into her hand then dragged over another chair to sit next to her. "It's like the police officer said. Our energy would be better spent figuring out who would have a vendetta against you and why."

"*Our* energy?" Maggie sniffed and swiped the towel under her nose. "You sure didn't sign up for this when you agreed to be my contractor."

"Maybe not, but I'm signing up for it now," he said. His jaw hard, he motioned to the window. "Matt Hooper said the writing looked like it had been done in glass paint, so I think it's safe to assume that whoever did this probably planned to mark up your car, then changed their mind when they were able to jimmy the lock on the trailer. Any ideas who that might have been?"

"Like I told the sheriff…," she began, and then paused.

Ian clasped her hand. "What?"

Her phone rattled on the tabletop where she'd laid it, and Maggie glanced at the screen to see who was calling. "It's Gwen," she said, picking up the phone. "My agent."

She stood and stepped outside before answering. "Hey, Gwen."

"Maggie! Thank goodness. I've been trying to reach you all morning."

"I had my ringer off and forgot to turn it on after church," Maggie said. "Listen, Gwen, now isn't a good time. Would it be all right if I—"

"It's about Rhett."

She fell silent.

"He's done, Maggie. Finished. Apparently, you weren't the only one he was stealing from—only this time, a couple of musicians filed charges against him."

When Maggie didn't answer, Gwen pushed on.

"Do you know what this means? They have proof. No one is going to believe anything he said about you now."

"That's good," Maggie said.

"Good? It's great. By this time next week, I'll have you booked on a tour."

Maggie tightened her grip on the phone. "Where's Rhett now?"

"I have no idea." Gwen paused. "Does it matter?"

"Maybe." Maggie sucked in a breath. "Do you know if he still drives that silver Mercedes he bought after he signed with the label?"

"Wh—no. Maggie, what in the world is going on with you? It's like you're not even hearing what I'm saying."

"I'm hearing you, Gwen, trust me." Maggie glanced back at the trailer. "Give me a couple of days to figure things out, will you? I'll call you when I can."

She didn't wait to hear Gwen's response, but ended the call and spun to find Ian.

"It's a long shot, I know," she said, when she finished telling him about Gwen's call, "but the car I saw on the street my first day here could have been silver, so if not Rhett, then who?"

"I agree, it's worth talking to Matt. I'll give him a call and let him know." He shoved away from the sink where he'd been standing and pulled her into a hug. "In the meantime, pack an overnight bag."

Maggie started to pull away and opened her mouth to protest, but Ian stopped her with a touch to her cheek.

"It's not safe for you out here by yourself," he said quietly, "not with some guy running around with an axe to grind. If you won't check into a hotel, my parents have a guest room you could use. It's that, or I spend the night in a sleeping bag outside your door."

He meant it. She could see it in the stubborn set of his jaw. "Fine. I'll check into a hotel, but just for tonight. Tomorrow, I want to finish cleaning up this mess and then install locks on the doors and windows of the schoolhouse so I can stay there."

"That'll work."

His quick agreement caught her off guard. She blinked and crossed her arms. "Wait, you're okay with that?"

"Sure. If you're staying in the schoolhouse, I can stay out here, in the trailer." He grinned and spread out his hands.

Rolling her eyes, Maggie feigned exasperation when, in reality, his protectiveness left her feeling more attracted to him than ever. "Just give me a second to grab a couple of things," she said, turning her face away before he could read the truth in her eyes.

Later, after Ian had said good night, Maggie sat alone in her hotel room, the TV droning a documentary in the background. Was it still only Sunday?

She rubbed her hands over her face wearily. It was hard to believe, given everything that had happened. Realizing she hadn't told her parents about the break-in, Maggie snatched her phone from the nightstand, then laid it back down when she saw the time. It was late, and there was nothing they could do about it anyway. No sense worrying them.

After kicking off her shoes, Maggie pulled back the covers and climbed into the bed, then climbed back out again to check the locks on the door. She'd told Ian she was fine, and it was true when he was standing next to her. Now, alone in her room, she wasn't so sure. Except…she wasn't alone. Not really.

She padded back to the bed and wriggled under the covers. "I don't know what Your plan is in all of this, God," she whispered, scrunching her eyes shut tight. "But I'm going to trust You. At least, I'm going to try. And if You could help me out when that trust lags a little, I sure would appreciate it."

It was a weak prayer, but that was okay, because as her mother said, God was in the business of meeting people in their weakness.

Chapter Thirteen

With the wiring finished on the panel and the inspection completed Monday afternoon, Maggie's hope of moving into the schoolhouse became a reality. The first time she turned on a light switch with actual power, she nearly shouted in relief. She didn't even mind the smiles from Ian, Cesar, and the work crew because, somehow, she sensed they were as happy for her as she was for herself.

"You've got lights and insulation, now how 'bout we get you some walls?" Ian said, pointing to a stack of drywall.

"Never thought I'd be so happy about drywall," Maggie said with a laugh, "but yeah, I'd love that."

Because the drywall involved scaffolding and heavy lifting, Maggie had decided to leave the work crew to it and find out what she could about Rhett. Despite their problems, she still wasn't convinced that he'd been the one to break into the trailer or lock her in the basement. It wasn't his style. Still, other than Betty and a mother she'd never met, she didn't have many options.

Ian gave last-minute instructions to Cesar then joined her at the door. "Ready?"

She tucked her hair behind her ear and sighed. "You really don't have to babysit me, you know. I'm perfectly capable of taking care of myself."

"I know you are," he said, no hesitation in his voice. "But some-times it's okay to accept a little help from a friend." He nudged her shoulder with his. "Makes the burden not so heavy."

"Well, when you put it that way…"

Maggie smiled and headed out to his truck. Their first stop would be the police station, and then she planned to make use of his computer and printer, followed by a few phone calls to see what she could learn about the charges against Rhett. If that failed to turn up any clues, they'd agreed to track down Betty so they could ask her a few questions. Secretly, she hoped it didn't come to that, because if she planned on living in Nameless, she certainly didn't want a war with the neighbors.

At the police station, Maggie filled Matt in on her history with Rhett and what Gwen had told her yesterday about the charges brought against him. Matt had agreed it was worth looking into in case Rhett was desperate and hoping to intimidate a third person from speaking out against him. After his promise to keep them updated, they headed for Ian's place, a small craftsman-style home midway between Nameless and Granville.

Standing in the entrance, Maggie couldn't help but stare. All the interior wood had been redone, the walls painted in traditional col-ors, and period furnishings added to enhance the overall charm.

Running her fingers over the satin finish on the stair railing, Maggie sighed. "Oh, Ian, this is beautiful."

He dropped his keys into a bowl on a table next to the door and smiled. "It's a work in progress, but I'm happy with it so far. Mom helped with all the decorating." He pointed to the railing. "Do you like that? I was thinking about doing something similar in the schoolhouse."

"Really?" Maggie glanced at him and then back at the solid newels and gracefully turned spindles. "I love it."

The front parlor had also been carefully restored, as had the dining room. When she finished exploring them, Ian pointed to another room down the hall. "The office is back here. I'll get the computer booted up for you and leave you to it."

"Thank you."

While the front rooms evidenced his mother's feminine touch, the office was strongly masculine. Next to two black, four-drawer filing cabinets, a wire crate made for easy access to a host of rolled blueprints. In the center of the room sat a giant desk with more house plans scattered on top, and on the windowsill, a small plant begged for water.

"Here, let me just…" Ian scooped the plans off the desk and dropped them onto a metal folding chair. "Like I said, a work in progress."

He rolled a leather office chair on squeaky wheels to the desk then stepped back and invited her to sit.

"Thanks." She looked at him expectantly.

"Can I, uh, would you like something to drink? Water or coffee?"

She smiled and set her purse on the floor next to her chair. "Water would be nice."

"Coming right up." He lingered a moment longer, and almost as though he wasn't sure what to do with his hands, he combed his fingers through his hair then nodded to the doorway. "I'll just…"

Maggie's smile broadened as he disappeared down the hall. He was acting nervous, as though having her in his place put him off-kilter. Thinking back to their first encounter, she knew exactly how he felt.

Drawing in a breath, she turned her attention to the computer and finding out what she could about Rhett. Thirty minutes later, she took a sip from the bottle of water Ian had brought her and read over the headlines she'd gathered.

COUNTRY MUSIC STAR DIMMED BY ALLEGATIONS

ROCKY ROAD AHEAD FOR SINGER SMALLEY

But the one that struck her hardest said simply, CAUGHT.

Wasn't that what she'd wanted—for Rhett to be caught in his lies about her? So why did the picture of him next to the bold print only make her sad?

Startled by the ringing of her cell phone, Maggie jumped then scrambled through her purse until she found it. "Hello?"

"Maggie Lange?"

"Yes?"

"This is Matt Hooper from the sheriff's office."

"Oh yes. What can I do for you?"

"Actually, I have some news for you."

Already? Maggie barely had time to think before he went on.

"Turns out Mr. Smalley was arrested for disorderly conduct in a bar outside of Nashville Saturday night."

"Wait…Saturday?"

"That's right. He was released yesterday afternoon after making bail."

"But that means he couldn't have broken into the trailer."

"Afraid so."

"I see. Um, thank you for calling."

"Yes, ma'am. If you think of anything else that can help us, give me a call."

"Will do. Thank you."

She ended the call and looked over at Ian, who had come to stand in the doorway when he heard her phone ring.

"Everything okay?"

"That was Matt." She told him what he'd said then motioned to the computer. "So much for this. It's a dead end."

Ian walked over to the desk and picked up one of the articles she'd printed then looked back at her. "I'm sorry, Maggie. I gotta admit, I was kinda hoping it was him."

"Me too," she said then added quickly, "but not because I wanted him to be guilty. I just really want to know who's behind all the stuff that's been happening."

Ian replaced the paper on the desk and motioned toward the door. "How about we head into town for some lunch and then see what we can find out about Betty? Maybe we'll have better luck there."

Maggie agreed, and once she'd shut down the computer and stopped to give the plant on the sill some water, they headed back out to the truck and made the short trip into Granville.

"I know a great sandwich place," Ian said, slowing to wait for a light to turn green before swinging off the main road onto a side street.

"I'm beginning to think you know all the good places to eat," Maggie teased.

Ian shrugged and laughed. "What can I say? I'm a contractor, not a cook. I didn't show you the kitchen, but you would have seen it's the last part of the house left to finish."

"I'll have to go back once it's done," Maggie said, then stopped. She didn't want him to think she expected anything from him. She gestured out the window. "So where's this sandwich shop?"

"Just up ahead. Oh, and I should tell you, if you're not in the mood for a sandwich, they have some of the best homemade soups around."

Though she hadn't thought she was all that hungry, her stomach rumbled at the thought of a bowl of cheesy broccoli, something her mom made whenever the weather turned chilly. They had just gone inside and were approaching the counter when Ian grabbed her arm. "Hey, there's Brian McBride."

"Who?" Maggie looked toward where he pointed.

"Otis McBride's son. He must have come into town when he heard his mother was sick." Ian smiled down at her. "I told you we'd have luck after some lunch. Come on, I'll introduce you."

Grabbing her hand, Ian wove past several customers at the counter to the checkout, where a tall, handsome man with a short, military-style haircut was collecting his change and a brown bag of food.

"Thanks, Marcy," he said to the cashier then glanced over at Ian, his eyes widening in surprise. "Well, hello there, Ian."

"Hey, Brian." The two shook hands, and then Ian pointed to the bag. "Is that for your mom? How's she feeling?"

"Oh, she's better today. Thanks for asking." He patted the bag then grinned and stuffed his wallet into his back pocket. "I figured

I'd pick her and Dad up some soup instead of stuffing them with my lousy cooking."

"I'm sure they'll appreciate it. Tell them hello for me, will ya? And let Norma know I'm praying for her."

"Will do. Thanks, Ian."

"Of course." Ian stepped aside and drew Maggie forward. "Brian, I'd like to introduce you to a friend of mine. This is Maggie Lange. She bought the old schoolhouse in Nameless."

Brian's eyes rounded as he stared at Maggie. His mouth gaping, he stumbled back a step. "What? Who?"

That was all he said. A second later, the bag slipped from his hands and landed with a splat on the floor.

Chapter Fourteen

Ian reached out to clasp Brian's shoulder. "Hey, are you all right?"

Brian's gaze dropped to the floor and the soup seeping out of the edge of the bag. "Oh my."

"Don't worry about it," the cashier named Marcy said. "We'll get someone to clean that up and get you a fresh bowl."

"Yes, okay. I'm so sorry."

"It's not a problem." She smiled and patted his arm then hurried away.

Ian's hand fell from Brian's shoulder. "Let's sit down for a second, okay?"

Brian nodded, but his gaze remained fixed on Maggie. Finding a table, he sat then leaned toward her across the table. "They say everyone has a doppelganger, but I never believed it until now. I'm sorry about my reaction a moment ago. It's just, the resemblance is uncanny."

"Resemblance to who?" Maggie asked at the same time as Ian.

Brian opened his mouth, closed it again, and then motioned to Maggie. "I suppose we should start with some introductions."

Now that Maggie's heart rate had settled some, she was able to talk. She told Brian her name and what she was doing in Nameless. "But I'm curious who you thought I was when you first saw me. I look like someone you know?"

"Used to know," he clarified softly.

Along with the return of her voice, Maggie was able to take in more of Brian's appearance. He was tall and lean, with a chiseled jaw and brown eyes that looked directly at a person when he talked to them. Wrinkles feathered the tanned skin around his eyes and mouth, as though he smiled a lot, an idea that instantly put Maggie at ease with him.

Resting his elbows on the table, Brian pulled a napkin from the dispenser and used it to dab his forehead.

"You all right, Brian?" Ian asked him again.

"I'm fine now. Just startled a bit." His gaze shifted to Maggie. "I dated a girl who looked a lot like you before I went off to the Marines. Just for a second, I thought you might be her, but I realize now that couldn't be."

"I didn't know you'd dated anyone," Ian said. "Was she from Nameless?"

"Not Nameless, Nashville. Her parents were wealthy, but you'd have never known it meeting her. Her name was Josie Obermann. She was as sweet and down-to-earth as they come." He gave a small shake of his head. "Nothing at all like her mother."

"If you don't mind telling me, what happened between the two of you?" Maggie asked. "I assume you broke up?"

"In a way."

Marcy brought Brian's soup, and he waited until she'd bustled off before he continued.

"Her parents didn't approve of our relationship. Somehow, they convinced her that things would never work between the two of us. Next thing I knew, she was gone. Just up and left without a word to anyone."

"That must have been tough," Ian said.

Remembering what *he'd* been through, Maggie laid her hand on his arm.

"You can say that again." Brian's voice roughened. He cleared his throat and continued. "Anyway, not long after she left, I enlisted in the Marines. I figured it was the only way I was going to be able to move on with my life."

"You never heard from her again?" Maggie asked.

Brian smiled sadly and grasped the rolled-down top of the paper bag containing the soup. "For a long time I hoped she'd change her mind and come back. I wrote letters to her. Hundreds of 'em. She returned them all, unopened."

"I'm so sorry," Maggie said. "I can see why meeting me was such a shock." For a split second, she wondered if this woman could be her mother, then shrugged the thought away. Her mother's name was Sylvia. But could she be a sister?

Maggie leaned forward. "Brian, did Josie have any siblings?"

"She was an only child." He sighed and shook his head. "Anyway, enough about that. Ian said you bought the old schoolhouse?"

Maggie hid her disappointment with a smile. "That's right."

"I'm so glad someone did. That old place was going to ruin sitting there empty."

"That's what I told her," Ian said.

Maggie nodded. "Ian and I were going through some old records we found in the basement, and we came across some with your dad's name on them. He was a student there?"

"Sure was." The lines that had appeared on his face when he talked about Josie smoothed with his smile. "Dad says the years he spent in that old schoolhouse were some of the best of his life, though you know you're going back quite a ways, talking about that. He met my mother there."

Ian's brows lifted. "I didn't know that."

Brian nodded, his smile broadening. "Dad's always telling stories about that old place. You remember the Williams family that used to live on Sawmill Road?"

"Bucky? Yep, I remember him," Ian said.

"Bucky was the youngest. He had nine brothers, and all of them went to that school. The oldest one, Roger, had a thing for my mom."

"You're kidding."

Brian shook his head. "Dad swears he had to arm wrestle him for her affection."

Ian laughed and Maggie with him.

It sounded like Otis remembered quite a bit about those years. Maggie's hopes lifted.

"Brian, do you think I could talk to your dad about the schoolhouse? The reason I'm asking is because I think my birth mother may have been from Nameless. She would have been too young to attend the school, of course, but I thought maybe Otis might have known her parents…my grandparents."

"If she was from Nameless, it's a possibility," Brian said. "They might've even gone to school together."

"That's what I was thinking," Maggie said. She reached into her purse and withdrew the picture of her mother and held it out to him. "Does this woman look familiar? She's my birth mother. I believe her name was Sylvia."

Maggie watched as the color drained from Brian's face. He took the picture, stared at it for a long moment, and then slowly lifted his gaze to hers. "Where did you say you got this picture?"

Maggie glanced at Ian in confusion and back at Brian. "My adoptive mother gave it to me. She found it in my baby things. Why? Do you know her? You know Sylvia?"

"I do," Brian said, his jaw hardening as he handed the picture back. "But that woman isn't Sylvia. That's Josie. Sylvia was her mother."

CHAPTER FIFTEEN

Ian leaned forward and held up the picture. "Brian, are you sure? This is Josie, the same girl you dated?"

Brian's hands shook as he took the picture from Ian. "I've seen her face a thousand times in my dreams. This is her." He looked at Maggie, the confusion on his face painful. "So, she…met someone? That's why she never answered my letters?"

For a long moment, no one spoke.

"There could be another possibility," Ian said quietly, meeting Brian's gaze. Understanding passed between them, and then Brian nodded and pushed up from the table.

"I have to know. If there's even the slightest chance…" His gaze dropped to Maggie.

Her knees shook, and she didn't quite trust herself to stand. Could it be? Was Brian McBride her father? She licked her lips. "How do we get in touch with Josie?"

He blew out a breath. "That I don't know. I haven't heard from her in years. But I believe her mother still lives in Nashville. She would be the one to ask." Despite the moisture gathering in his eyes, his chin lifted, and he held out his hand to her. "We should talk to her, for both our sakes."

Drawing a breath, Maggie took his hand and stood.

"We'll go now," Ian said, rising with her. He looked at Brian. "Will you lead the way?"

"Of course."

That settled, the three of them left the restaurant and headed for their vehicles. A few minutes later, Maggie and Ian hit the highway behind Brian, the only sound the hum of the tires on the pavement. She startled when Ian reached for her hand.

"Are you all right?"

She opened her mouth, shut it, then opened it again. "To be honest, I'm not sure. My whole life, I thought my mother's name was Sylvia. Now I know it's Josie. I just wish I knew why she left...."

She motioned out the window, but deep down, she meant something else. She knew it, and by the way Ian was looking at her, he did too.

His grasp on her hand tightened. "We'll get the truth, Maggie. We'll find her, and we'll get the truth."

Knowing he would help her eased some of the ache in her chest. Neither one spoke the rest of the way to Nashville. Only when they passed the glittering lights and windows of the city and stopped in front of an imposing brick structure on the outskirts of town did Maggie voice her doubts.

"What if they won't see me?" She dragged her gaze from the window to Ian. "What if I tell them who I am and they send me away?"

"Then it will be their loss," he replied, cupping her cheek. "Maggie, I wish I could tell you what's going to happen when you walk up to that door. I can't. I wish I could protect you and make it all go right. But I'll go with you, if you want. I'll stand next to you and hold your hand. And I'll be praying for you the whole time."

"I know you will." Maggie's eyes filled with tears.

"Are you sure you want to do this now?"

Maggie hesitated as Brian climbed out of his truck and looked back at her, and then she reached for the door handle. "I'm sure. I have to know."

She looked at Ian for affirmation because as much as she thought she wanted the truth, she also feared it.

"Let's go," he said, his voice low. "I'll be right next to you."

She gave a slow nod, then pulled on the handle. Brian was there to open the door for her. As she stepped out, she looked up at him. His eyes were reddened, his jaw rigid and lips white. This was hard on both of them. She laid her hand on his arm.

"I have to ask you something."

He looked back at her steadily.

"I'd like a chance to talk to her alone first, before we ask who... if you..."

He grabbed her hand. "I understand. I'll wait here."

"Thank you," she whispered, then turned to give a nod to Ian.

The walk from the street up the driveway to the house was the longest she'd ever taken. Twice, she started to turn around, but Ian's strong fingers curled around hers kept her moving forward.

At the end of the drive, a silver luxury car was parked inside the garage. The door was open, as though the owner had just returned. At first, Maggie was barely aware of it, until something else caught her eye.

White paint on the bumper.

"Oh no." She froze, dragging Ian and Brian to a stop with her.

"What is it?" Ian peered into her face and then in the direction she stared. "What's wrong?"

She didn't have time to answer. The door inside the garage leading into the house opened, and a tall, slender woman dressed in black pants with a matching black-and-white-striped blouse stepped out. She froze when she saw them. Meeting her gaze, Maggie instantly knew.

"You're Sylvia Obermann."

The woman said nothing.

"You're my grandmother," Maggie continued.

At this point, Sylvia seemed to collect herself. She closed the door behind her quietly and moved out of the garage toward them. Ian pressed closer and slightly in front of Maggie.

Sylvia ignored him and focused on Maggie. "How did you find me?"

"It wasn't hard, once I knew your name."

Sylvia swallowed and folded her arms over her chest. "Well, you shouldn't be here. The records were sealed for a reason."

Her words, her attitude—both were like blows to Maggie's heart. She dropped her gaze then dragged it up again.

"I'd like to know what happened to my mother."

Sylvia blinked, and her jaw, already rock hard, tightened. "Your mother gave you up for adoption. That's all you need to know. I'm going to ask you to leave now. Leave, and never come back."

She turned, but as she neared the house, the garage door opened again.

"Mother, is everything all right?"

"Go inside!"

For the first time, the impeccable aplomb slipped, and Sylvia nearly ran to the door. What else was she hiding, or was it...who?

Maggie dropped Ian's hand. "Josie Obermann?"

Sylvia froze, one hand holding someone at bay just inside the door and the other outstretched toward Maggie. "Don't come any closer. I mean it. I'll call the police."

"No, you won't," Maggie said, surprising herself with the conviction she heard in her voice. "You won't, because I'll tell them about the bottles of paint in the trunk of your car."

"What is she talking about? Who is that?" the voice from inside the house said.

"She's...no one," Sylvia said, but the cracks in her demeanor were already widening. She turned her attention to the person inside the house. "Sweetheart, please, go up to your room and let me deal with this. I promise, I'll tell you all about it once she's gone."

Maggie held her breath, waiting. She could call out, but somehow knew she shouldn't. So she waited. Aching. Dying. Hoping.

There was movement inside the house.

"Josie," Sylvia said, but there was nothing she could do. Her daughter pushed past her and stood inside the garage, staring out at Maggie. Maggie stared back at her.

Slowly, Josie took one unsteady step toward her, and then another, stopping several feet shy, as though she dared come no closer. Her lips moved, but for a long time, no sound came out.

"Margareta?" she said at last.

Every fear, every doubt, every longing and heartache Maggie had ever felt was reflected in Josie's eyes. Maggie couldn't speak, couldn't find the words. She nodded.

And then watched as Josie Obermann crumpled to the ground.

CHAPTER SIXTEEN

Maggie was only mildly aware of a ragged voice calling her birth mother's name, and then of Brian flying past her to scoop Josie up from the ground.

"Open the door, Sylvia," he said.

Sylvia didn't move, but in her defense, Maggie wasn't quite sure she could.

Ian brushed past her, past Brian holding Josie, and pushed open the garage door. Maggie followed blindly, half expecting Sylvia to protest and relieved when she didn't.

Inside, Brian carried Josie into the living room and laid her oh-so-gently down onto a floral-covered couch. Kneeling next to her, he smoothed her limp hair from her forehead and whispered her name.

"Josie? Can you hear me? Wake up, sweetheart."

"I'll get some water," Ian said, and disappeared back through the kitchen the way they'd come.

Maggie remained rooted. Everything was moving too fast, and no matter how hard she tried, her mind just couldn't catch up. Ian returned with the water and passed it to Brian.

"Josie?"

This time, her eyes fluttered open and fixed on the man at her side. "Brian? Is that you?"

"It's me, sweetheart."

She recoiled, her expression broken and hurt. "But you…I don't understand. You left me."

"I would never leave you." He brought the water closer. "Here, drink this." He helped her rise then held the glass to her mouth. Josie took a sip then pushed it away, her head swiveling frantically until she caught sight of Maggie.

"Oh." The word slipped like a sigh from her lips. She looked at Brian then slid her legs off the couch and tried to stand. She accomplished it but only with Brian's help. Coming closer, she held out her hands to Maggie's face, but didn't quite touch her.

Sensing she sought her permission, Maggie closed the last small distance between them and pressed Josie's hands to her face. It was as though that move released something in Josie, and in Maggie too. Tears rolled down both of their faces, and then Maggie was holding Josie, comforting her the way a mother would her child.

Behind them, Brian stood rigid. When at last they pulled apart, he looked at Josie. "She's your daughter?" he asked, voice hoarse.

"Yours too," Josie whispered. "I wanted to tell you, but then you left and I never heard from you again. I thought it was because you didn't want me. Didn't want the baby." Her breath caught, fresh tears slipping down her cheeks.

Brian's gaze fixed on Maggie, his own brown eyes filling with tears. "I didn't know."

"I know you didn't," she whispered.

Her gaze slid to the door, where Sylvia had appeared and now stood, silent and pale, watching them. How many lies had she told over the years? How many more had she created to cover up what she'd done?

Suddenly, Sylvia didn't look so imposing. Instead, Maggie felt sorry for the life of deception and bitterness she'd led.

She tore her gaze away. "We should go."

"No!" Josie's head jerked up, and she stared, pleading, first at Maggie and then at Brian. "Please, I can't lose you both again."

"You won't, sweetheart," Brian said, stepping closer to pull her gently from Maggie's arms. "You're coming with me. I'm taking you both home."

CHAPTER SEVENTEEN

It had been three months since Maggie had learned that Josie was her birth mother. Three months since she'd learned about everything Sylvia had done to keep Josie and Brian apart—first convincing him that Josie wanted nothing to do with him, then lying to her daughter and telling her Brian had abandoned her when he enlisted in the Marines.

Josie's devastation at that news hadn't fazed Sylvia back then. In fact, it had played into her plan for Josie to give their baby up for adoption. What she hadn't accounted for was that Josie would hide a photo of herself in the baby's things or that Maggie would one day seek out the attorney who'd handled the adoption and come looking for her mother. It was he who had warned Sylvia of Maggie's presence, all of which had set in motion the things that happened after, including Sylvia doing some digging of her own. She'd learned about Rhett's accusations against Maggie, which is why she'd painted "liar" and "cheat" on her windows in the hopes it would drive her away.

"Well, sweetheart? What do you think?" Maggie's mom and dad stood on either side of her, looking up at the completely renovated schoolhouse.

"I think it's gorgeous," Maggie said, slipping an arm around each of their waists. "Thank you so much for all your help." She gestured toward the RV her parents drove up to stay in while they finished with the renovations. "We couldn't have done it without you."

"Don't just thank us," her mom said, giving a nod to the couple exiting the front doors. "They had a hand in it too."

Watching Josie and Brian draw near, Maggie couldn't help but smile. They hadn't been apart for a moment since being reunited. Now, feeling the way she did about Ian, she understood why.

"So?" Maggie asked, reaching for Josie's hand. "Do you like it?"

"I love it. It's beautiful." Josie paused and cupped her hand over her eyes as she stared down the road at a small green sign in the distance. "It was very close to this spot that I took the picture of us. I'm so glad I did. It led you back to me." She smiled up at Brian. "To us."

Maggie recognized his smile. She saw it every time she looked in the mirror. He motioned back to the schoolhouse. "Ian is inside. He's waiting for you."

Maggie looked at her parents, all four of them, smiling at her, loving her, urging her on, and suddenly her heart was so full, she almost couldn't hold it all. She took one step, then another, and before she knew it, she was running, up the stairs and through the doors and into Ian's arms.

"Whoa there," he said, laughing as he scooped her close and swung her around. "You weren't supposed to look yet."

"I couldn't wait," she said, breathless from excitement and eager to tell him everything that was in her heart.

In her back pocket, her cell phone chimed a message. She ignored it and pulled Ian's head down to press a kiss to his mouth.

"Aren't you going to look at that?" he said, his voice rough.

"No," she said between kisses. "I already know it's Gwen. She's been calling and texting to tell me she got me a tour."

Ian's body went taut, and he pulled away to look at her. "And?"

"And I don't want it. Not anymore. I realized it when we drove to Nashville to confront Sylvia. There's nothing there for me anymore." She snuggled against his chest and sighed with happiness. "I've decided I'm going to get certified to teach music."

"So, you're staying in Nameless then," he said, as though he couldn't quite believe she would choose to give up the lights and fame of Nashville.

Maggie lifted her head but didn't quite leave the circle of his arms. "I'm staying, Ian," she said, placing her hand on his cheek. "Everything I want is right here in front of me."

He searched her face for a long moment, then let go of her and crossed to the hall closet. "Well then…"

Opening the door, he pulled out the violin case Maggie had found in the basement. "You're going to need this."

Maggie's eyes rounded. "Is that your mom's fiddle?"

"It is."

"But it's been in your family for years. I couldn't take it, Ian. It should stay with you."

"It *will* stay with me. That is…" He dropped to one knee and held the fiddle up to her. "If you'll have me."

Maggie stared into his beloved face, unable to grasp all that had been given to her in such a short span of time. "Ian…"

"I'm asking you to marry me, Maggie. I love you. I have from the first moment I laid eyes on you. I promise, I'll do everything in my power to love you and care for you. If you say yes—"

"Yes."

Ian blinked and lowered the fiddle. "What did you say?"

"I said yes. I will marry you, Ian." Tears formed in Maggie's eyes and spilled down her cheeks. "I love you too, Ian. I always will."

Jumping to his feet, he pulled her into a one-armed hug and kissed her soundly, then lifted the fiddle over his head and let out a whoop.

The front door opened a crack, and her mom poked her head in. "Does this mean what we think it means?"

"It does," Maggie said, laughing when all four of her parents, plus Ian's mother and father, came flooding through. For several minutes, it was laughter and chaos as everyone oohed over the house and ahhed over Maggie and Ian. Finally, he pulled her into a quiet corner for another kiss.

"You're sure about this?" he whispered against her hair. "It can't be easy giving up your dreams of Nashville."

"I'm not giving up anything," she replied, tilting her head to look at her fiancé.

"Mm-hm. You're not fooling me, Maggie Lange," he teased, placing a quick kiss on the end of her nose. "You just want me for my fiddle."

"Well, it *is* a very nice fiddle," she teased back.

Ian laughed. It was a sound Maggie knew she would love hearing for the rest of her life.

Across the room, the message on the chalkboard caught her gaze. Closing her eyes, Maggie whispered, "Thank You, Lord."

Jeremiah was right. His plan had been better along.

Dear Reader,

Every story I write contains pieces of me in it—whether it be places or memories or people I've met who've left a lasting impression. This story, in particular, is intensely personal because of the struggles the main character, Maggie, faced. Her internal desire to somehow make a name for herself is something I long struggled with, until the day I heard my heavenly Father whisper, "Fear not, for I have redeemed you; I have called you by name, you are mine."

Suddenly, I understood that I already had a name. It was Daughter. And it was better to be chosen than anything I could earn in my own strength.

I knew immediately this would be the theme for my story. What I did not know was that at the same time God was revealing this to me, He was speaking the same message to Leslie's heart and impressing the same verses upon her.

Now, some would say this was coincidence brought on by the name of the town where our stories are set. I believe it happened more by Divine appointment, because the Lord had a story He wanted written, to beloved children who needed the reminder.

Leslie and I both pray our stories speak to your heart and soak into the broken places in need of healing. May you find rest and peace in knowing you have a heavenly Father who loves you and has called you by name!

Sincerely,
Elizabeth Ludwig

✍ About the Authors ✍

Leslie Gould

Leslie Gould is the number-one bestselling and Christy-Award winning author of over forty novels. She's also won two Faith, Hope, and Love Readers' Choice Awards and has been a finalist for the Carol Award. She and her husband, Peter, live in Portland, Oregon, and enjoy hiking, traveling, and spending time with their adult children and grandbaby.

Elizabeth Ludwig

Elizabeth Ludwig is a *USA Today* bestselling author whose work has been featured on Novel Rocket, More to Life Magazine, and Christian Fiction Online Magazine. She is an accomplished speaker and teacher, often attending conferences and seminars where she lectures on editing for fiction writers, crafting effective novel proposals, and conducting successful editor/agent interviews.

Elizabeth was honored to be awarded a HOLT Medallion in 2018 for her book, *A Tempting Taste of Mystery*, part of the Sugarcreek Amish Mysteries series from Guideposts. She was named a finalist in the 2020 Selah Awards for *Garage Sale Secret*, part of the Mysteries of Lancaster County series from Guideposts.

Along with her husband and children, Elizabeth makes her home in the great state of Texas.

Story Behind the Name

Nameless, Tennessee

There is not a whole lot known about Nameless, an unincorporated community in Jackson County, Tennessee. In fact, except for the debate over the origin of its name, not much has happened there that most people would say is of any particular note.

At its peak, Nameless had a population of about 250. It consisted of a school, a general merchandise store, and a small post office which most think can be credited with giving the town its name. According to legend, when the residents applied for the post office, the line for a name on the application was left blank. It was returned by the US Post Office Department with the word "Nameless" stamped on the form, a moniker given by accident but which stuck through the years.

Others believe a local official sought to name the post office "Morgan" after the attorney general but was turned down because of associations in the minds of people with the Confederacy and General John Hunt Morgan.

Whatever the truth might be, what is notable about this place is the people who inhabit it. Four times a year, the owners of the J.T. Watts General Store reopen its doors to host a town party for anyone who wants to join. Along with MoonPies and cold Coca-Colas served in glass bottles, the people enjoy reminiscing about times past and sharing each other's company. It is quintessential small-town America and is well deserving of a visit.

Apple Stack Cake

Cake Ingredients:

5¼ cups all-purpose flour

1 teaspoon baking soda

1 teaspoon baking powder

1 teaspoon salt

1 teaspoon ground cinnamon

2½ cups brown sugar

1 cup vegetable shortening

2 large eggs

2 teaspoons pure vanilla extract

½ cup buttermilk

apple filling (see below)

confectioners' sugar, optional

Directions:

Preheat oven to 425 degrees. Grease and flour 9-inch cake pans. (Reuse pans as needed.)

Combine flour, soda, baking powder, salt, and cinnamon. Set aside. Cream brown sugar and shortening two to three minutes. Then beat in eggs and vanilla.

On low speed, beat in flour mixture alternately with buttermilk, beginning and ending with flour, until just combined. Divide dough into seven ¼ cup portions. Each ¼ cup is one cake layer.

Bake each layer 10 minutes or until golden brown. Remove from pans and cool completely on wire rack.

Apple Filling Ingredients:

5 cups water

1 pound dried apples

2 cups packed brown sugar

2 teaspoons ground cinnamon

1 teaspoon ground nutmeg

½ teaspoon ground cloves

¼ teaspoon salt

Directions:

Bring water to a boil. Chop dried apples and add to water. Cook uncovered over medium heat until all water is absorbed, about 20 to 25 minutes. Add sugar, cinnamon, nutmeg, cloves, and salt. Simmer 15 minutes, stirring frequently.

Assemble:

Stack cakes with apple filling between layers. Cake is best if you let it stand twenty-four hours before serving. If desired, sift confectioners' sugar over top of cake before serving.

*Read on for a sneak peek of another exciting book
in the Love's a Mystery series!*

Love's a Mystery *in*
HAZARDVILLE, CONNECTICUT
by BETHANY JOHN *&* GAIL KIRKPATRICK

The House Love Built
By Bethany John

He heals the brokenhearted and binds up their wounds.
—Psalm 147:3 (NIV)

Hazardville, Connecticut

June 1894

It's quiet.

Emma Cooke had been waiting for this moment for weeks. Looking at the calendar, marking off the days, almost like a child would count down till Christmas. All her lessons had been taught. All her tests had been graded. The recitals were done.

The students she taught at Dixon Academy for Girls had all gone home for the summer.

It's finally quiet.

There was no more giggling or silly gossip or singing hymns off-key. There was no transporting girls to their fitness class or dining room duty to attend. Her schedule was blissfully clear.

It was too quiet.

Emma had thought she would enjoy this day. It was the end of her first year at the prestigious school. The academy was founded to promote a strong sense of self, individual achievement, and the highest moral and spiritual standards in young women. Emma had attended many schools like it when she was a girl. Her father was a music master, a brilliant instructor who played piano, flute, and clarinet. He gave private lessons to girls from wealthy families all over the United States. And at every illustrious school in which he taught, he made sure his contract included the provision that his daughter would be provided an education at that institution.

It was a smart move. He never would have been able to pay for her schooling otherwise.

He had been gone six years now.

Her father had done so much for her. She thought of him whenever she walked into the beautifully appointed music room in the school. She thought of him on Sundays when she sat in church and heard the first notes of a hymn as the organist started to play, for her father had played the organ masterfully as well. She thought of him Saturdays and holidays and every day. She missed him.

Especially today. Most of the other teachers who lived at the inn had left shortly after the girls. They were off to see their families for the summer holiday. Only she and Mary remained.

Mary was like her. No parents. No one to visit on the holidays. They had both stayed in Hazardville during the Christmas break. It wasn't so lonely then. They attended church together and went caroling with some locals.

Almost everyone in town worked for Hazard Powder Company. Everyone knew each other. There was a closeness in this town that Emma wasn't used to. Mama died when Emma was four, lost while giving birth to a brother who also did not make it. Her father and she had moved a lot. Going from city to city, from one school to another, never staying more than three or four years in one place. Father always said it was exciting, but a new place meant leaving behind friends they had made, leaving behind familiarity and comfort, and starting afresh each time.

She had wished for this quiet. This stillness, but maybe it didn't suit her. She'd been on the move her entire life.

"Emma?" There was a knock at her door. She would recognize Mary's soft voice anywhere.

"Come in," she called to her, glad for the distraction from her thoughts.

Mary walked in, her pretty, reddish-blond hair piled high on top of her head, a few tendrils escaping and framing her face. Her cheeks were pink. She looked happy.

"I'm sorry to bother you. I know you were looking forward to your quiet time. The girls were very excitable this week."

"Oh no! Please don't be sorry. I'm glad to see you. I'm not used to quiet anymore. I almost don't know how to handle it. Please, sit down."

Mary eased into the armchair next to the bed. "It's glorious outside. I've just come from a walk along the river. Forgot my hat. My grandmother would have kicked up a storm if I ever pulled that around her. She is probably in heaven fussing to whatever angel will listen to her. I've never understood why being hatless is such a bad thing. Fresh air and sun are good for the soul. Why would God create such a perfect thing if he wanted us to hide from it? It seems almost sinful to me."

Emma smiled at Mary. Her friend was so plainspoken, the Maine accent still slightly gripping her words. It was almost hard to believe that she was the foreign-language teacher and spoke the most beautiful French, Latin, and Italian. "I should get outside." Emma stood up and looked out the window. A beautiful sugar maple, its leaves gently dancing in the breeze, greeted her. "Today seems like the perfect day for a picnic." A memory took hold of Emma. "Remember the day we took our afternoon classes outside for lessons? And how that bumblebee landed on Gemma Alexander?"

"Of course I do! She screamed and screamed and *screamed*. She kept boasting about the expensive French perfume her mother had sent her. The bee probably took her for a flower."

"She was a trying little thing at times, but I will miss her." Emma sighed. "I will miss them all." She looked back at Mary, suddenly feeling a wash of melancholy flood over her. "I thought I was looking forward to this time, but I must admit I don't know what I'll do with myself."

"You could come with me to Boston. My cousin works for Harvard. I'm going to meet his soon-to-be wife and her family. I hear they are fancy people. I'll have to remember all the lessons I learned from the ladies here to try and impress them."

"Thank you for the invitation, Mary, but I couldn't intrude on your family time. I know how close you were to your cousin growing up. You should spend time with him and not worry about me."

"But we are family, Emma. We orphaned, unmarried, educated ladies must stick together."

Mary was right. There weren't many women like them. They'd both gone to college and earned degrees. The idea of educating women was a dangerous one to some. Most women their age were married with two or three children. It was simply what women did.

Emma's father didn't want that for her.

I don't want you to be tied down. I want you to have choices.

Her father's words always clung to her thoughts. He had made sure she learned from the best. She'd received private lessons from some of the world's best math minds.

She was educated. She earned her own wage. She was supporting herself. Emma had recently begun to wonder if her father knew he wasn't going to live to see her become a woman. She tried not to think about it, because if he had known and he kept it from her and robbed her of all of the extra moments she could squeeze in with him, she would be very angry with him. She didn't want to be angry with her father. So she tried not to think about it.

"We are a family," Emma said to Mary. "I say we go on a family outing to the shops today. We deserve something sweet for all the hard work we put in this year. It's my treat, and I do not want to hear any arguments from you, Mary."

"No arguments from me!" Mary stood up. "I've been dreaming about pudding for days."

"But do grab your hat this time. I would hate to have your grandmother fussing again," she said with a smile.

Mary went to get her hat, and the two of them walked to Main Street, where the shops were located. They got delicious custards and chatted with the new shop owner's wife. Hazardville had been a company town for many years, but after the War Between the States, the Hazard Powder Company's business started declining. Many people had moved on, but there were new people in town too. There was a new public school and a large, gorgeous church. There was community here. Emma liked Hazardville and often wondered what her life would have been like if she had grown up in a place like this. Or just one place instead of many.

She and her father had moved from big city to big city. New York. Boston. St. Louis. San Francisco. She didn't have roots. She never realized how much slower life could be until she came to Connecticut.

Of all the places in the world she thought she might end up, Connecticut wasn't one of them. There was a beauty here she hadn't expected, and people were more open about educating young women.

"I'm not sure about the color of this fabric I bought." Mary glanced down at the bag she was carrying as they walked back to the inn. "Do you think it's too much?"

"Of course I don't. Lilac is a beautiful color. I think it will look lovely with your hair."

"I've never liked my hair. Such an in-between color. Not red. Not blond. My mother had dark brown hair. Almost as dark as yours. I've always thought dark hair was so beautiful."

"We all seem to want what we don't have. I've always thought my dark hair was too plain."

They returned to the inn, chatting about everything and nothing at the same time. It was nice not to have to rush back and prepare for their next lessons or worry about where the girls were supposed to be next. As they approached the steps of the inn, Emma saw a man in a dark suit standing on the porch, a briefcase in one hand, a packet of papers in the other.

"Miss Cooke?" The man looked directly at her, seeming to already know who she was.

Immediately her heart started to beat a little faster. No one ever came looking for her. In fact, most of her life she felt quite invisible. "Yes?" She swallowed and glanced at Mary, who looked just as perplexed. "How can I help you?"

"I'm Collin Reed. I'm with Caldwell and Wickers."

"Caldwell and Wickers," she repeated. "You're a lawyer?"

She knew the name. She'd seen the ornate sign every day when she'd lived in New York City. The building was across the street from the school she'd attended until she was fourteen. It was one of the most prestigious firms in the country. Only wealthy clients could afford their services.

"You know our firm?" he asked with raised brows.

"I went to Spencer Academy."

He nodded. "We have clients whose daughters attend that school. I have heard fine things about it." The slight smile dropped from his face, and he was all business again. "Is there somewhere we can go to have a conversation? I have important information to relay."

"Maybe I should leave you alone to discuss your business." Mary took a step away, but Emma caught her hand and held on tightly.

"Maybe you shouldn't. I have no secrets from you." Emma looked back at the lawyer in his very dark suit. "Is there a reason, Mr. Reed, that Mary cannot hear what you are about to tell me?"

"No. I'm sure she would learn the news soon after I leave anyway. The whole town will know shortly."

"The whole town?" Emma shook her head. "No one is suing me, surely. I do not have a penny to my name."

"You are not being sued, miss."

Her head spun as she tried to think of a reason such a high-profile attorney would need to see her. "Both my parents have passed penniless. I have no other family."

"If we could go somewhere private, I would be happy to tell you why I am here."

Printed in the United States
by Baker & Taylor Publisher Services